ALLISTER
BOONE M.D.

TORVI TACUSKI

TORVI TACUSKI

Cover Art by GrandFailure | iStock

Torvi Tacuski | ALLISTER BOONE
Fiction | Contemporary Fantasy

Contents

A Message From Torvi Tacuski

I am not a psychiatrist, or any other professional certified to give mental health advice. I am just an author who has struggled most of my life with depression and anxiety. The story you are about to read should never be used in place of professional help from a mental health provider. If you are sensitive, struggling with depression, anxiety, low self-esteem, PTSD, suicidal thoughts, or any other emotional problems, this book may not be for you. To give it to you blunt and short: Allister Boone is a fictional asshole, and you are beautiful and loved and needed and wanted, even if you don't believe it yet. One day you will. Just give it time.

Please seek help from friends or family, or reach out by calling the National Suicide Prevention Lifeline: 1-800-273-8255.

THE GAME

1

"Name one thing—only one—that you dislike about yourself," I told my newest patient fifty-three seconds after she entered my office.

I always asked the same question. It was how I broke the ice. It was how I tested them. Most would mull over the things they hated about themselves, trying to decide which one was *the one*. And then they would choose one and leave it at that. But every now and then I got someone like Margot Henry who just couldn't help herself.

"I-I uh…well, I hate that I'm overweight," she said, looking down at her hands on her lap. "But I, uh, also don't like—"

"I said *one*, Miss Henry"—my index finger sprang up—"One means one, not two, or three, or *but also*. By the looks of you, I know it must be difficult for you to comprehend the meaning."

Her cheeks turned red. I knew she wanted to leave the room right then, to waddle down the long stretch of hallway and into the restroom and shut herself off in a stall and cry into her hands. But Margot Henry was a doormat. And she wasn't going anywhere until I told her she could leave. She ripped a tissue from the square box on my desk and dabbed the corner of one eye, sniffled and kept her gaze down like the submissive little—big—woman she was. How pathetic.

Margot had nice hair. I liked her hair. It was brunette with blond highlights, clean and silky and smelled of fancy salon shampoo. Unfortunately for Margot, it didn't go well with her face. The stylist did a fine job on the hair, but it was better suited for someone else. Another face. Slimmer and more confident. Any face but fat Margot Henry's face.

And her outfit—hmm. She wore a hideous pink blouse and a pair of matching dress slacks. I loathed it. Of course, I only loathed it because every person who saw her in the building my office was located, loathed it. But I'll get to that later.

"So," I began, "you dislike the fact that you're two people rolled into one—I don't blame you."

She raised her head and looked right at me.

(Did he really—How could he say something like that?)

She blinked several times, and then she just stared at me. Dumbfounded. Wounded. *Pathetic.*

(Arrogant piece of shit. I have to get out of here…)

"I'm going to tell you something, Miss Henry," I said, leaning forward and interlocking my fingers on my desk. "I'm going to tell you a lot of somethings over the course of however many days you choose to come here. You can listen, or you can tell me to fuck off, call me an arrogant piece of shit and threaten to sue me—as always, it's your choice. But first, before you decide, let me ask you one more question. Is that okay?" Sure it was—she was the poster child for desperation.

She nodded.

I leaned my back against the leather chair again and made myself comfortable, then looked across the neatness of my desk where nothing was ever out of place, and at Margot who still had her gaze fixed on me, waiting for me to make it all better.

"Why did you choose to see me?"

"I, uh…"—she swallowed—"I-I needed someone to talk to." She didn't seem confident in her answer.

3

My left eyebrow hitched up, and I nodded as if to say "Yeah, and—come on now Miss Henry, my rates aren't cheap" and I waited impatiently for her to get her shit together.

She tangled her fingers on her lap, getting the hint.

Then suddenly:

"Why *else* would I come here?" she snapped, and I grinned deep inside my skin where she couldn't see it because I knew the bitch had a backbone somewhere underneath all the layers of fat. "You're a psychiatrist, Mr. Boone. Why does *anyone* choose to see you?"

The grin found it's way to my eyes—the pink outfit was looking better on her.

"I didn't ask why anyone else comes here," I said. "I asked why *you* came here. What did *you* hope to get out of my services? What were *you* thinking when you held the phone in your hand for five minutes, staring at my number on the screen before you finally hit the call button? Why do *you* hate yourself so much that you're willing to pay an 'arrogant piece of shit' like me three hundred dollars an hour to make you hate yourself even more?" I swept a hand in the air at her. "Why do *you*, an overweight, spineless, walking, talking bottle of Pepto Bismol, need someone to talk to?"

There went her backbone; it slipped right out of her like a calf being born.

She swallowed again and couldn't look me in the eyes anymore.

"Answer the question," I instructed. "Why did you, Margot Henry, choose to see me?"

She glared at me, gritted her teeth behind a pair of pretty mauve lips. Too bad the courage wasn't enough she could speak her mind. Instead, she answered flatly: "I chose to see you so you could help me feel better about myself, Mr. Boone. To help with my anxiety. I chose to see you so maybe you can..." She sighed, reluctant, "...so maybe you can make me believe I have something to live for." Her eyes fell away from mine again.

"Are you suicidal, Miss Henry?" No, she wasn't suicidal, but to look like I was doing my job as any human would, I had to ask.

Margot Henry often thought about suicide, but the majority of people unhappy with their lives think about it every now and then—thinking about death is as common as daydreaming about winning the lottery. *Maybe I'm better off dead. I wonder if anyone would miss me if I died. I'm so tired...I wonder what death is like.* Thinking about suicide and planning it are two different things. Planning it and acting on it are also two different things. Margot Henry was still at Level One, where most remain until something positive happens— because it always does—and they can abandon the Three Levels of Self-Destruction.

She shook her head slowly, which was her way of saying yes by saying no. Which was her way of subliminally trying to get me to feel sorry for her. But I didn't take the bait—I didn't feel sorry for anybody.

"Good," I said. "Now that we've gotten that out of the way." I leaned forward again. "I am here for three things, Miss Henry: to listen to your troubles and provide advice as I see fit, write a prescription if needed, and to diagnose you. If you're willing to accept me as I am, I'm willing to take your money. Is your throat dry? Would you like some water?" Her constant swallowing was distracting.

"Yes," she answered, nodding with that pitiful look she wore so well. "Thank you."

I motioned toward the mini fridge in the corner next to the microwave and coffee pot.

Margot's eyebrows crumpled in her forehead.

"You should probably get it yourself," I told her. "You could use the exercise."

Her face turned red again, but this was an entirely different shade. Fuck-You Red. Fury-And-Rage Crimson. Had-It-Up-To-My-Fucking-Eyeballs-With-Your-Shit Scarlet.

She crushed the tissue in her fist and then shot into a stand, tossing her purse over her shoulder.

"You know what?" she said, gritting her teeth. "You *are* an arrogant piece of shit. And you really *can* go fuck yourself."

The chair she had been sitting on tipped sideways in her furious march toward the exit, but it settled back down without falling over. Thinking about how that chair had more control over its existence than Margot Henry had over hers, I shook my head.

A few seconds later, the door to my office swung open; Nancy, my secretary, stood in the doorway with a hand on her hip and a scowl on her face.

"What did you say to that woman?" she scolded. "Second one today, and it's not even noon."

"Physician-patient privilege, Nancy," I reminded her, and then stood up; I took my suit jacket from the coatrack and slipped my arms into it.

Nancy's scowl deepened; she crossed her arms over her small breasts and stood in the doorway, blocking my escape. I really did want to escape. Nancy was an intimidating woman; she was forty-six and had a body like a marathon runner; there wasn't a thing in the world she feared, including me—especially me. I had gone through eleven secretaries before Nancy came along. She was the only one who could put up with my "abuse"; she was the only one brave enough to call me on it; she was terrifying and so-so beautiful in that almost-fifty, overly-muscled marathon runner sort of way, but most of all she was full of anger at the world and was one of few people whose soul I actually looked forward to reaping when her time came.

She glared at me.

"Your next appointment is at two," she said.

"What happened to my one o'clock?"

She smirked. "Cancelled, of course. One o'clock was nine o'clock's best friend." She shook her head and chewed on the inside of her cheek. "I used to wonder why in the hell I stay here, but now I know. I'm the one of us who makes sure these people who come to *you* for help, don't walk out those doors feeling like *everybody* in this world is against them."

"Well, maybe you should be doing my job," I suggested nonchalantly.

"No thanks. I wouldn't want that kind of responsibility." She stepped aside to let me pass. "Be back in time for your next malpractice lawsuit," she said.

"Yes ma'am."

I'd been sued several times, but most of the cases never made it off the lawyer's desk. It's difficult to sue a psychiatrist. Or maybe it's just me—I can't lose.

I walked past Nancy and made my way to the elevator. I doubted I would be back by two o'clock. Time was never on my side. Literally.

In fact, Time was a bigger asshole than I was.

I caught a cab and went to meet him at Brisbane's Bar & Restaurant on South Street.

2

I wasn't in the habit of drinking before noon, but Time, also known as Morty Finch, liked Brisbane's and rarely ever wanted to meet anywhere else. He was an old man with the temperament of a spoiled child, and unless I wanted a tantrum—or for him to cheat at our Game—then I knew I had better give in to what Morty wanted. It was always what *Morty* wanted.

We were as different as summer and winter. Where Morty was erratic and stubborn, my temperament rarely changed; where Morty was a "pervert", I considered myself a gentleman; while Morty enjoyed playing games—mostly with mortals—I preferred to watch from the sidelines; Morty was old, I was fairly young—in appearance, not in age, of course; we are the same age—and lastly, Morty liked The Beatles, and I was a Rolling Stones guy.

But it was the ways we were alike that put us on equal ground in the universe: neither of us could be defeated; we were Inevitable; nothing living could ever escape us, and neither of us could die. Or so we'd been told.

And because of these very special likenesses, we were a team. I despised it, having to work with Morty, because he was an insufferable bastard. But it was mandatory and I had no say in the matter. It was the way things were, the way things would always be.

I pushed open the glass-and-wood door and entered the dimly-lit atmosphere of the bar. As expected, there were only a few people inside at this early hour: Frank the bartender, who was so used to Morty and me that he hardly batted an eye at our "bizarre" conversations anymore; the cook who rarely ever emerged from the heat of the kitchen, one waitress, three or four customers having lunch, and, of course, Morty Finch. He always sat on the same barstool, the one with the best view of the flat-screen TV mounted on the wall; and there was always a cloud of smoke around his head because he liked generic full-flavored cigarettes about as much as he liked the ladies and was rarely seen without one. It was strange that he was by himself today, but I didn't care much, and wasn't about to ask.

"Allister!" he called out from across the room, waving his cigarette at me to join him; it was illegal to smoke inside public buildings but Morty could do whatever he wanted, being who he was and all.

I walked over, preparing myself for what I knew would be an exhausting meeting with my dearest and oldest friend and enemy.

"It's good to see you Allister," Frank, the bartender said. "What'll you have?"

I shook my head. "Nothing today, thanks."

Morty sighed irritably and his bony shoulders fell into a slump underneath a white button-up dress shirt.

"Come on and have something," he insisted. "It's been over a month since our last meeting. I've missed you!" His voice was deep and rough like a man who'd smoked three packs of cigarettes a day for thirty years.

I turned on the barstool to face Frank instead.

"I'm not drinking anything today, Morty." I reached for a peanut and cracked the shell in my fingers. "So, what did you want to talk to me about? I'm a busy man these days, a working man; you wouldn't be trying to interfere, now would you?" I popped the peanuts into my mouth.

His old, shriveled head with a puff of white hair drew back, and a little burst of breath pushed through his lips.

"You calling me a cheater, Allister Boone?"

I looked over. "Sure I am. But why bother; you know I'm going to win; it's just a matter of—." I stopped myself.

Morty grinned, and I wanted to wipe it right off his face.

"Nice choice of words there, Allister," he said, cigarette dangling from his lips.

"Yeah, I put my foot in my mouth, I know, but I'm still going to win, and you know it."

Morty laughed and pulled the cigarette from his mouth; smoke circled his head. He brought his glass up and drank down the rest of the whiskey, then slid it across the bar toward Frank for a refill.

Morty shook his head. "I dunno, Allister, you scared away two patients today." He smacked his palm on the bar and laughed. "Margot, the fat one, she left the building with some intense images in her head."

"What kind of images?" I could've looked myself but I didn't care.

"Oh, you know, the jump-off-a-bridge kind."

"Margot Henry isn't suicidal, Morty."

"She wasn't when she went in there," he said. "But you know how fickle mortals are—think about it; you were probably her last hope. Woman makes the decision to finally see a psychiatrist after years of depression and societal abuse, only to have the psychiatrist abuse her too!" Laughing, he smacked his hand on the bar again. "You can't make this shit up. She'll be a point for me, I guarantee it." He pointed a gnarled finger at me.

I cracked another peanut shell, hardly ever looked at Morty on my right.

"Maybe so," I said, "but when this is all over, I will have beat you Morty Finch."

"How many more days we got?" he asked, looking at his watch as if it could tell him—yes, Time wore a watch, because even he had a hard time keeping up with himself.

"Two hundred twenty-three," I said.

He smiled, his bright dentures on display.

"That's a lot of days and a lot of deaths," he said.

"We'll see." I turned on the barstool to face him. "Now tell me—why are we here?"

Morty crushed his cigarette out in the ashtray and swiveled around on the stool to face me, his black loafers propped on the spindle. For someone who could have and be and do anything he wanted, Morty didn't care much for style. He liked cheap whiskey and cheap cigarettes and cheap hookers, and he drove a cheap car. The only thing that had to be top-notch for Morty was his fancy silver money clip; no significant reason for it as far as I knew. He just liked it.

"What's the current score?" Morty asked.

"You know the score."

"Yeah, but I want to hear you say it." He wiggled his bushy white eyebrows.

"You want to hear me tell you that I'm winning, Morty?" I found that odd. "Okay, the score is my twenty-four to your five. That's a big gap."

"Yeah, yeah, I'm tailing you, Allister, I know, but that's why I wanted to meet with you today." He leaned in closer, pretended to care if anyone might be listening, and then he said, "I can't be losin', Allister, you know that. I never lose. I always win. I always catch up. Eventually."

"I never lose, either. We're incapable of losing—*you* know *that*. And this conversation already happened one hundred forty-two-days ago, Morty, so I'm not really in the market to buy into it again. It was ridiculous the first time around."

"Umm, why don't you two humor me?" said Frank the bartender, batting that rare eye. "What kind of game are you playing?" He slid the refilled glass over in front of Morty.

Both of us looked at Frank. Then Morty looked right at me. He smiled and sucked on a tooth, waiting for me to be the one to answer. Because just as I was incapable of dying or losing, he knew I was also incapable of lying. It was part of the Balance. Along with the inability to be biased or to feel empathy—basically I would exist forever, but never really live, and I had power I was powerless to use. Except on certain occasions.

Morty's balance was more complicated.

"You want the truth?" I asked Frank.

Frank leaned on the bar.

"Sure I do," he said. "Can't be any weirder than all the other stuff I hear you two always talking about. Lay it on me; I can handle it." He gestured a hand at the nearly empty bar. "It'll be dead in here for another hour at least, so I've got time."

I glanced over at Morty, wondering if Frank had time because Morty had given it to him, just to watch me squirm.

One corner of Morty's wrinkled mouth hitched up into a grin.

I shook my head, cracked another peanut shell and popped the little nuggets into my mouth. I dusted off my hands.

"All right," I said, buying into it again anyway, and I folded my hands together on the bar. "It all started…"

One Hundred Forty-Two Days Ago…

I hadn't seen Morty Finch in about sixty years; we usually did our jobs far apart, but still very much together, you see. We couldn't work without each other. Time and Death come as a pair, like a golfer and his caddy. A hitman and the cleaner. Morty would decide when someone's time was up, and I came in afterwards to reap the soul.

"So…"—Frank looked mildly confused—"…Death isn't the one who kills?"

"No," I said, mildly offended. "There are a lot of things you people get wrong—can I continue the story?"

Frank nodded, amused.

Anyway, I was strolling along the Steel Pier in Atlantic City when I heard a voice call out over the sounds of carousel music, whirring helicopter blades, and distant screams of terror and laughter.

"Allister! Allister Boone! That really you? Ha-Ha! I can't believe my eyes!"

Morty slipped through a crowd of people, careful as always not to touch them first, and made his way over to me.

I slid my hands into the pockets of my dress pants and sighed.

"How long's it been?" he said.

"Not long enough."

He snorted, and then slapped me on the shoulder. "Always so bitter, Allister," he said. "One of these days I'm going to take offense; might start to believe you really hate my guts."

I raised a telling brow; he brushed it off like he always did.

The truth was that I never really hated him and he knew it. Morty could be good company when he wanted. But that was rare. I just preferred the solitude of my existence, and with someone like Morty around, there was no such thing.

"What have you been doing with yourself?" he asked.

"Same thing I always do," I said. "Wandering the earth, cleaning up your messes."

He shrugged, and right about that time a woman walked up and draped her arm over the back of his neck. She was long-legged and skinny in that meth-addict sort of way. Her high-heels were too tall and made her look like a giant— though Morty was quite short—a looming skeleton of a woman with smeared lipstick and a dazed look in her eyes. She leaned over, her breasts spilling over the top of her tight blouse, and she planted her lips in the top of his white hair, his hand hooked at her waist.

A mother with two children walked by, and she looked Morty's companion up and down with revulsion. She pulled her children to the opposite side as they passed, as if the extra distance was enough to keep them from catching whatever diseases she carried.

(So nasty. There are kids out here for Christ's sake!) the woman thought.

"Same thing you always do, eh?" Morty echoed. "Well, it ain't my fault you're so doom-and-gloom all the time." He pulled the woman closer and squeezed her hip in his hand. "You don't see me moping around, wasting eternity away. I know how to have fun, Allister! You should try it sometime." He plucked a cigarette from his shirt pocket and wedged it between his lips.

"You can't waste eternity if it's eternal," I reminded him. "And I don't mope. You have to somehow care about something to mope. I am content with my existence. Except when I see you, of course."

"Ouch!" Morty said, feigning offense. "I resent that, Allister, I really do."

No, he really didn't.

"Well, still"—he shrugged, puffed on his cigarette— "I may have all the time in the world, but that don't mean I gotta act like it."

"Morty knows how to have a good time," the woman said sultrily, pressing her breasts against his head. "Duncha *papi?*" she cooed.

"No one asked you," I told her. "Where'd you pick up this petri dish of STDs anyway, Morty?"

The woman snarled.

"Souls a gettin' to yah again, I see," Morty accused. He glanced around at the passersby. "Or is it the living?"

I never answered.

He walked with me to the edge of the pier; the petri dish followed.

"Let's have a chat," he said.

"I'm really not in the mood."

"Oh, come on," he insisted, and patted me on the back. "For an old friend."

Resting my arms on the railing, my hands dangled over the water, I gazed out at the ocean and contemplated for a moment.

"I suppose it has been a long time," I finally said. "Sure, let's have a chat."

It *had* been a long time since we'd seen one another, since we got together like long-lost brothers with starkly different lives who lived on opposites sides of the world; since we had done anything together, like catching up or drinking in a bar or plotting the death of someone famous so we could watch the during and after of the mortals it affected—that was our Broadway show, our front row seats at the Super Bowl. I couldn't deny that, as much as Morty was a disruption to my solitude, I did miss our brief moments together. *What could it hurt?* I told myself, knowing it could hurt very much. But Morty was right: the souls were getting to me again—*and* the emotions of the living—and I needed a change. And there was no one better to shake things up than Morty Finch.

Of course, like being hungover the day after, I regretted the night before.

3

Morty patted my back again, delighted, relieved. Probably because he didn't have to work as hard as he did sixty years ago for my cooperation.

"So, I was talking with an old friend of ours not long ago," he said, "and I won't bore you with the details of the conversation, but I had an epiphany that day."

"Who was it?"

"Gluttony," he said with the dismissive wave of his hand. "I tell you I had an epiphany and you ask with who?"

I shrugged.

"Right. Okay." He stopped and turned to the woman standing behind us. "Be a doll and find me a chili dog, will yah?" He dug into his pocket and slapped a twenty into her hand.

"Sure thing, Morty," she said, kissed his cheek, and then sauntered off in those too-tall high-heels that made her look like a newborn fawn trying to walk for the first time.

He turned back.

"Gluttony and I were going on about the deep things in life," he said with the twirl of his wrist, "you know, all the stuff mortals contemplate but will never know until long after they're dead: Why are we here? What's the meaning of Life? Stuff like that. I mean, who really knows if their questions will ever be answered, but that's beside the point." He rolled his eyes.

"I thought the conversation wasn't the important part?" I reminded him.

Morty chewed on the inside of his cheek.

"Just givin' yah a little rundown, Allister—come on, don't be a party-pooper so soon in the game."

"Okay, Morty," I said, listlessly.

"So, that stuff led to other stuff, which led to you and me," he went on. "Just like mortals contemplating their mortality and their place in the universe, I realized that even though I am what I am, that I can do and be whatever I want, that I—and you too—aren't that different from them."

"I'd say we're very different from them, Morty."

He pushed himself into my personal space, his old eyes alight with determination. "In every way but one, yes. Like them, we are forced to exist regardless of what we want or how we feel about it. Like them, we go to work every day, a never-ending cycle of monotonous chores that lead to…what?" He opened his hands.

I raised a curious brow.

When I didn't answer, he answered for me: "We don't know"—he threw his hands in the air—"that's just it; like them, *we-don't-know*." He pointed at me, squinted one eye. "Will Time really go on forever, Allister? Is my existence truly eternal?" His left caterpillar brow hitched up, and he looked at me as if about to ask for the answer to the most complicated puzzle ever constructed. "Do I really exist *at all*? Uh-huh, it's a good question, ain't it? Am I really standing here in front of you, buzzing around your head like a fly that you just can't swat? Or, are you crazy, Allister Boone? Have all those souls you've reaped since the Beginning finally taken over? Have the sheeple's wool been pulled so far over your eyes that you only see the Illusion anymore, just like them? Has the wolf finally become the sheep?"

I sighed and gave my eyes a little roll—leave it to Morty to complicate the complicated. Of course, he didn't believe any of the things he was taunting me with. No, Morty firmly—vehemently—believed in his existence and his

17

superiority, and although it was okay he joked about it himself, it was never okay that anyone else did.

Which was precisely why I did it.

"Can you remember Time before Time?" I asked.

"What do you mean?"

"Think back as far as you can," I told him. "What's the first thing you remember?"

He thought about it for a few seconds, his deep-set eyes squinted in concentration.

"The bright light," he answered, "and the heat."

"But you don't remember anything before that?" It wasn't necessarily a question as it was a statement.

He rubbed his chin in his fingertips.

"What are you gettin' at?" he asked suspiciously.

"You haven't been around forever," I told him. "There was a Time before you. Probably a Death before me. Which probably means that we *can* die, and that one day we *will*. And then Time and Death will be born again. But not Morty and Allister, of course."

"Don't mess with me, Allister," he warned, his voice sharp and unforgiving. "You know I don't like it when you mess with my head." He gritted his teeth, and his eyes filled up with retribution.

I smiled, close-lipped, and then turned back to face the ocean again, my hands dangling over the railing.

"Time has *always* existed—*I* have always existed," he ripped the words out. "If your stupid little theory is even remotely correct, then maybe we do die—maybe we have died—but we're always reborn. But ain't been no other Time or Death before us."

"How do you know?" I asked, still 'messing with his head', and enjoying it like a fine wine.

"Because I know!" He slammed his fist down on the railing. "You know better than to test me, Mr. Boone."

A man glanced over his shoulder at the commotion as he walked by.

I looked at Morty, a grin dancing at one corner of my mouth.

Morty, realizing what I was doing, released all of his anger in one long breath.

"Fine. I'll give you that one," he said. "But you should be more careful."

"Is that a threat, or a request?"

"It's both," he said, crossing his arms and pouting like a petulant child. "You know how sensitive I am about that stuff."

"Yeah, Morty, I know."

"You just better be careful," he repeated, "or I might have to work a little overtime this month."

"All right, all right," I gave in, pretending like I didn't care about his threat when we both knew I did. I very much cared.

Morty knew how much I detested reaping souls; it was really the only thing he had over me. I had something over him too—the Balance and all. I could undo what he did and send a soul back to the world of the living, if I wanted. But I rarely ever "wanted" to, and when I did, it had always been under special circumstances. But more significantly, I *was* the Balance. I was who kept death from running rampant; it was my job to keep it in check. There had been times throughout human history when I'd failed, and my failure led to mass deaths in the forms of war and disease and natural disasters.

As I mentioned, Morty Finch was the opposite of me. Where my personal emotions were limited mostly to the indifferent ones, Morty's were more involved. It was precisely why—in mortal's eyes—some mortals who deserved to die, lived, while those who deserved life, died. It was why mortals believed "only the good die young". It wasn't that he favored "bad" people over "good" people—like Death, Time is unbiased to that sort of thing—he was just bored easily, and gave more attention, more *time*, to mortals who *kept* his attention. But don't think of him as a terrible, heartless being.

Not entirely, anyway. In the eyes and opinions of mortals, he probably needed to straighten out his priorities, but he couldn't help the way he was, as much as you or your nosey next-door-neighbor can help the way she is. Morty liked to have fun, and, in this world, fun tended to be the bad stuff.

Church—*bor-ing*.

Drinking—fun!

Structure—*bor-ing*.

Chaos—fun!

Morty ended lives, yes, but he wasn't, and never had been the direct cause of any death. That job went to someone else, a million or more someone elses.

The Someone Elses gave a person cancer, caused a car accident, influenced a man to murder his wife, and hardened a person's arteries. The Someone Elses were the "bad ones", the ones who mortals should blame for life being "unfair". Not Morty or myself.

I know what you're thinking: But what about kids? How could Time be so cruel to children?

Nobody knows this about Morty Finch, but he has a soft spot for children. There is a reason so many die at such young ages. Because Morty knows that what's on the Other Side waiting for *them*, is what their parents make themselves believe. It's true. The Afterlife—for children, not everybody—is, literally, Paradise, Heaven, whatever you prefer to call it. And this world, this life, this reality, is not that far from being Hell. When a child dies, he or she gets a one-way, all-expense-paid ticket to bypass the place the rest of you go when you die. Because they're innocent, and the rest of you are mostly tainted pieces of shit.

Frank pushed air through his lips. "And you know this *how*, where kids go and such?" Frank jumped off the fictional train a long time ago, but he was being a good sport. I liked Frank.

I popped another peanut into my mouth, and answered, chewing: "Because I've seen it. I take them there every day."

Frank's brows rose and he nodded in slow-motion. *(Wow, I really have heard it all—Looney. Fucking. Toons.)* "Ah, well okay then," he said out loud.

So, Morty forgave me that day for riling him up about the one thing that bothered him the most: the truth about his existence. He did it all the time—riled me up, per se—just by being who he was, or leaving certain kinds of souls for me to reap that literally made my skin crawl. We were like brothers who were also rivals: we were close, but we always hit the other where it hurt most.

"So," I said to Morty, "what did your 'epiphany' have to do with me?"

Morty smiled, the kind of smile that claimed to have just thought of the Best Idea Ever.

"Well, I figured since there's so much we don't know, because *Some*one"—his eyeballs rolled upward toward the sky—"is too selfish to tell us, that maybe we should test the boundaries, play a little game to see for ourselves if what we've been led to believe is true."

I turned around with my back and elbows against the railing—Morty had finally gotten my attention. I may have been the opposite of Morty Finch, a prude even by his standards, but I certainly wasn't a fossil.

"What kind of game?" I asked, very interested.

Morty's face brightened and darkened simultaneously. Brightened because he knew he had me where he wanted me. Darkened because...he knew he had me where he wanted me.

He leaned against the railing.

"No one can beat either of us, Mr. Boone," he began. "No one can escape us. In the end, we always win, you and me. They can run, but we always catch up to them. They cheat us every now and then, but we *always* win." He looked over. "So, if that's true, that neither Death nor Time can ever be beaten, then why don't we compete against *each other*?" He leaned in closer—my head was spinning with the possibilities; I couldn't even look at him.

"If we are truly equals," he said at last, "then no matter what we do, no matter how we play the game, there can be no winner."

After a moment:

"I'm listening."

About that time, Morty's companion reappeared with a sloppy chili dog nestled in a paper cradle. Irritated by the interruption and put-off by her presence, I couldn't help myself. "Get rid of the whore, Morty," I grumbled. I looked right at her then. "You don't wear your skin well, honey; it's too loose on you, like that chasm of a hole between your legs. No one will ever love you, few even want to touch you, and the ones that do only do it because they're as repulsive as you are." I stepped closer to her, my eyes fixed on hers as they shrank under a veil of anger and humiliation. "Now, give Morty his chili dog and go find a pipe to smoke."

She didn't move for a moment; only her rapidly blinking eyes.

And then—*smack!*—her hand fell across the side of my face so hard that Death actually saw spots.

"Bastard!" With gritted teeth and one balled fist, the woman threw Morty's chili dog at his feet, turned on her sky-high heels and stomped away without tripping. I watched as a small crowd of onlookers parted for her.

That was one of my problems, you see: my "emotions" were often affected by those of the living—technically, they weren't my emotions at all, but theirs. Mash that together in a bowl with a quarter-cup of my inability to tell a lie, and you get someone who says all the things you've ever wanted to say but were too afraid to. Someone you never want to meet, because he will tell you all the things you already know about yourself, but you've spent a lifetime trying to ignore.

The things I said to Morty's companion were not just the thoughts and judgments and emotions of the crowd, though—they were mostly *her* thoughts and judgements about herself. The reason this part is important to the story is that it became an integral part of The Game, how my emotions were dictated by others, and how my inability to tell a lie or sugarcoat the truth would be my second greatest challenge. Next to my...deteriorating condition.

Morty looked down at the sad heap of chili oozing into the crevices of the floor.

"Welp, that's unfortunate," he said matter-of-factly.

Then he turned and propped his arms on the railing again; the onlookers finally went back to enjoying their Family Day at the pier now without Morty's unacceptable-in-society companion scarring the eyes of their children.

"What are you proposing?" I asked, eager to know about this idea of his, and intolerant to anymore interruptions. "What kind of game?"

He smiled over at me; the cigarette he had been smoking now burned to the filter, dangled from his mouth.

"What kind of death am I incapable of choosing its time?" he began.

"Suicides," I answered.

"Precisely!" He pointed his index finger upward. "I can't do anything about the ones who take their own lives, the ones who die before their time."

"Okay..." I wanted him to get to the point.

"But I *can* influence their decision," he went on. "Just like you, I can persuade mortals; I can fill their heads with thoughts enough to put us on level playing ground."

I already knew this; I wondered why he was telling me.

"I don't follow."

He placed his hand on my shoulder.

"Let's see how many lives you can save," he whispered near my ear, looking out at the ocean, "while I work against you to end them."

23

All right, so maybe Morty *was* a terrible, heartless being. But Morty was Morty, and he wasn't human, so in a way he got a pass. I did say he liked to play games with mortals. They were chess pieces to him. Besides, if you were forced to work the same job for eternity, you'd probably find a way to make scrubbing toilets more interesting, too.

"Wait a second," I said. "Why am I the one who needs to save them? Better yet, how am I supposed to do that? Do I look like someone who rushes to the aid of a suicide?"

Maybe I was as heartless and terrible as Morty Finch.

"I have no misgivings about cutting a cord, Allister," he said. "But you, on the other hand, would rather I didn't most of the time. You feel violated with all those souls creeping around inside of you, so I figured you'd jump at the opportunity to try and prevent it." He shrugged. "And I have a few ideas about how you can pull it off—no superhero cape required."

"Hmm." I thought about it. "What kind of ideas?"

The grinding snap of a lighter was brief as he set the end of another cigarette aflame; the ember glowed and crackled as he took a long drag.

"Well," he began, "you could disguise yourself as their loved ones, use the body so you can talk some sense into them."

"Absolutely not." I shook my head and slashed a hand in the air in front of me. "I don't like touching them, and you suggest I *wear* them like a *suit*? The one I'm wearing is bad enough. You're as cracked as you look, Morty Finch. Besides, even if I did that, I'd have to *act* like the loved one, and, well, I think we both know that's not going to play out well."

Morty chewed on the inside of his cheek contemplatively. And then he nodded. "Yeah, I guess you're right. For someone who feels no love, *as* a loved one, you're more likely to drive them to their death than steer them from it."

Both of us stared into oblivion for a few minutes, the gears in our heads grinding. The greasy stains on the floor faded in and out of my vision as my mind tried anxiously to find the answer. I had already been sold on the game—Morty could sell bibles to the Devil—so I was determined to make this idea work. After all, I was bored with scrubbing toilets.

"What about you just go to them as you are," he said, "tell them the truth, and then try to convince them that life's worth livin'?"

I shook my head.

"As they are fickle," I explained, "they're also delicate and weak, even the strong ones. They don't believe in such things, and to show them can be traumatizing. Besides, the whole thing would turn out to be about me doing magic tricks to prove to them I am who I say I am. They'd start with the damned questions: *What's the meaning of Life? Why are we here?* I'm not interested in becoming the interviewee."

"No superhero cape?"

"No," I grumbled.

Another minute in oblivion.

And then:

"What about a psychiatrist?" a sultry, familiar voice said.

4

Vanity stood against the railing as if she'd been there all along. She *had* been, I realized, because she knew all about the conversation. It didn't surprise me; Vanity enjoyed spying, but she enjoyed butting-in even more.

She sashayed toward us; long, black hair tumbled over her left shoulder, leaving her plump cleavage exposed in the skin-tight red dress she wore that hugged her curves to her thighs. She was tall and lithe and beautiful and I enjoyed her company about as much as I enjoyed Morty's. Maybe less than.

Morty stepped up, took her delicate hand into his and pressed his lips just above her knuckles.

"Always a pleasure to see you, my dear," he said.

"Oh, I know, Morty," she said. "I *am* quite the pleasure." She held her head high to appear as important as she felt.

A group of young women stopped to admire their reflections in the cameras of their cell phones. "Ohh! Ohh! Selfie!" one of them said, and they huddled together in front of the phone like the irresistible beauties they knew they were, pooched out their lips and had sex with the lens before the shot was frozen in time for all of social media to see.

Vanity smiled, always proud of how easy and *fabulous* it was to be her.

Then a couple walked by; the girlfriend stared Vanity down.

(God, I wish I looked like her.)

In the three seconds they took to glide by, admiration turned to jealousy, and with a disapproving sneer the girlfriend gripped the boyfriend's hand.

(That bitch should put on some clothes), the girlfriend thought.

"You should put on some clothes," I told Vanity.

She dismissed me with the roll of her eyes.

"And you should change your name from Death to Conformity, you accommodating little monster." Her demon tongue snaked out and licked my cheek two-feet away.

I breathed in deep and just let it go. Provoking Vanity wasn't one of my favorite things to do, because the narcissistic souls of the mortals she infected were one of my least favorite to reap.

She turned her stunning blue eyes on Morty, the one of us who liked to feed her gargantuan ego. She circled him like a cat around its slave's legs, purring and rubbing herself against him, knowing she could get him to do anything she wanted.

"A psychiatrist, you say?" Morty asked eagerly. "*Do* tell." He hooked a hand at her waist and inhaled deeply of her scent. I wondered if Lust was around somewhere, too, waiting for the opportunity to stick his nose in where it didn't belong—yes, Lust is a male, believe it or not.

Vanity smiled like the serpent she was.

"Of course," she said. "It's the *per*fect disguise"—she glanced at me—"especially for someone like Death."

"Someone like me?"

"Someone who cannot love or feel love," she said. "Someone who is unbiased and can offer a truthful, unbiased opinion, but most of all someone who knows the inner-workings of mortals more than anyone." She pointed at me. "Am I wrong in saying you are more intimate with them than any of us are? I mean"—she grinned—"you *are* the only one of us who carries those poor, pathetic souls around with you long after we've wiped our hands and scrubbed our eyes clean of them." She shook her head and clicked her tongue. "I do so feel pity for you, Allister Boone."

She felt pity like I felt love.

Morty's eyes were wide and filled with wonder; he massaged his chin with his rough fingertips again, and he paced; the lightbulb above his head glowed brighter and brighter.

He stopped. "She's right," he said. "It's the perfect setup. I was thinking you could just meet these people in a bar—you know all the sad souls who go to bars to drown their sorrows in whiskey—but you'd have to go to them, and that'd probably get awkward real fast. Nobody goes around offering a shoulder in bars—they're there to drink!"

"And, as we all know," Vanity put in, "Allister isn't known for his…social skills." She smiled.

"Right," said Morty with one hard nod. "As a psychiatrist, you won't need to fake social skills to mingle with people—they'll come to *you!*" Morty's face lit up. "And with their sad problems for you all laid out like a deck of cards in Vegas!" He looked me right in the eyes. "All you'd have to do is pretend, listen, and then play the hand accordingly."

I had to admit, I liked the idea. Maybe not as much as Morty and Vanity, because there was one blaring kink in the plan.

I pushed away from the railing. "You seem to forget," I said, pacing, "that I cannot lie. This 'perfect' plan might actually be the *worst* plan. Maybe neither of you understand the job of a psychiatrist—they are expected to *help* people off the ledge, not send them right over it."

Morty looked to Vanity. "He does have a point."

Vanity stepped up to me, brushed the back of her fingers along my jawline. "You're smart, Allister—almost as smart as I am," she said as she walked around me. "You'll figure it out. I know it'll work. But if you can think of something better"—she opened her hands in front of her and tilted her head to one side—"then by all means."

When I didn't respond to her *marvelous* explanation, she crossed her arms underneath her breasts and smirked. "I have to say, I never took you for the type who backs down from a challenge."

I knew Vanity was trying to manipulate me, but I had made up my mind to do it three seconds after she'd arrived— even despite the blaring kink. Maybe I was just bored, desperate even, to step out of the monotony of my existence, I didn't know, but I would do it. And I knew, too, that my personality put me at a disadvantage, and would pave the road for Morty to jump ahead of me early-on in the game. And it did. I lost two people in the first few weeks of my new position in the universe as Allister Boone M.D..

But as I stood there, contemplating a decision I'd already made, I thought about how ridiculous it all was. And how familiar. Morty and I had participated in some outlandish ideas in the past: a failed one that resulted in the Mandela Effect, which didn't have the effect we were going for (Frank, the bartender, was actually from a different reality, but that's another story); Tachypsychia; and our little stunt with the 2015 Large Hadron Collider test that threw the dimension off track and, inadvertently, resulted in the 2016 United States presidential election, and the unusually long list of celebrity deaths that followed.

Throughout our existence, Morty and I have always competed with one another, but never with any real intention of beating the other. Something like that never crossed our minds because it was impossible, unheard of. But to actually test the boundaries, see if we could prove that what we had been led to believe since the Beginning, was true—Oh, I was all for it!

Frank had been wishing he'd turned on his cell phone's voice recorder back when I told him about how I'd seen the place mortals call Heaven; he stood there now, a blank look on his face that did not do well to hide the thoughts behind it.

(This guy is a fucking nut-job. Seriously. A fucking nut-job! Ha-Ha!)

"So…I take it you agreed?" Frank asked out loud. He believed none of this nonsense, but he liked his job as a bartender more every day, because he was never bored— maybe I should've been a bartender.

"Of course I agreed," I answered. "And Vanity was right: it *was* the perfect idea." I looked over at Morty and smiled victoriously. "Because, despite what they thought— and I was sure they thought I was setting myself up for disaster—I am, for lack of a less-stinging word, *winning*."

Morty grumbled something under his breath, swigged down another shot, and set the empty glass on the bar. Frank went to fill it again, but Morty put up his hand.

He went for another cigarette instead.

"Okay," Frank said. "So, then how does it work exactly? And were there any rules?" He believed none of it, sure, but he couldn't deny himself the pleasures of the story.

Mortals and their fiction—they love it more than "reality". Most spend more time daydreaming about things they'll never have, places they'll never see, events that will never happen, worlds that can never exist. They are often lost in these places inside their heads; they read books to escape, watch movies, play games, dress up as furry animals. Mortals are always pretending to be someone else, some*thing* else, some*where* else. If you ask one thousand people if they're happy with their lives, or if they could be somebody else who would they be, or if they could go anywhere in the world where would they go, approximately two would answer: I'm perfectly happy; I wouldn't want to be anybody else; there's no place I'd rather be than home. And those two would be liars.

"Rules were simple," Morty said. "Any death involving the suicide of one of his patients is considered a point for me. And no bringing anybody back to life."

"And how it works," I began, "is that Morty chooses the targets and sends them to me. Because it's not his job to inflict a mental or emotional disorder, he must choose those who have already been inflicted by the Someone Elses."

"But can't he just...end their time before you can change their minds?" Frank asked.

"No—weren't you *listening*?" Morty cut in; clearly all that losing was affecting his mood. "I ain't got no say in someone who chooses to end it before their time."

"But why not?" Frank asked.

"I don't *know* why," he said. "It's just the way it is. They choose their own time."

"So...then you don't have power over them...?" Frank's brow hitched up.

Morty slammed his fist on the bar; the whiskey glass vibrated.

Oh boy, Frank was treading dangerous waters.

Morty did everything he could to keep from throwing a tantrum or touching Frank and watching him fall to the floor like a slab of meat. Frank had a bad heart, and it was only a matter of time before it gave out on him—it was only a matter of Morty. But Morty liked Frank, and as I mentioned, his favorite bar was Brisbane's, and since Frank owned it, killing him would mean Morty would have to find another favorite bar. I suspected Frank was safe also because, despite the outburst, Morty was in a fantastic mood. I hadn't forgotten how complacent, smug even, he was when I'd first arrived. It concerned me somewhat, whatever it was he'd wanted to meet me at Brisbane's about, but I figured I'd deal with it when he got around to that part.

Frank found Morty's outburst amusing; he raised both eyebrows, pursed his lips.

"So, he chooses the targets," he said.

I nodded. "He influences them to seek 'help'," I explained, quoting with two fingers. "Inserting my name into their heads to steer them in my direction. They set up an appointment and I take it from there."

Frank's index finger moved back and forth between Morty and me, as did his eyes. "He sends them to *you*, then *you* try to convince them that life is worth living, while *he* works against *you* to convince them that they should just end it."

"Yes."

"And if one offs themself, Morty gets a point."

"Yes."

"And if they live, you get a point."

"Yes."

"But what if they die before their time *later*? How long do you have to wait before you can count a point as a point?"

"If I can change their minds enough that they are clearly better off than when they came to see me, then it counts as a point for me. If they slide later, and decide to end it, then I lose the point."

Wrinkles of confusion tightened in Frank's forehead. "But something like that could go on...forever. I mean—"

"We set the deadline at three hundred sixty-five days. One mortal year," I said. "At the end of the three hundred sixty-five days, we'll tally up the score." I glanced over at Morty puffing on his cigarette. "A score that, so far, is leaning heavily in my corner."

Morty smirked.

"But not for long," he said. "Now to the reason I brought you here."

Yes, I was concerned, but I pretended otherwise.

I motioned a hand, palm up, offering him the floor.

He took it.

"You've been winning, yeah," he said. "So, to make things more interesting, I've employed help."

"You mean, you're trying to cheat," I accused.

"It's not cheating," he said, and his smug, complacent smile returned. "There was never any rule that said either of us couldn't get outside help."

Metaphorically, I kicked myself because that was true.

"Okay, so then who's helping you?"

His smile stretched across his wrinkled face like the sun on the horizon of a new day.

"The Someone Elses," he revealed, and my empty black heart sank into my anal canal.

"Elses as in *plural?*" I asked.

He beamed. "Elses as in plural," he confirmed.

I shook my head, then tapped the bar with my fingertips. "I think I'll have that drink now, Frank."

"Sure thing."

I should've known better than to trust that Morty Finch could get through this without some kind of shortcut.

"Okay," I said with a sigh, "when does the cheating begin exactly?"

Morty laughed. "The first *perfectly legal piece* has already been put into play," he said. He hopped down from the barstool, lit another cigarette. "Gluttony is working on your girl as we speak."

"My girl?" I slid off my barstool too.

"Margot Henry," he said. "Gluttony is with her right now, helping her down a gallon of mint chip. Afterwards, they might hop over to Red's for a burger and free refills on fries. When Gluttony's done with her, I'll ease my way back into her life, and whisper sweet nothings in her ear."

"Why can't you just play fair?"

It was unfair because Morty knew my chances of also employing the Someone Elses were exceptionally low. The Someone Elses' jobs were to end lives, not to save them. And they loved their jobs like priests love little boys.

"Nothing in the rules says you can't hire someone too, Allister."

I tightened my lips and shook my head at him.

"And just who exactly would I get to help me?"

Morty shrugged, grinned with the cigarette dangling from one corner of his mouth. "Dunno," he said, and then walked past me. "But you better figure it out soon"—he tapped his finger against his watch—"Time always catches up, Mr. Boone."

The little bell above the door jingled as he exited the bar.

"So, he brought you over here just to tell you that?" Frank asked, wiping the bar down with a dishcloth. "Couldn't he just call?"

"No," I said as I fingered the cash in my wallet and set a twenty on the bar. "Morty likes to show off; he always has. And he wouldn't miss the chance to see the look on my face when he told me."

"So, what are you gonna do?" Frank took the twenty and stepped over to the register.

"I'm going to find a way to up the ante. Keep the change, Frank."

I left and went back to meet with my two o'clock, already expecting it to end like my eleven o'clock. Because I was Death, blunt-force-trauma, and my tongue was a bag of hammers, and I really had set myself up for disaster when I agreed to this.

THE PIECES

5

Jason Layne was a twenty-five-year-old man who recently quit his job at a truck-stop convenience store. Alone except for his dear sister's loving company, which sometimes suffocated him but he'd never tell her that because he was afraid she'd leave him like everybody else had in his life. His mother died when he was eighteen. His father abandoned them on Jason's eighth birthday. His first girlfriend cheated on him with his only best friend. His second girlfriend left him for a woman. He had no third girlfriend or a second best friend, and his trust issues were so deep he was afraid to leave his shopping cart outside the restroom in the grocery store because he just knew someone would steal it.

And Jason was dying. Stage Four prostate cancer. He'd known something was wrong long before his diagnosis, but because the internet—and even his doctor—told him that prostate cancer was unlikely because of his young age, he was never screened. And, like so many people, his "knowing something was wrong" wasn't enough to convince him to go to the doctor until after it had started to spread. For months, Jason consumed large amounts of cranberry juice and popped Cipro and Macrobid and later D-Mannose because the people on the Natural Remedies web site told him how much safer it was than antibiotics. Now his hair was growing back after several failed rounds of chemotherapy, and the only thing left in his arsenal of meds and natural remedies anymore were the end-of-life kind.

He brought a calendar with him to our first session, but he wasn't ready to explain its significance yet. And even though I already knew what was in it, I did not press him. He would get around to it eventually, I was certain.

He sat across from me in what I had secretly dubbed The Electric Chair. He was pale and skinny and his hands looked like bones with a layer of cheese cloth draped loosely over them.

I knew somebody like him, with no hope left, would never spend their last days talking with somebody like me. I could do nothing to help change his life, make it better, steer him in a more promising and rewarding direction. There were no medications I could prescribe that would prolong his days. Jason Layne was going to die. And there was nothing anyone could do about it.

So then why was he here, staring at the wall in my office, that important calendar on his lap caged like a bird beneath his skeletal fingers? Because he *was* suicidal. He literally had nothing left to live for but a short prison sentence of pain that would feel like a lifetime's worth. And also, because Morty had a terrible sense of humor.

I pitied Jason Layne. Of course, I only pitied him because everyone in the building who saw him on his way to my office, pitied him. None knew what was wrong with Jason, but mortals tend to know when one of their kind is dying. And death tends to bring out the best in people. He'd received the silent condolences and stares of compassion on his way up the elevator, and as he sat in the waiting room, out of breath from the long walk down the hall, Nancy briefly left her job as my secretary to become Jason's personal assistant. She brewed a fresh pot of coffee for him, helped him fill out the paperwork, and then followed closely beside him on his way to my office.

Before she left me alone with him, she stabbed me to death with her eyes as she stood in the doorway.

But Nancy didn't need to worry. Much. Because of my—well, hers and everybody else's—pity for Jason Layne, my bag of hammers would stay closed for the most part.

"Tell me, Jason—it's okay I call you Jason?"

He nodded. "Sure. No one has ever called me Mr. Layne before, so that might be a little weird."

I nodded, too.

Folding my hands together on my desk, I leaned forward.

"Why did you choose to see me today?" I went off script for him.

He blinked. And then like most do, his eyes scanned my desk for the paperwork he'd painstakingly filled out moments earlier, in precise detail, so we could skip this part and get to the solution. But for Jason there was no solution, and he did not have the energy to complain, to ask why he wrote all that stuff down just so he'd have to repeat it verbally.

"I'm dying, Mr. Boone. Cancer," he answered in short-hand.

"I see." I pulled away from the desk and rested my back against the leather chair. "Well, then I suppose my next question would have to be what you think I can do to help you with that?" My inability to lie also meant that sometimes I had little perception of tact or sensitivity.

I expected Jason to react as most would: offended, if not hurt, but he didn't even flinch. I dug around inside his head, assuming he was just good at hiding his thoughts, but there were none of note on the matter. He simply did not care.

"I really don't know, Mr. Boone," he said. "I'm not even sure what I'm doing here. I-I don't feel like I need or *want* help. I-I mean, what could you possibly do, anyway?"

"Technically, nothing," I answered. "But you came here for *something*. Perhaps you know the reason deep-down, or maybe you don't know it yet and hope I can help you figure it out?" It was a question as much as it was an observation open for discussion.

He had come to see me because Morty Finch had basically told him to. But Jason Layne, like all mortals, could only be influenced to the extent they allowed it. If there was not some microscopic part of him, buried so deep not even he knew it existed, that wanted help, Morty's sweet nothings about visiting Allister Boone M.D. wouldn't have made it past Jason's ears, and I would've reaped his soul by now.

I scanned Jason's handwriting in front of me where he listed his family history and personal information; my eyes moved down to the yes or no checkmarks listed in different sections. *Have you ever heard voices that other people cannot hear? Have you ever felt that your thoughts were being read by other people? Have you ever felt that your mind was being taken over by someone else? Do you have any special powers that normal people lack? Do you feel that anyone else is to blame for your suffering? Have you had thoughts of ending another person's life? Do you feel hopeless about the future? Do you feel fearful about the future? Have you had thoughts of ending your own life? Do you feel lonely? Do you feel depressed? Do you feel angry? DO YOU FEEL ANYTHING AT ALL, JASON LAYNE?!* He answered no to everything. Though his checkmarks were inconsistent on "hopeless" and "fearful"; the pen didn't mark as hard, as if he was reluctant to check no, but decided to anyway.

Jason Layne was not the kind of person who felt sorry for himself; he didn't like to bring attention to his problems; he accepted everything in his life no matter how "unfair", and he believed he was owed nothing, that he was just a man with cancer and that it was nobody's fault. Next to Nancy's, his was the kind of soul I most liked to reap. Because it was so unlike all the rest.

People like him were as close to innocent as an adult mortal could be. Not sinless, because no mortal is sinless, but just innocent. He wasn't a murderer or a child molester or a manipulator or a sex addict; he wasn't violent, or greedy, or jealous, or lazy, or vain, or gluttonous, or vulgar or vile; he wasn't full of hatred or vengeance. He wasn't odd or perfect or too high or too low. His soul was…calm. Kind. Peaceful. Accepting. In a word, Jason Layne was a rarity. And a soul like his would make me feel more at peace, it would help to hush the voices in my head, calm the chaos. I wanted— needed—him to die. But not by suicide, because I don't keep suicide souls. So, it was just one more reason to save him from himself.

For someone like Jason, so accepting of death, he had to be here for something. I knew what it was, because I could feel it as he clutched that calendar—I could always sense when someone feared Me—but I still wanted him to be the one to tell me. It was all part of playing the role of his psychiatrist.

"Tell me about the calendar, Jason." I glanced down at it, and his fingers tightened around its worn edges.

He hesitated. He swallowed.

"Could I…do you have anything to drink?" he asked.

"Sure," I said, and got up myself to get it for him.

I broke the seal on the cap and set the water bottle in his reach on my desk.

He opened the bottle and took a sip; it was the first time he didn't have at least one hand clutching the calendar. After tightening the cap and taking his time about placing the bottle back on the desk, he reluctantly set the calendar down next to it and opened it to October. The Grand Canyon, spread out under a yellow-orange sunrise was the photograph of the month.

"The doctor gave me six months," he said, and he set his fingertip on the number three encased in a black-lined square; fluorescent-green highlighter marks filled the space unevenly. "October third will be exactly six months to the day when he told me."

I started to speak, but Jason was not finished, and this surprised me because he didn't seem much the talking-type and I thought I'd have to do most of it.

"But I know it's going to happen before October," he said.

He pulled back one page to reveal September. Lake Tahoe.

He pulled back another page. August. Yellowstone National Park.

July. Bryce Canyon National Park.

He stopped on June.

"I did a project on Crater Lake in elementary school," he said, looking down at the caldera lake with reflections of the cliffs that surrounded it. "I think I'm going to die in June." He left his hand on the calendar. "In two months. Not six."

"What makes you think you're going to die in June, Jason?"

"I just feel it, y'know?"

He sat back in his chair, and his hand fell away from Crater Lake and back into his lap. For the first time since that calendar walked into his life, he felt free of it. He had been waiting for a long time to tell someone what he was about to tell me.

"I've never been to Oregon," he began, "and I've never even thought much about that place throughout my life. It's one of those states you rarely hear about in the news, like Arkansas or Idaho. Anyway, I don't know why I chose Crater Lake in fourth grade. I could've picked anything. I didn't even know what Crater Lake was until that day I looked through the geography book in the library to decide on my project." He paused, looked off in thought at the window overlooking the city. "But the moment I saw it…it kind of…took hold of me, y'know?"—he balled one hand into a fist with conviction—"I worked hard on that project. I used lots of foil, and my mom bought some of those tiny trees from the hobby store. I didn't win. Lacey Devony won with Mount Saint Helens, and it was good; she deserved it. I didn't even win third place, but I didn't care, I was proud of my work and I took it home and set it on a milk crate in my room and I looked at it every night before I fell asleep. After about a week, I had forgotten it was there. After about a month, it had gotten knocked over at some point and I didn't bother to pick it up. And then one day I came home from school and saw that my room had been cleaned and that Crater Lake was gone. I never asked about it. But for the next sixteen years, I don't know why but it would always pop into my head." He stopped and licked the dryness from his lips, his gaze strayed from the window behind me and fell on the photograph of Crater Lake. "I never forgot it. Of all the things in my life, the one thing I consistently remembered and thought about was that project. Crater Lake."

He raised his eyes to mine.

"Isn't that strange?" he asked, but he wasn't necessarily looking for an answer.

"Why do you feel that Crater Lake has some kind of significance in the timing of your death?" *Are you planning to go there to commit suicide in June, Jason?* It was the real question, but again, I wanted to let him tell me in his own time, and in his own words.

Jason sighed, and he thought about it before answering.

"I had just left the doctor's office," he went on. "I was in shock. I couldn't drive myself because I couldn't see straight and I didn't want to kill anybody in an accident, so I hailed a cab and left my car on the parking deck. The cab dropped me off at the corner of Wilkes and Wilshire and I walked across the parking lot to the Walmart. I just didn't want to go home. So, I walked around the store, aimlessly, looking for nothing in particular, and hardly noticing anything or anyone except for the bright lights in the ceiling. I was almost run over by a lady with her shopping cart. Then another one. And then another. I felt like I was standing in the center of a busy intersection and cars were swerving to miss me; they honked and yelled at me to get out of the way. Somehow, I found my way out of the flow of shopping carts, and I stood there in a safe zone, catching my breath. I noticed

I was in the aisle with the framed art. I looked down and saw Crater Lake in black-and-white staring back at me." He paused to breathe; his expression grew more intense; he wasn't looking at me anymore but reliving that day. "I stared at that framed picture for the longest time. And then I ran out of the store."

He stopped.

I waited for him to go on but saw he needed help.

"What happened after that, Jason? Where did you go?"

He looked up.

"I went home," he said. "I don't even remember how I got there. Everything was different; nothing was the same anymore, not even the cozy atmosphere of my apartment. It seemed...darker. The bright-white walls seemed gray; the air freshener my sister had plugged into the outlets no longer had a smell—it would usually hit me in the face whenever I opened the door after being gone for eight hours. Everything was different, almost...fake."

It is *fake, my friend.*

Jason jumped ahead a little.

"I was sitting on a barstool in the kitchen when my sister came home. She didn't know about the cancer yet. She was humming a song as she walked through the living room with three plastic store bags on one arm, her purse on the other. She smiled at me as she set the bags on the counter. I smiled back. I think. I wasn't really sure. She told me about her day and asked me about mine. I told her my day was fine."

Jason looked lost in thought again, the corners of his eyes creased with focus.

I waited patiently.

"But it was like something else was there," he went on, "some*thing* or some*one* distracting my sister, because she always knew when I was sick, or aggravated about something at work. I always hid it but she always knew. It was strange that she didn't detect the slightest change in me when the most devastating thing in my life had just taken place a few hours before." He looked right at me. "Isn't that weird?" he asked, again not necessarily expecting me to answer.

"She started taking things out of the bags while she talked," he continued. "A new pair of scissors, a box of allergy medicine, batteries for the remote, cleaning stuff. And a calendar. *That* calendar"—he looked at the one between us, but he didn't touch it; he was done touching it—"I picked it up, and my sister's voice faded into the background. I opened it to October, and I stared at the number three until my eyes hurt. I flipped the pages back, and when I made it to June, I knew then. I knew that I would not make it to October."

6

Jason's story was finished, but he was not. He had questions, dozens of questions I hoped most he wouldn't ask because then I'd have to tell him the truth. I was banking on him being in a psychiatrist's office and realizing that some of those questions might make him seem "crazy". But if I had to answer any of them, then *I* would be the one who seemed crazy.

"Do you believe in fate, Mr. Boone?"

"Ah, yes, Fate," I said. "I do believe in Fate."

Jason waited for me to elaborate, but I was not going to unless he directly asked.

"Why do you believe in fate?" he directly asked.

I rested my elbows on the chair arms and interlocked my fingers above my lap, my right ankle propped on my left knee.

"Why do you believe in *me*, Jason?"

He looked confused.

"Well, because you're sitting in front of me?"

"And I believe in Fate because I've seen them. Because I've sat across from them."

"Them?" he asked, his eyebrows gathered.

I nodded.

"There are three. Unbearable puppets, if you ask me."

Now he looked *thoroughly* confused—and I was beginning to look "crazy" to him.

I waved my hand in a dismissive gesture. "Fate is ridiculous," I told him. "If Fate were a human, they'd be the one sitting in my chair."

Jason just looked at me. "So...then you think it's ridiculous to believe in fate?" He was trying desperately to wrap his head around my answer.

"Yes, I think it's ridiculous to believe in Fate the way you people do."

He pondered it, and slowly his mortal mind gathered the illogical pieces to put together a logical explanation.

"Why did you ask me that particular question?" I said, turning the spotlight back on him.

His bone-white hands moved restlessly on the chair arms; he looked down into his lap, and then at the wall.

"Because it...well, it just seems strange. Crater Lake following me all my life."

I sighed.

"It followed you all your life, Jason Layne, because it was the first thing you loved about yourself, the first thing you coveted, the first event in your life that meant something to you, no matter how small and insignificant it seems to you now." I leaned forward on my desk, looked him in the eyes. "You *were* angry that Lacey Devony won first place, that you didn't even win third, because you worked *so* hard on that project. But you were a nice boy, brought up right your mother, and it wasn't hard for you to push that anger and jealousy down, mask it, make yourself believe sixteen years later that you were never angry or jealous at all. But that was the moment in your life that the *course* of your life changed, the moment when you lost your Innocence. That is why you've remembered it all these years." I pointed at the calendar on the desk between us. "That is why you're associating Crater Lake and the month of June with the timing of your death. Because it's natural for humans to grasp at straws when they're desperate, when something seems 'strange' or 'weird' or 'impossible' and you need to make sense of it, or when you know you're going to die and you want to understand *why*."

Jason stared at me blankly. A part of him was angry with me for not agreeing with him, for not believing in the one thing he'd so carefully constructed around himself to make him feel better about dying. He wanted to believe that fate existed, that because he was so close to death now, maybe somehow God had opened his mind a little more to the Unknown he was soon to face. He wanted to believe that because he was dying he was worthy to know more than those around him.

All mortals are born innocent. They grow up innocent, until the influence and strain of being surrounded by so much sin tears down their fragile walls as thin as the Earth's atmosphere, leaving them exposed to all the things that make them...unworthy. Their one-way tickets to Paradise ripped out of their hands. Gone forever.

The Crater Lake project was the moment when Jason's innocent child mind became open to the grown, guilty world around him. And now, as he sat there across from me, as I took away his feelings of worthiness, his *purpose*, he experienced what many do when on their deathbeds: animosity towards God.

(Why me? What did I do to deserve this...?)

But being a rarity, Jason immediately felt guilty afterwards, and he tried to erase what he'd thought.

(No, that's not right.) He shook his head, ashamed.

I folded my hands on the desk and leaned forward.

"Do you plan to travel to Oregon?" I asked.

He paused, glanced at the calendar.

"No, I uh...well, I hadn't thought about it before..."

He was lying.

"But now you're considering it?"

He paused again.

"No," he finally answered, deciding in that moment.

"Why not?"

"Why would I?"

To commit suicide.

"Fate?" I said out loud.

"But you don't believe in fate," he said, puzzled.

"This isn't about me," I told him. "What I believe has absolutely no bearing on your life, Jason. You, like everybody else, create your own path, your own fate, your own reality. How *you* see it is how you shape and mold it."

I stood up.

"Tell me," I began, pacing, "what were your thoughts on fate before you asked my opinion of it?" His eyes followed me. "What did you hope my answer would be, and why?"

"Well…I…I guess I did believe in fate," he began. "I mean I *do*. But not the you-can't-escape-it kind, a set path for everybody, an all-roads-lead-to-the-same-destiny"—he shook his head—"I don't believe in that because it doesn't make any sense." He gestured his hands. "If there is a God, or just somebody up there moving us all around like chess pieces, what point is there in walking a path that can't be changed? What's the point of playing a game you already know the end results?"

I nodded, agreeing.

"But I do believe in…"—he struggled to find the right words; he reached up and scratched the back of his head—"…signs, Mr. Boone. Small, but monumental events. It's *fate* we see them, that they can lead us to the answers, but it's up to us to notice them, to try and understand them, and to *find* the answers." He lifted his back from the chair and added with conviction: "And I believe that Crater Lake has more meaning in my life than a milestone that marked the descent of my innocence."

I was impressed.

Jason Layne had taken back the control. He felt worthy again, and this time it would be harder to convince him otherwise.

But that was a good thing—I wasn't *trying* to convince him otherwise. His unexpected surge of energy and strength played in my favor. Because it meant he was less-likely to end his life before his time. He wanted to understand the things he called "signs", to unravel the clues, and he couldn't do that if he was dead. I just had to convince him to keep trying. Because he was still suicidal, despite what he wanted. The tightrope he walked was as thin as a strand of hair.

"What did you hope my answer would be, and why?" I repeated.

"I don't really know," he said.

"You wanted me to agree with you," I told him. "You needed validation from someone else so you'd feel more confident in your own belief."

"Yeah. I guess that's it."

I sat down on the end of my desk in front of him and I looked at him.

"That makes you pathetic," I said, and he blinked. "Needing validation from others makes you as weak and simple-minded as everybody else. Mortals are like dogs— except dogs are innocent and more deserving than humans will ever be—they don't do anything without permission; they're always following in someone else's shadow; they beg to be fed and watered and loved and paid attention to; they are loyal to those who own them. In your last days, Jason, don't be a pathetic, weak, simple-minded mortal. Free your mind from the collective and be yourself. Think for yourself. Believe in yourself. And stop wasting the fucking air."

Blink. Blink. Blink. Blink.

Jason's gaze strayed toward the large window overlooking the city again. He thought long and hard about my comments. He wanted to be mad, to feel offended, to point a Margot Henry finger at me and tell me to go fuck myself. But he couldn't, rarity and all.

Then he looked at me and nodded slowly. "You're right," he said. "So, what do you suggest I do, Mr. Boone?"

"What are your intentions?" I countered. "Why did you come here to speak with me?"

Are you suicidal, Mr. Layne? Do you plan to kill yourself at Crater Lake in June, Mr. Layne? I still wanted him to be the one to say the words.

He swallowed again, but it wasn't because his throat was dry.

"I had planned to go to Crater Lake," he began, "in June. And…well, I was going to…"

Yes?

Just say it. I will not have you committed; it's not as easy to do as most people think.

Hellooo? Is there anybody in there?

"I was going to kill myself," he finally answered.

"How long have you been planning to do this, Jason?"

"Not long. A week. Maybe."

I stood from the end of the desk and went back to my chair on the other side.

"Is that what you think your signs of fate were about?" I asked, sitting down. "To kill yourself? Does it make sense to you after twenty-five-years of life, to end it early, to walk a path that can't be changed, play a game you already know the end result?"

Insight dawned on his tired face.

But then he countered: "But I'm already walking a path that can't be changed—I'm going to die, no matter what I do."

"You're *all* walking that path," I said. "You're *all* going to die no matter what you do. But none of you know when, or technically how; none of you know what will happen between that time and now, therefore you're not walking a path that can't be changed or playing a game you already know the end result. But if you kill yourself, you *will* be."

"But death is always the end result."

"Then it's everyone's *fate* to die, and that's all it means. And you believe in fate, but it's the you-can't-escape-it kind, the set-path for everybody. And those signs you spoke

50

of mean nothing, therefore Crater Lake means nothing, and you have no purpose, Jason Layne."

His mouth snapped closed. He looked down at his hands.

My movements and a sharp breath changed the atmosphere in the room as I reached for my notepad on the desk. "I want you to do something for me," I said as the pen scratched the surface of the paper. "I want you to spend the next two months here, in New York. And I want you to pursue five things you've always thought about, but never pursued, things like Crater Lake. I'm not talking about taking a trip to Italy, or riding the world's scariest rollercoaster, or skydiving—remember, they have to be things *you've* always thought about, not things everybody else generally wants to do. It doesn't matter what it is, big or small or even illegal— do it, seek it out." I continued to jot down my instructions.

"You want me to do…a *bucket list*?" He scratched his temple with a fingertip.

"Sure, if that's what you want to call it." I tore the sheet from the notepad and slid it across the desk to him. "But don't think of it as a list of things to do before you die; it's more a list of things you've always *thought about* but never pursued further."

"Isn't that basically the same thing?"

"Is Crater Lake the same thing as looking at beaded tits in the French Quarter?"

Finally, he understood.

"So, you want me to…pursue other potential signs?"

"Are you looking for validation again, Mr. Layne?" My eyes locked on his. "Just. Fucking. Do it."

He took the paper, looked at it, contemplated it.

"Why two months?" he asked.

"Because after two months is over, it'll be July. And July is Bryce Canyon National Park. Not Crater Lake."

I stood, changing the atmosphere in the room again with my sudden movements.

"Seems our hour is up," I said.

51

"Wow," he said after a moment, "where'd the time go?"

Yeah, Morty, where'd the time go? I could almost hear him laughing.

Jason stood, folded the paper once and stuffed it in the pocket of his jeans. He wasn't sure yet what had just happened, but he couldn't deny there was something about it he liked.

With any other patient, that would be a good sign, giving them something to look forward to, giving them hope for the future. But nothing like that was going to change the fact that Jason Layne would die before he turned twenty-six, and that his last days would be painful.

I could only hope the assignment I'd given him would keep him busy long enough...just long enough.

Nancy opened my office door just as Jason and I were stepping out. She had a look of warning on her face, but it had nothing to do with Jason Layne this time.

"You've got a visitor," she said, holding open the door for us. She waited until Jason passed by to whisper: "And you deserve whatever you get from this."

Margot Henry stood in the waiting room, chunky arms crossed tightly over her double Ds, a sheet of paper clutched in her hand. She glowered at me, and her puffy cheeks were red with splotches that spread down her neck like a rash.

She held up the paper. "Care to explain this?" she demanded.

Nancy shot me a look, and already knowing what to do, she urged Jason to the reception desk.

"I'd like to see Mr. Layne again in one week," I instructed.

While Nancy tended to Jason's next appointment date trying to keep him occupied, the livid Margot Henry was on the verge of making a scene. I gave Margot my full attention.

"Would you like to talk about it in my office?" I offered, hand out, gesturing toward the door.

Margot smirked. "Oh, sure," she said, and strutted toward me. "Don't want other patients to know how much of an asshole you are."

Jason Layne pretended not to have heard, but a deaf person could've heard.

I escorted Margot into my office and closed the door.

7

It had been one week since I'd seen her at our first—and I thought our last—session together. Seeing her today was a sour surprise.

"How can I help you, Miss Henry?" I went around my desk and sat down. "I have about fifteen minutes before my next session."

She waddled over and slammed her hand on the desk, the paper crumpled underneath her palm.

I glanced at it long enough to acknowledge it.

"You had the nerve to send me a *bill?*" She opened the paper all the way and set it in front of me, tapped it with her fingertip in emphasis. "I was here all of five minutes before your arrogant, insensitive, poor-excuse-for-a-psychiatrist ass ran me *out!*" Her voice cracked.

"It's not my fault, Miss Henry, that you chose to leave early."

"*Chose?*"

Blink. Blink. Blink. I considered keeping eyedrops in the office along with the tissues for my clients.

She pressed her palms against the top of my desk and leaned forward, her eyes swirling with ire.

"Yes," I said. "You agreed to the time, you knew it would last one hour, you arrived and then you *chose* to leave early. No one here, certainly not me, forced you to leave."

She gritted her teeth.

54

"But I wasn't here for the full hour—I shouldn't be charged for it."

"The session you agreed to," I explained calmly, "was also a reservation, Miss Henry. A reservation is a time in which you *reserve*, meaning no one else can fill that slot, which means you are responsible for the bill in-full."

Her face turned blood-red; I thought if she grinded any harder that her teeth might break off in her mouth.

I pointed at the wall behind her. "There is a notice in the waiting room, in big, bold, black letters, Trebuchet font, that states: **A 48-HOUR CANCELLATION NOTICE IS REQUIRED, OR YOU WILL BE CHARGED IN-FULL FOR YOUR RESERVED SESSION FEE**. The same notice was on the paperwork that was mailed to you the following business day after you called and scheduled the appointment. And four days before your appointment, my secretary, Nancy, gave you a courtesy call to remind you of the appointment, and also of the required forty-eight-hour cancellation notice."

Her eyes grew the width of the sockets; her nostrils flared.

"How was I supposed to know beforehand," she said, leaning forward on the desk, "that you were going to be the biggest asshole I've ever had the displeasure of meeting in my life? And I've met some serious assholes, trust me."

"I'm well aware," I told her matter-of-factly. "You hate yourself so much that you attract 'assholes' like you attract dress sizes. Why didn't you settle this with my secretary?"

She slammed a fist down on the desk, rattling the pens jutting from a coffee mug that read "Keep Talking, I'm Diagnosing You" on the side.

"That's *it!*" She hit the desk again. "How *dare* you disrespect me! You're a *psychiatrist* for Christ's sake, in a field where people's lives hang by a thread every day. People come to you for help, not to be treated like shit, talked down to and made to feel even worse about themselves. You should be *ashamed* of yourself, Mr. Boone! You should—"

"Strength looks good on you, Miss Henry"—I opened my hand, palm up, and motioned toward the Electric Chair for her to have a seat—"just imagine how confidence would look. It might almost make you fuckable."

Her face said she wanted to knock my teeth down my throat, but shock rendered her motionless.

Brow raised, I gestured at the chair again.

(He's crazy...He actually thinks I'm going to...Is this guy serious? What the...)

She sat down, crossed her arms, her bulky red purse pressed beneath them; she cocked her head and chewed on the inside of her cheek.

"You practiced this in the mirror before coming here, didn't you?"

No answer.

"You've wanted to tell me off since you walked out that door last week," I went on, "and you haven't been able to get it out of your head. For seven days I've taken up more space in your mind than you could bear, and that's why you came here rather than calling, demanded to speak with me rather than explaining your problem to my secretary outside that door." I pointed at the door. "Because the only way you could be free of me, the only way you were going to have any kind of control over your life again was to put me in my place, to tell me what you're too afraid to tell the men in your life who come and go through the revolving door between your legs and leave nothing for you other than a string of broken promises and a thousand-pound weight of regrets pressing on your shoulders that threaten to crush you every day"—I leaned forward, my eyes boring into hers—"But the little control you thought you had over your life, the control you came here to reclaim, is just an illusion. You're the only person in this world who *doesn't* have control over you. Men control you. Women control you. The step-father who raised you and fondled you when you were a little girl, controls you. The mother who fat-shames you, controls you. The child you aborted controls you. Margot Henry controls nothing. Margot

Henry is a subservient sheep to society desperately seeking some shred of satisfaction in her self-proclaimed tragic life of...*sorrow*."

Silence. It stretched across the room like plastic pulled tight over a victim's face.

But the silence was the calm before the storm; two seconds later and Margot Henry's head was buried in her hands, her body quaking with sobs, her pudgy fingers pressing against her eyes.

I pulled a tissue from the box on my desk and handed it to her.

"Oh...so I'm...worth...a t-t-tissue now?" she cried, her breath catching between words. "A week ago, I...wasn't worth...a...b-bottle of water!" She snatched the tissue from my hand and swiped under both eyes, and then the snot from her nose.

"My two o'clock will be here in a few minutes," I told her, tapping my watch. "I'm willing to speak with you further, if you're willing to schedule another appointment. I never pass up a challenge." *Yeah, and that's what got me into this mess.*

Her mouth fell open with a little burst of air.

"O-Oh, and I suppose you still expect me to p-pay for the fifty-five minutes I never used, too?"

"Technically, forty-five," I said. "You just used ten minutes of my own time. But yes, I still expect you to pay for it."

Miss Henry got up; her purse strap fell over her shoulder but she barely noticed. She went toward the door, defeat washing over her.

"I'll make a deal with you," I spoke up before I lost her.

She stopped. And she kept her back to me.

"You come to my office every Tuesday, same time you came today, and I will allow you to make up that forty-five minutes with my fifteen minutes of freedom *(from the ridiculous perils of mortals)* to help you gain control of your life."

She turned and looked at me, the tissue still crushed in her hand.

"*Real* control, Miss Henry, not the kind you settle for."

Her thoughts grazed my offer with little to no actual consideration.

And then she turned and walked out.

When Nancy brought in my two o'clock minutes later, I stopped her before she closed the door.

"Did Miss Henry say anything to you before she left?"

Nancy glanced at my two o'clock, wanting to be herself and tell me off like she did every hour, but she couldn't for the sake of the patient.

"She paid her invoice," she answered. "She didn't say anything of note. Was she supposed to?"

"No," I said. "Thank you, Nancy."

She left me alone and I got to work on unintentionally ruining another person's life.

8

Morty Finch and his entourage of Someone Elses were working hard against me. In only two and a half weeks since I'd met Morty at Brisbane's, four more of my patients ended their lives before their time. Jason Layne and Margot Henry were not among the dead, but I could only contribute that to having had the opportunity to plant my seed of hope deep enough the Someone Elses couldn't so easily dig it up. Well, Jason Layne, anyway. I had no idea what was keeping Margot Henry alive. She didn't take my Tuesday offer and I hadn't seen her since she walked out of my office. Maybe it was because she wasn't suicidal despite what Morty told me. I never sensed it before she left; her thoughts only told me how much she hated me, and how much she hated herself. But there was nothing in her head about suicide, or death at all.

But the Someone Elses were, even by my unbiased, unsympathetic standards, cruel and brutal and went straight for the jugular. No thought. No remorse. No regrets. They were, after all, only doing what they were created to do. I had no problems with them before; they did their jobs and I mine; we stayed out of each other's way; I was used to it. I never liked reaping the majority of souls they doomed, but it was what it was, and I knew it always would be. Or so I thought.

Things were different now.

Working for Morty, thrilled at the chance to be a part of The Game—because even the Someone Elses got bored—they were working double shifts, and I was, literally, in a race against Time.

I had to do something to even the playing field.

But who in hell would ever help me? I was Death, trying to *save* lives—everything about that sounded ridiculous and contradictory. And I didn't exactly have any "friends" in the inner circle, at least none that would ever go along with my side of things. I was a loner, per se, and even the *Other* Someone Elses—the Seven Heavenly Virtues, the Angels—weren't exactly for saving lives, either. They were for saving *souls*. They were even more eager for mortals to leave this world and enter the Next Phase than the Seven Deadly Sins and their countless collaborators were.

In a word, I was *fucked*.

"You're fucked, Allister Boone," Pastor John Macon said.

We were sitting in the front row of his empty fifteen-thousand-capacity mega-church. It was 8:15 in the morning. A mass of living souls was already pressing in on me as they showered and dolled themselves up and put on their best jewelry and ate breakfast and had their morning coffee and got into their expensive cars and gossiped on the way to New Harvest Church in Dallas, Texas for 9:00a.m. service. I picked the worst day to come here. Sunday. The Day of Hypocrisy. The great gathering of sinners and doomed souls who thought they were buying their way into Heaven just by attending, and dropping a dollar in the collection plate to ensure Pastor John Macon and his wife could afford their ten-million-dollar home where they laid their heads at night, and their fifty-thousand-dollar cars that got them to church every week to spread the Word of God because God chose *this* man to preach His Word and would *never* choose a poor man with nothing, who wanted nothing, believed that *something* was too much, who traveled with *no staff, no bag, no bread, no money, not even an extra tunic*. I was by no means "religious", but I was amazed daily at the sheer weakness and gullibility of mortals, how easily they were deceived. And by how many didn't care they were being deceived because they loved their sinful lives and welcomed any excuse to keep living them.

Pastor John Macon, like most evangelicals, was an intelligent mortal who led but could not be led, a man who filled his pockets with his mouth—and he *enjoyed* it.

Don't get the wrong idea—unbiased remember? I rather enjoyed Pastor John Macon's company. To his devoted followers and the world, John Macon was their Savior's Right Hand, His lips and His eyes; he was the one leading them to salvation. But John Macon was the epitome of a wolf in sheep's clothing. He was scalping tickets into Heaven. He was a liar and a manipulator and was most surely going to the place mortals called Hell and he was fully aware of it. But to me, he was exactly who he was; he wore no mask and told no lies; he was someone I could go to for an honest opinion. No tricks or games or hidden agendas. But most of all, John Macon was human. He was one of few mortals who knew who and what I was, and it was nice to chat with someone with a human's perspective about the effect immortal entities such as myself had on the mortal world.

"That's some mess you got yourself into, Allister," he told me after I'd explained everything. "Morty never was one to play fair, you know that." He opened his hands. "Look at *me*," he said. "I've been on borrowed time for the past five years, and you know what he got outta me to pay *that* debt. 'Entertain me, *amigo*! Put on your Fool's hat and your pointy boots and dance for me!' That's what he said. I was all for it. Until I wasn't anymore. There's always a price, Allister Boone."

I looked around at the enormous building, the thousands of empty blue-velvet seats, the decorative carpet that stretched across the floors and climbed the steps all the way up into the balconies; the grand stage with light fixtures that rivaled any show any rock band had ever put on, and the tiny glass podium centered within it where Pastor John Macon performed his weekly ritual pretending to lead souls into Heaven when he was really just an actor putting on the show of his life to keep Morty entertained. And his pockets full.

Morty was not a happy camper when Jim Jones, Marshall Applewhite, and David Koresh ended their lives early. John Macon was basically one of their replacements. A more stable, levelheaded replacement, that was. There are two kinds of cult leaders: those who are perfectly sane and love wealth, and those who are perfectly *in*sane and love power. John Macon was the former. And Morty had had enough of the latter always offing themselves and ending the party early.

"Until you weren't anymore?" I inquired.

John nodded; he sat sideways on the seat beside me, his left arm propped on the back of the seat; he smelled like expensive cologne and cheap sex.

"Don't get me wrong," he said. "I'm not complaining about the rewards, just the work. It's *a lot* of damn work! Preaching to these people, feigning conviction, constantly having to come up with new ways to 'inspire' them, all while dodging the ones entirely unfooled by my performance. It's exhausting!"

I nodded. "I bet it is."

"So," John said with the curious tilt of his head, "whattya plan to do?"

"I was hoping you could help me out with that." Our voices were crisp in the vast, empty space.

"Me?" He chuckled, shook his head. "How am I supposed to help? Besides, the last thing I wanna do is get in Morty's way. There are way too many men out there like me—wouldn't want Morty looking to replace me, if you know what I mean."

"I'm not asking you to get directly involved," I said.

I wasn't sure what I had hoped to get out of John Macon. Maybe I expected nothing, and I just came for the conversation. Wouldn't be the first time.

John stood. He looked out at the massive building he owned, across a landscape of blue chairs and up at the balconies. He raised his arms out at his sides as if he were on the bow of a ship and the ocean winds were blowing through his hair. "*Look* at it," he said, looking at it. "The easiest way to make anybody want to stay in this Godforsaken world is with material things."

He dropped his arms at his sides and stepped into the aisle. I watched him, and I listened, because even though I was Allister Boone and one day I would reap his soul, too, Pastor John Macon was a man of many words that always made sense whether they were manipulative or honest. It was his greatest gift, his way with words, and as it was with all mortals, not even the *im*mortals were immune to the effects of their Gifts—it was their only weapon against us.

"Material," he went on. "That's what this world is all about, it's what holds it together. Money and all the things it can buy, power and all the people it can control, sins and all the emotions they can pleasure." He walked slowly toward the carpeted steps leading to the stage, his hands clasped on his backside. "Material is more than the things one can touch and taste and see—even love can be a material thing."

"Oh, please do explain, Mr. Macon," I insisted, eagerly—like I said, I enjoyed his conversation.

"Love," he said as he walked up the steps. "It's like me, Mr. Boone—a liar in a suit." He paced. "Suzanne Wilkes wants to be 'loved' so badly she cries herself to sleep at night. She dreams of picnics in the park with the *love* of her life, the clichéd proposal, the sparkling ring, walking down the aisle in her wedding dress. She doesn't want wealth or fame or any of that 'greedy' stuff—she just wants *love*! And she's so *angry*, Allister"—he turned on the top of the stage, a fist balled in emphasis in front of him—"because she just turned thirty-five and she's still single. She's so terribly depressed; she's jealous; she wonders why her friends are all married or engaged; she wonders what she's doing wrong, if she's ugly, if her blowjobs are up to par. She's angry that everybody else has what she doesn't have, what she wants the most, what she believes will make her happy—what she *deserves.*" He shook his fist, looked down at me, and he smiled. "Love is a material thing for Suzanne Wilkes because she views it as a possession, and just like a new car or a big house or a ten-thousand-dollar wedding dress, she wants love to fix her, to fulfill her, to bring her happiness, to make her feel pretty"—he pointed his index finger upward—"And what's the keyword in everything I just said?"

"Her," I answered.

"Exactly!" His eyes were alight with excitement. "*Her.* She wants love for herself, the same way a working-man wants a man-cave, or a rich socialite wants a new dog she can carry around in a fur-lined purse, or an Olympic skater who wants to win a gold medal." He waved a hand in a dismissive gesture. "Love, happiness, even knowledge become material things the moment any one of us want it or need it for ourselves. Doesn't matter how innocent it seems, or if we believe our 'heart is in the right place'"—he quoted with his fingers—"it's greed and envy and pride no matter how you look at it."

"You are correct," I told him, crossing one leg over the other and resting my arms on the back of the seats on either side of me. "Too bad you don't tell your devoted followers this stuff. Could be buying your own ticket into Heaven."

He rolled his eyes. "Reign in Hell. Serve in Heaven"—he opened his hands at his sides, palms up, and tilted them like scales—"And all that jazz, Mr. Boone."

If only you've seen Hell, Mr. Macon.

"But why the sermon, John?" I asked, going back to his speech.

He pointed at me.

"Because if you want to keep those patients of yours alive," he said, "then maybe you oughtta entice them with the things mortals love the most."

I shrugged, not sold on the idea.

"You need to cater to their wants," he went on, "not their needs—it's *so* much easier. Let one win the lottery. Send one a husband. Turn a dead sperm into a live one and give Sarah that baby she's always wanted. You have that power, Allister. And it might keep them alive long enough for you to win against Morty."

"I'm a psychiatrist, not a genie in a bottle," I told him. "And I'm unbiased, remember? I don't get involved like that. Just because I'm not limited to the boundaries that mortals are doesn't mean I should cross those boundaries. I just balance death and reap souls. It's what I've always done. Besides, I wouldn't...feel right about that."

John stood on the stage above me, wrinkles trying to set in his plastic Botox forehead.

"What?" I asked, confused.

"You wouldn't *feel right* about it?" He cocked a curious brow and looked at me sidelong.

I sighed, realizing. But I didn't elaborate because I didn't need to. And I didn't *want* to, either—the truth about my condition was always a tough pill to swallow.

"Souls are getting to you," John said, just like Morty had said.

I hated that. Not only that they were right, but that it was so damn obvious.

"Yes, I suppose they are. Hazards of the job." I stood up, slid my hands in the pockets of my dress pants. "But also, it feels like lying, and you know I never lie."

"Letting poor Sarah get pregnant is lying?" John asked.

"Sure it is," I answered. "It's not my job to make that happen; it's not my place to forcibly change the course of her life. It's cheating, just like giving someone the winning lottery numbers. And cheating rides the lying horse."

"Well," he said with pep in his step, "I say that's your ticket to the finish line, my friend. Morty will play whatever cards he has in his hand, *and* the ones up his sleeves"—he pointed at me—"It's probably time you break out of that committed repetition, Allister. Death gets cheated all the time. Maybe it's the hour Death fought back."

John Macon made a good case— evangelicals were a lot like lawyers, always finding the loopholes—but I still wasn't convinced. Thing was, I thrived on structure: I was a serial killer with OCD, a CEO with a Master complex, a strict mother with a germ phobia. I agreed to play the role of a psychiatrist, to try convincing my patients that life was worth living, to try fixing them with facts and the power of suggestion and influence, which was perfectly legal. I never intended to play dirty. And I sure as hell never intended to get my hands dirty, either. It was bad enough that my condition was worsening, that my connection to the souls I reaped was bleeding over into my unemotional self. To break out of myself that much more by becoming Morty Finch and the Someone Elses—*and* the mortals—wasn't an option. It was, well…suicide.

Wait—was that what Morty wanted? For me to push myself over the edge?

Hmm.

"You did say you didn't want to get in Morty's way, John. And here I thought you were an honest liar, my go-to-guy for when I needed mortal advice." I shook my head.

"What are you talking about?" he asked.

I walked up the steps and joined him on the stage. I looked out at the rows of empty seats, wondering if he was there, hiding in a shadow somewhere.

"All right, Morty!" I called out, my voice echoing across the room. "I know you're here somewhere! Are you threatening John, or just pulling the puppet strings?!"

I expected Morty to make his grand appearance, smiling and eager to see my face now that I knew I stood no chance at winning The Game, but he never showed. Because he was never there.

As my confidence drained out of me, I turned to face John Macon on my right, my shoulders slumped.

"Paranoia doesn't suit you, my friend," he said, shaking his head.

"Why are you helping me then, John?" I didn't want to talk about paranoia; I wanted to wash myself of it.

John shrugged, and then slipped his hands in his pockets like me, and we walked side-by-side down the length of the stage.

"Maybe I'm just…getting tired, y'know?" he said. And then he laughed. "Not of the money and the big house and the trips all over the world—hell, I even get off a little on how much these people admire me"—he leaned toward my ear—"you wouldn't believe how many women in this congregation want to fuck me. We're in *church*, for God's sake! And I get the sex-eyes from women in the audience all the time." He laughed harder, even threw his head back once. "It's a man-in-power fetish, I get that, but it only proves my point."

"What point would that be?" I asked.

"That humans are animals. Unevolved. I'm not like them. Never have been. And it's why I do what I do. I get a kick out it. I'm entertained, *appalled* by their stupidity, their naivety, how simpleminded they are—they're goddamn primates, Allister! And I'm the fucking poacher."

"You know, dictators and serial killers often have that mindset."

"I guess they do," he agreed, and glanced over at me. "But I haven't killed anybody."

"You've killed them all, John," I said. "They just don't know it yet."

Pastor John Macon smiled close-lipped, and a quiet moment passed between us.

"But really, Allister, a part of me is getting tired of this circus."

I listened.

"It's like playing the same song over and over again. I don't care how much you love it the first six hundred times you hear it, you *will* get tired of it eventually." We stopped next to the glass podium and he waved a hand at the empty seats. "I've played this song about five-hundred-ninety times, and I'm finally starting to see the inevitable end. I'm not ready to die just yet, I admit, but I can't borrow time forever. And it's not like I can just take my money and leave, because Time always catches up." He patted me on the back. "So, I may as well help out an old friend before Morty checks me out of this psychiatric ward."

I smirked. "Are you trying to wheel-and-deal with Death, John Macon?"

He grinned. "Why not?" he said. "After Morty is done with me, you're who I see next."

9

"You know there's nothing I can do," I said. "I'll reap your soul and take you where I take them all."

"And where is that exactly?" he probed, grinning.

"Nice try, John, but I never tell the living about That Place."

"But I asked you directly," he said. "Aren't you supposed to tell me the truth?"

I shook my head. "I can choose not to answer any question—it's just difficult for me not to most of the time. But when it comes to that…"

He sighed.

"Well, you did lie just now, y'know."

I looked at him, waiting.

"When you said there's nothing you can do. You can bring me back to life after Morty pulls the plug. You have the power to put my soul back into my body."

"That wasn't a lie, John," I said. "It was…well, it's complicated." I turned to face him, and I rested my hands on his shoulders, looked him in the eyes. "Let me rephrase it: There is nothing I *will* do other than reap your soul. And there is nothing you can offer me, no advice or help you can give me, that will ever change that."

He chewed on the inside of his mouth nervously. "Well, then you could keep my soul instead of—ah, never mind; it was worth a try."

69

We both looked up as the first of many sheep trickled into the auditorium.

Before we could be seen, John insisted I follow him through a side door on the stage, and we slipped out of sight.

"If you're willing to risk your life by 'getting in Morty's way' by helping me, why would you want to come back? Why risk it at all if you're not even ready to go?" I pursed my lips and added with sarcasm: "I know you don't love me *that* much." I also knew something else was going on here.

We stopped in the brightly-lit hallway just off the stage; it stretched many feet and was lined with doors on either side. Voices funneled to us from the auditorium as more people arrived. The doomed souls were suffocating me; I wanted to get farther away, but the only distance that would've made any real difference was leaving the church entirely, and I wasn't done with John Macon yet.

Before he could answer, the answer hit me in the face.

"John," I said, suspiciously, "you sold your soul, didn't you? That's how you...*obtained* all this." It was also what he meant when he mentioned I could just keep his soul "instead of". Instead of *what?*

His set-in-cement brows tried so hard to draw together.

"I resent that, Allister," he said. "No, I didn't sell my soul"—he waved a hand in the air—"I have all this because I'm *that* good. There wasn't anything otherworldly involved in the success of my empire, that's for sure."

"Then what did you do?" I insisted. "Because you did something."

I could've just read his mind to find out, but that would've taken the fun out of it. And I was worried—I *wanted* his soul. A man like John Macon, who, in his own words even, wasn't like the rest of the "unevolved primates", was a soul I looked forward to reaping. Like Nancy, and Jason Layne, John Macon's soul was one of my favorite kinds. Intelligent. Evolved.

70

His gaze strayed; he looked discouraged.

Then he sighed and said, "I didn't sell it. But I did gamble with it, and there's a chance I'm going to lose."

"Ah, I see." I crossed my arms. "What was the bet?" I didn't need to ask with whom he gambled his precious soul—there was only one, other than me, who dealt with them.

The only difference between Lucifer and myself when it came to reaping souls was that he could do whatever he wanted with them afterwards, and I was eternally stuck with them.

I *needed* souls like John Macon and Jason Layne—accepting, insensible, non-contentious, fearless, genuine, innovative—to balance the overabundance of distressing, piteous, idle, melancholic emotions the world was full of.

"Well, the bet isn't important," John said dismissively. "It was stupid, not even worth the conversation, but—"

"Tell me anyway," I insisted. I needed to know what I was up against, because I wanted John's soul and I intended to have it.

John sighed, defeated.

"You *really* want to know?" He just *really* didn't want to tell me.

"What was the bet, John?" I narrowed my eyes.

After a moment, he answered, "That you would lose."

Ah, so it all made sense then.

I shook my head and looked at the white-tile floor; a disappointed sigh cut through the silence.

"I take it everybody knows about The Game Morty and I are playing?"

John nodded. "*Every*body," he confirmed.

"And you bet against me." I admitted, I was surprised.

"Sorry, Allister," he said, "but I'm a first-hand loser when it comes to Morty Finch. If anybody knows how dirty he plays, it's me. You don't stand a chance."

He might've been right, but I hadn't lost yet.

71

More than that, I realized in that moment the answer to the reason I came here in the first place: Who in "hell" would ever help me? Lucifer, of course.

"Then why were you trying to bargain with me?" I asked. "You said there was a chance you'd lose—so which is it?"

John laughed.

"There's always a chance. And I'm always covering my bases, Allister," he said. "I do think Morty will win, but in the off-chance he loses, and I lose my bet with your brother, I wanted to bargain with you as a backup."

"So, even if you lost, you would still win by default," I said, "because all souls must pass through me before they get to him." I shook my head and laughed under my breath. "You're on borrowed time with Morty, but going behind *his* back to help *me*, hoping *I* would bargain with *you* to save your soul from a bargain you made with Lucifer, yet you bet *against* me and you *need* me to lose—you're a devious, complicated little man, John Macon."

"Yes, I suppose I am."

"And what makes you think I won't just let him have the soul he won fair and square?" I pointed out. "I do it all the time. If you people are dim enough to sell it to him, or to gamble with him, then you deserve whatever you get. That's something else I don't interfere in."

John smirked. "Oh, come on now," he taunted, "we both know what kind of souls you most like to reap. It's why you enjoy my company so much."

He was right, and he knew that I knew it.

So much for no tricks or games or hidden agendas; John Macon had covered all three by the time I was ready to leave.

I had to give him credit though; I still preferred his treacherous company to that of almost everybody else in the world and the one beyond it. I dreaded going back to my office nestled in that big city full of emotional pollution. But it's where I had to be bright and early Monday morning.

72

"So, whattya say, Allister?" John tried one last time.

"No deal."

"But…don't you want my soul?"

"Of course I do," I said with a nod. "But I intend to win against Morty. If I make a deal with you, it's the same as admitting I believe I will lose"—the bustle of the crowd carried through the auditorium; I looked at my watch— "Don't you have a show to put on?"

John Macon smiled, and sucked on a tooth.

He walked out onto the stage and voices rose like a tidal wave moving over the audience. I was the shore, where the waves crashed onto the rocks repeatedly, drowning, suffocating, violently thrashing, eroding the top layer. But I stuck it out, one palm braced against the wall for balance. Sweat beaded on my forehead; my mouth felt stuffed with cotton; the heat of my body blurred my vision. *Fools!* I thought as I tried to gain control of myself. *Damned fools!* I resented having to walk the Earth in such a body. A human body. It made the human emotions that much harder to bear; they were like a flesh-eating disease.

The living were as damaging as the dead were, especially in numbers like these, all gathered in a group, all sinning the same sins, believing the same lies, following the same devil. Fifteen thousand doomed souls. Fifteen thousand unsuspecting lives soon to be washed against the rocks for the final time, battered into nothing. And then I would be eternally stuck with them. I wouldn't be able to leave them behind like I would do on this day.

John Macon's voice rose over the auditorium through the speakers in the ceiling.

"…and I tell you, as you sit here today in the Lord's House, I tell you that we will not let the America we once knew fall at the feet of the heathens!"

The crowd cheered and clapped and praises rose and voices carried their words of agreement and devotion.

"…our great America has become the modern-day Sodom and Gomorrah…"

And he went on and on, pouring his sermon into the ears of his followers like poison into their morning coffee.

I had had enough.

But like a man who could only conquer his fear by facing it, I faced the crowd on my way out rather than go out a back door, unseen.

Thousands of eyes were on me as my feet carried me slowly over the hardwood floor of the stage. And as I made my way down the steps, they followed me. And as John Macon continued his sermon—now with a knowing grin in his eyes—they followed me. And as they praised the Lord with John, their hands raised above them, they followed me.

I looked at each in my line of sight, the eyes of Death passing over the eyes of the blind. Women wanted to fuck me. Men wanted to be me. Children wanted me to tell them who I was because they knew I was not like them. The dying felt a chill. Those still with plenty of time felt a flicker of reality I knew they would dismiss the second I was gone.

And I left the House of John and went back to the Office of Allister.

10

Contrary to popular belief, finding Lucifer had never been an easy thing to do. It wasn't like I could just snap my fingers and he'd appear; I couldn't sit around a pentagram of candles and summon him. Lucifer was a busy guy, and, like anybody needing time with a successful CEO, one had to schedule an appointment.

Fortunately, being his brother, I didn't have to schedule six months in advance. My appointment was this Friday, three days away, and I was certain I'd lose a few more patients between now and then, but it was what it was. Meanwhile, I would be doing what I could to save them, which felt more and more like absolutely nothing now that the Someone Elses were more heavily involved.

Straight for the jugular, just like I said.

Prime example: Ann Singleton. Young woman with *actual* depression, not the kind people think is depression when really, they're just unhappy with their lives and want the label to wear around like a nametag on a shirt so everyone will feel sorry for them, give them the attention they desperately need.

Ann Singleton would be one of my toughest cases. Because she was truly sick; she had a disease that affected her emotions and her mood and her personality and her will to live, and I could talk someone onto a different path, but I couldn't take away their disease. I was Death, not a miracle-worker. Sure, as John Macon pointed out, I could alter a mortal's life in "miraculous" ways, but it was against The Rules to forcibly undo what the Someone Elses did. It was cheating. And I did not cheat.

Ann Singleton and Jason Layne were equally difficult cases, but different because Ann stood a chance, and Jason would definitely die. Odd how Jason was, so far, easier to help. I had to be careful with Ann. And I knew that would be almost as hard as helping her.

Actual Depression is much more difficult to treat than Fallacious Depression. Just as malignant cancer is more difficult to treat than a benign tumor. And as Actual Depression is more difficult to treat, it is also more difficult to diagnose because of the overabundance of Fallacious Depression cases—the signs and symptoms are mostly the same. And those who aren't genuinely depressed often romanticize it, making it harder to distinguish, or believe, those who actually need help—it is one of the most destructive instances of crying wolf. But I was no ordinary psychiatrist. I knew when someone was bullshitting me, or when someone thought they had depression because they had been brought up to believe that the natural little bumps along the road in life warranted antidepressants, or that simply being unhappy was a disease.

Ann Singleton was not unhappy—she had a potentially fatal illness.

She sat across from me in my office; thirty minutes had gone by and I'd managed not to say anything offensive or hurtful. But that was mostly because she didn't care about much of anything. She wasn't "sad" or seeking an ear to tell her troubles to; she wasn't looking for pity. She was here only because her husband talked her into coming. She did it only for him, because she loved him. And because she didn't want him to think it was his fault after she was gone; she wanted him to live with some shred of peace that he had done all he could do, and it wasn't his fault that it just wasn't enough.

I had never experienced much frustration in my existence, aside from the random emotional frustrations of the souls I'd reaped and the living I lingered around. But I was experiencing it now. Because I didn't know what to do. *Me*—Death, didn't have the slightest clue about how to fix a being inferior to me. It was embarrassing. With Jason, it was a no-brainer: there was nothing I *could* do, so there was no sense getting frustrated over it. But with Ann, there *was* an answer, there was *some way* to help her, but I couldn't quite put my finger on it.

"Here's a prescription for an antidepressant," I said as I tore the square of paper from the pad and slid it across the desk toward her. "It's different from the last few you've tried, but we'll find the right one for you."

"Yeah, I've heard the speech before: It's not a one-size-fits-all disease." She sighed and stuffed the prescription into her purse with no intention of getting it filled. "Look, Mr. Boone..." she began, paused, and then said instead: "Have you ever been tired? I don't mean sleep-deprived, I mean...*tired*, you know?"

This was her way of indirectly asking about suicide.

"I'm tired right now," I answered with honesty. "Every day of my existence, forced to walk this Earth with the weight of billions of tortured souls pressing in on me from all sides, I feel myself slipping away, slowly but inevitably crushed into the soil and out of the universe from which I was born." I nodded once. "So, yes, Ann, I am very fucking tired."

After four sessions with Ann Singleton, it was the first time I'd really gotten her attention, the first time she showed the slightest interest in living longer, even if only a few minutes longer, just to know more, to hear my fresh take on being "tired", because she could somehow relate. She sat there, her lips parted slightly, her face blank, her heart pounding for the first time since the Someone Elses upgraded her debilitating disease to Stage Four. And it was unintentional. My answer wasn't part of her therapy; I never expected it to make any difference, but there we were, Ann and I, in a draw.

I had fought with her for one month, and I was ready to face defeat and give this point to Morty when Ann came to my office today. Because last week I'd read her thoughts and she had made up her mind; she already had a plan in place, a method, a time and a date, and it was supposed to happen tomorrow on her birthday. She never told me these things.

But now I had her attention.

(So strange...why would he say that? What did he mean? Is my psychiatrist...suicidal? So strange...)

She wanted to ask questions, but she wasn't sure how, or which questions to ask. She'd seen several counselors, one psychologist, and a family therapist with her husband before seeing me. She'd struggled with moderate depression most of her adult life, until recently when the Someone Elses turned up the heat on her burner. But the professionals she'd seen in the past had all read from the same script, prescribed her the same medications she felt were the *real* professionals. Just as my secretary led my patients to me, the counselors, psychologists, and therapists were the Nancys leading them to the drugs. Ann felt like they were passing her off to a bottle of pills, sending her home, and forgetting about her the moment she left their offices. She didn't care they didn't seem to care about her, she just thought it unfortunate that other patients, who *did* care they would be forgotten, would come in after her.

But I was different. I intrigued her—a little, but in her case a little was a lot. Apparently, Ann Singleton thought I was inadvertently opening up to her, and she didn't know what to think about that. I was still throwing a prescription in her lap like all the professionals before me—that part was only adhering to mortal's expectations of what a psychiatrist is expected to do, and I thought it would help her about as much as telling her to take two Skittles every morning. Some patients respond well to medication, but Ann Singleton was not one of them.

(He's...different. There's something...off about him.)

After a moment, Ann cut the silence with a Samurai sword.

"Why did you become a psychiatrist?"

Great—a direct question in which the answer could have severe repercussions.

"You want the truth?" I asked, dancing around it for as long as I could.

"Is there something wrong with the truth?"

"Depends on how you look at it."

"Okay," she said, "then let's see how I look at it."

I nodded slowly, leaned my back against the chair, my hands loosely locked above my lap.

"It was a bet," I told her. "With an old friend. A game, actually. I have to—"

If you tell her the truth she'll think you're crazy, Allister. If she thinks you're crazy, you won't be able to help her.

I might've thought it was my own voice inside my head—I talked to myself a lot—but I knew that voice anywhere. Lucifer.

(Did I close the bathroom window before I left? Shit. I think I left the window open. Marvel might get out.) Ann looked to her left, in thought, a little dazed as if the Devil had just distracted her from her curiosities about me.

Then she turned back, snapped back into the moment.

"I-I'm sorry," she said, shaking her head. "It's none of my business. And you're the one supposed to ask the questions, I know."

I waved a dismissive hand in front of me. "No, it's fine," I told her. "If you want to ask me questions, I don't mind."

What the hell are you doing, you idiot? Again, Lucifer.

"I could tell you the long, drawn-out story of why I became a psychiatrist," I said to Ann, "or you could ask me the questions you really want to ask. It's your choice."

I know what I'm doing, I told Lucifer.

You better know what you're doing, he said. *If you lose, I lose too.*

"Yeah, I uh," Ann said, "I guess I do have a question or two."

Never doubt my ability to manipulate my way out of a crisis, dear brother. Me.

"Ask me anything," I told Ann.

I know what I'm doing even when I'm worried. Me.

"Are you suicidal?" Ann asked.

The Samurai sword just cut off my fucking head.

You were saying? Lucifer, with a smirk in his voice.

11

I cleared my throat.

Let's see you manipulate your way out of this one. Catch you on Friday! Lucifer laughed, and then he was gone; his abrupt absence felt like a swimmer on the edge of a pool heaving himself out of the dark waters of my mind.

I felt Ann's eyes on me, her patience, her expectation.

I took a breath and dove into the deep end.

"Yes," I answered with honesty. "I am suicidal. But it doesn't mean the same thing as you might think."

She arched a curious brow. "Oh?"

I shook my head, straightened my tie.

"I don't want to be here anymore," I began, "and, in many ways, I guess you could say that I'm a danger to myself. But I've already accepted who and what I am, and what role I have to play in this world, this reality, therefore I'm not looking to leave it in any particular way or time of my choosing." *And as far as I know, I can't.*

"Then how are you a danger to yourself?"

"I'm reckless," I told her. "I do reckless things against my better judgement: I gamble and bet with my very existence; I'm a masochist; I tend to torture myself just so I can feel something that is mine and not what belongs to everyone around me, crowding me, suffocating me. But I've never been able to tell if my emotions are, in fact, my own, or if I am, truly, incapable of emotion. I walk this Earth in a body that isn't mine; to everyone else it looks like it fits, but to me, I'm constantly slipping into corners to pull my underwear out of my ass; my skin itches and I sweat profusely for no apparent reason; I make myself vomit every time a woman touches me sexually, and I vomit without assistance every time I take a shit because it's disgusting. Humans are disgusting. Foul. Diseased. Cesspools of filth and barbarism. And I resent the fact that the skin of one is my uniform."

She just sat there for a moment, thought about it; I was surprised by her non-reaction.

"Why don't you just quit your job?" she suggested— naturally, she took everything I'd said as metaphor.

"Because I don't quit"—absently, I clenched a fist— "There's a *reason* for all of this."

"Like fate?" she probed, mildly intrigued.

"No," I answered. "There are no set paths, Ann. A wise man once said: 'What point is there in walking a path that can't be changed? What's the point of playing a game you already know the end result?'"

She tilted her head thoughtfully.

"So, you…stay here even though you want to leave because you feel like your existence has a purpose, yet you don't believe your purpose is fate?"

Who's the psychiatrist here—you or me?!

Was she toying with me? Was her question the bait to hook me and prove I was being contradictory? I couldn't tell. And strangely enough, I was having trouble reading her suddenly.

"Fate is as fickle as it is subjective," I said. "It changes with you, your movements, your thoughts and actions and deeds. You create our own fate, Mrs. Singleton. You use the Gifts you were given to do not what you were *meant* to do, or to accomplish, but what you have the *capability* of accomplishing—it's all up to you: your life, your future, everything. If you're strong enough to make it through to the end, no matter what obstacles are thrown in your path, then it was fate that you made it that far, that you served your purpose; but always on your own terms, the end result a creation of your own doing, and *not* a set path created by some 'higher power'." I paused, searched her impenetrable thoughts. "But if you give up before you make it there, throw in the towel because you get hit too many times in the face, then you will never know what your purpose was, or the great things you could have accomplished, therefore fate does not exist." I leaned forward.

Ann looked down at her hands. I still couldn't read her, and I found that more intriguing than anything.

"So, you think everyone on Earth," she began, "has some grand purpose? I don't believe that."

She stood and walked to the window, and that, too, intrigued me. It showed not that she was comfortable in my presence, but that she wasn't inferior to it. None of my patients had ever taken it upon themselves to leave the designated chair they paid me hourly to occupy. I was the "doctor", and patients always feel inferior in the presence of doctors, sitting obediently on the little transformer bed, the aggravating crackle of roll-out sheeting beneath them, listening with absorbed interest and due respect to someone who may or may not know what the hell they're talking about. Ann's action, although seemingly insignificant—and unknown to her—was a sign of superiority rather than obedience, of intelligence rather than conformity. Ann Singleton was human but, not in the offensive sense of the word.

Looking out at the city under a bright-blue cloudless sky, she put off an energy I had rarely ever felt. I wasn't ready to accept it yet as being what I suspected, but I listened…with absorbed interest and due respect.

"If billions upon billions of people all had a grand purpose," she said, "that would create chaos, Mr. Boone. It would be like putting a thousand fighters in a tiny arena to fight to the death, but not one of them would die; the fight would go on forever." She glanced back at me, her arms crossed. "And I do think this life is like one big fight in some

83

otherworldly arena, and God—or whatever—is up there laughing at us as we kill each other."

A smile slowly crept over my mouth.

"We're not special, Mr. Boone," she went on. "We're ants in a colony, all moving back and forth from the resources and the home base. Not one of those billions of ants is ever going to do anything in its tiny lifespan that's going to affect anything in the universe. We're so small we practically don't exist. We are nothing, in a vast, endless Everything that will go on forever whether we're stamping our little feet in it or not."

My suspicions were correct. Ann Singleton, young, married woman with Actual Depression, was in a way like Jason Layne—a rarity. But she was even more-so because she thought beyond the veil pulled over most mortal's eyes.

But she was, however, still only human, and I was not.

"Have you ever been bitten by an ant, Mrs. Singleton?"

She shrugged. "Sure I have," she said and stepped away from the window.

"How many ants do you think you've been bitten by in your lifetime?"

Her eyebrows drew together. She shook her head. "I don't know, not many, I guess. Maybe ten or fifteen."

I waited a moment, gave her time to think about it.

She thought about it.

"There are over seven billion people in the world," I said. "And for every human being, there are approximately one to two million ants. The number of ants living at the same time as you are is in the quadrillions, yet, despite how small and insignificant, you can still give me an estimate of how many ants you've been bitten by in your thirty-two years of life."

I stood up and she sat back down.

"They may be small, and seemingly insignificant, or as you described 'not special', but ten or fifteen out of *quadrillions* made enough of a mark that we're sitting here, in one of the most important moments of your life, having a discussion about them."

She stared off at the wall but probably wasn't seeing it.

"Every single person in this world has a purpose—and if you haven't noticed, the world *is* chaos—but for most, their purpose is simply...to exist. One life affects another, one person inspires another, one drives another mad. Every*one* and every*thing* living keeps The Wheel turning, paints the color of the wooden spokes, destroys and repairs the mechanisms that control it."

She still wasn't buying it, but she was intrigued.

"So then what *purpose* does a stillborn baby have? A ten-year-old with cancer? A sixteen-year-old in a fatal car accident?"

I shook my head.

"Just because someone dies before they really get a chance to live," I said, "doesn't mean they didn't serve a purpose. The time of someone's death has nothing to do with the impact that their life, no matter how short, has on the people around them." With my hands buried in my pockets, I paced behind her in the chair, but she kept facing forward. "They can't help it if they die too soon; the time of their death is not in their hands—not even child suicides, because they know not what they do—but all of them still serve their purpose by default. And only innocents get that privilege."

She turned to face me.

"And everybody else?" she asked, half-serious, half-expecting-me-to-show-my-oh-so-divine-credentials.

"Everybody else"—I opened my hands in front of me—"they know exactly what they're doing, they have a choice, they are the other quadrillion ants. Most of them will never see anything outside their habitats, their monotonous walks to and from the resources and the home base. They commit suicide without actually killing themselves simply by giving up, they waste their lives away wallowing in self-pity, dishing-out negative energy; they die leaving nothing behind but a legacy of worthless material possessions and self-regard, and they never fulfill any purpose beyond being a lesson, a warning the living should heed. But ten or fifteen will leave their mark." I softened my voice. "Everyone has a purpose, but not everyone succeeds in fulfilling it before—by choice—they fade away. And not everyone has a 'grand' purpose. But it's up to each individual to choose whether or not their purpose will be grand."

She sighed and faced forward again.

Feeling like I still hadn't opened her mind enough to give it much thought, I played a risky card.

"And you have a purpose, Ann. A *grand* purpose. It's why you were infected with this disease—because They're threatened by you. It's why your fight is harder than most, why you're so overwhelmed by your disease you feel the only way to make it stop is to end your life. Because that's what they want. It's what they convince you to do."

She laughed shortly under her breath.

"They who? And how could you possibly know something like that?" She wasn't asking; she was pointing out how ridiculous I sounded to her. Though, deep-down, she believed me.

"I'm sorry," she said, abruptly changing her tune, "I just don't…" She couldn't finish, and her self-doubt saved me from having to answer the questions.

I stopped in front of my desk chair and looked down at her. "The struggle is hard, unbearable—I know. But like everybody else, the only ant in that arena you're fighting, is yourself."

Looking at the desk, Ann shook her head, overwhelmed by the information, and not sure if she wanted to let it manipulate her. I still couldn't read her, but it was what I assumed judging her posture and her silence.

"You talk about this stuff as if you know it's true," she said, raising her head. "Your method of therapy is a little unconventional, don't you think?"

I sat down, looked her right in the eyes. And for the first time, she saw me. I don't mean she merely looked at me—she *saw me*. I could feel it, the cryptic recognition, the chill tapdancing on the back of her neck, that feeling everybody gets when in the presence of something preternatural, but they always dismiss what they don't understand.

Suddenly, I could read her again. Because she dismissed what she couldn't understand, and the light weight of Reality was again replaced with the heavy weight of The Illusion.

(I hope he's not some crazed religious freak. That's the last thing I need.)

Had I lost her? I worried that I had—or if I ever had her to begin with. I needed to bring her back, but I didn't know how. And I didn't want to tell her I *knew* the things I said were true because, as Lucifer had warned me, if she thought I was crazy, I would not be able to help her. Plus, how would it look if I admitted I knew the things I said were true, but I couldn't tell her her purpose, or even why any of us were here?

"Why do *you* believe we are here?" I countered my own thoughts. "I mean, other than God laughing at us."

"Look," she said, resigned, "all I know is that *I* don't like it here; all I know is that *I* don't live here, I just exist. I wake up every morning to the same joyless life, and I go through the entire day in a dark haze of thoughts that always bring me back to the same solution. I'm not sad, or unhappy, or feel like I've been cheated or betrayed or lied to; I don't care about material things, or fun things, or terrifying things; I don't feel like I'm owed; I feel little of *anything*, other than how much I don't want to be here. And I don't know how to make it stop."

"But you want to make it stop?"

She looked right at me.

"No," she answered after a pause. "Not anymore. Like I said...I'm just tired."

The pause was the only hope I had of saving her. The pause was a heartbeat of uncertainty, and it was all she had left.

"Looks like my hour is up," she said, and I hadn't even noticed myself.

She stood, shouldered her purse.

Before she could step away from the chair, out of desperation I did the only thing I knew to do. I touched her hand upon the desk.

Darkness coated my vision like storm clouds blotting out the sun; the breath of her life took the breath from my lungs, and every emotion she had ever felt, every pain she had ever endured flooded me like violent waves crashing over a ship and taking it down into the depths of the sea. I felt like I was falling, and in my mind, I scrambled to grasp at something to keep me standing but nothing was there. Only blackness. The Nothingness from where I came and where I believed someday I would be again. At rest. At peace. Knowing nothing, seeing nothing, hearing nothing, tasting nothing, feeling nothing, *being* nothing. Ah, the sweet lure of the Nothing, I did so yearn for it!

"Are you okay?"

I looked up, hurtled back into the moment. I was still standing, I realized, but there was enough in my face she noticed something was wrong. Then I looked down to see that my hand wasn't touching hers anymore; the overwhelming emotions of her living soul had flooded me in only a fraction of a second. It always happened that way: in a fraction of a second. I could only imagine what a longer touch would feel like. I'd been touched many times before—and I'd touched many, masochist and all—but souls like hers were the most powerful.

"Oh, I'm fine," I lied. *I lied?* Already I felt myself scrambling inside my head, desperate to fix the error: touch a doorknob five times, shave off my hair, cut out my tongue. Cut out my tongue...*Cut out your tongue...Cut out your fucking tongue, Azrael!*

Ann smiled at me, though it showed more in her eyes than on her mouth, and I shoved the voice inside my head—my own voice this time—into the farthest reaches of my mind.

Cut out your goddamned tongue!

I smiled back at her with the same level of placidity.

She walked toward the door and I followed. Before I reached out and opened the door for her, she turned to face me. She looked down at her hand with absorbed curiosity, the hand I had touched. And her small smile grew a little more, spreading away from her eyes to find her lips.

She had felt...something. Something other than nothing. Something other than pain.

"Same time next week?" she asked.

I nodded.

"Yes," I said. "Same time next week."

I opened the door and Ann Singleton left my office. I read her thoughts as she walked toward Nancy at the reception desk, and as she stood there for fifty-two seconds as she paid her bill; and I read them as she went out into the hall. *(I hope Marvel didn't climb out the window. Hmm, what should I make for dinner? Lasagna. Michael's favorite.)* No thoughts of ending her life. No thoughts of me being crazy.

I had bought Ann at least one more day—a brush with death had a way of doing that. But I knew it wouldn't last. At least not with someone like her. It was only a small brush, after all.

"Mr. Boone," Nancy's voice snapped me out of my reverie. "Margot Henry insists you told her to come at this time every Tuesday?"

And there she was, the missing but not forgotten Miss Henry, dressed in her usual solid-color, one-dimensional clothes, standing to the right of me, waiting with her arms crossed like sausages wrapped in hog casing.

Nancy waited with a raised brow.

"Yes," I spoke up. "I did tell Miss Henry that."

"Well, maybe next time," Nancy scolded, "you could let me know? I mean, I *am* the one responsible for the scheduling."

"Yes, I'll let you know next time."

Margot grinned; she got a kick out of my nuts being crushed in Nancy's hand.

"Does this mean I need to stall your two o'clock?"

"No," I said. "I will be on time."

She glared at me, shook her head, and then went back to work.

I opened my hand and gestured Miss Henry into my office.

"Right this way," I said, and she followed with a smirk.

12

The color for today was yellow. Yellow slacks, yellow blouse that hung from her like a parachute, yellow shoes at least one size too small so that her feet looked like baking bread, yellow purse, dangling yellow earrings, matching yellow bracelet and necklace—I felt like I needed sunglasses only because everybody who saw her on the way up felt like *they* needed sunglasses.

Miss Henry sat down before I offered her the chair. She tapped her fingers against the purse on her lap, a mixture of resentment and apprehension hot in her face. And defense. Margot Henry came prepared today; she would strike back at me with all she had, berate me like I'd never been berated. She wasn't even here for my help. She was here for revenge.

And I was ready and eager to see what she was made of.

"Well—"

"First off," she cut in, index finger pointing skyward, "you're not going to talk to me with such disrespect, Mr. Boone." She shook the finger at me then, her eyes narrowed. "No matter what you say to me, I'm not walking out that door until I get my fifteen minutes. You got that?"

"Sure," I said, and opened my hands. "That was what I had hoped the first time you came here."

"If you hoped I would stay," she said, "then why talk to me the way you did?"

"Because it's what you wanted."

Her narrowed eyes fell under wrinkles of confusion; I could've sworn I heard crickets.

"What I wanted?"

"Yes."

A long pause.

"Umm, you want to explain that to me?" She shook her head, gestured her hands. "I mean, because that's"—she scoffed and leaned forward—"the most ridiculous thing I've ever heard. Are you fucking *kidding* me right now?"

I sighed. "Miss Henry," I said, sitting down, "you are the way you are because you choose to be. You hate your life because you choose to hate it. And everybody around you sees you as a disgusting burden to society because you let them see you that way. Because you have no power. As I said before, you're the only person who doesn't have control over your life."

I waited, gave her a chance to speak her mind, to tell me I was wrong. But I knew she wouldn't; bewilderment was the only emotion she could feel in that moment.

But in the next moment, I could smell the salt of her inevitable tears like approaching rain. Thankfully, she held them back.

"Go on," she insisted, an outraged shudder in her voice. "Get it all out. Say what you've gotta say."

I opened the file drawer on the right side of my desk and produced her file, the one that told me all about her unfortunate childhood with a pedophile for a step-father, and a brutal, loveless mother. She used nearly every inch of white space on her six-sheet questionnaire, back and front, to explain in-short all the sad details of her pathetic life. She had wanted to say these things to someone for many years, to get everything out, if for nothing than just to feel the false sensation of the weight of it all leave her shoulders. Temporarily. Because it would always be there, no matter how much she talked about it or cried about it or invented reasons why any of it happened. It would always be there because Margot Henry refused to let it go. The vast majority of emotional pain is self-inflicted, after all.

Though her problems today may have stemmed from her problems growing up, they were not what made her what she became. Sure, she had rock-bottom low self-esteem because of her weight and her mother's verbal abuse; she was desperate to find someone to love her, to tell her she was beautiful, to accept her and all her baggage; every day she tried to fit into society's mold.

Margot Henry did not suffer from Actual Depression. She did not suffer from Post-Traumatic Stress Disorder, Bipolar Disorder, or any of the various mental disorders that *does* affect the chemical makeup of the brain. Margot Henry, like many—sad, happy, rich, poor, famous, hated, loved—suffered from Failed Societal Assimilation.

"I want you to picture for a moment," I said, "what your life would be like if you were thin, desirable, if you turned heads instead of stomachs—don't cry, Miss Henry, just do as I ask."

She swallowed and sniffled back the tears that had crept to the surface.

And then she did as I'd asked. I saw images of her walking through a crowd, as skinny as any A-list actress; heads turned as she passed, men eyed her with sexual need, women eyed her with envy. She was wearing blue from head-to-toe: blue slacks, blue blouse that clung to her hourglass form like a corset, blue high-heels, blue purse, dangling blue earrings, matching blue bracelet and necklace. Margot Henry loved her solids—she would be any fashion guru's worst nightmare—but she looked fantastic, because she felt fantastic.

"Is that what you've always wanted?" I asked.

Reluctantly, she nodded.

"Now, I want you to toss that visual," I said, "because that'll never be you—don't cry, Miss Henry, *please*, just do as I ask."

She sat there staring at me, wanting to put her hands around my neck, but at the same time, wanting to listen.

"That will never be you," I went on, "because by the time I'm done with you, you won't *want* that to be you."

And in that instant, I became the only person in Margot Henry's life whom she trusted, the only person she believed could help her, the only person she believed *wanted* to help her. She couldn't explain why or how or what exactly it was about me, the bastard she wanted to choke just moments ago, but she didn't care.

"Okay." Her fingers, clenched around the leather of her purse, loosened; her rigid shoulders relaxed and she swallowed.

"Would you like some water, Miss Henry?"

Suspicious of the offer, she held her breath and looked at me sidelong.

Finally, after careful consideration, she answered, "Yes. I would like some water."

I pointed at the mini fridge, but I did not get up.

"You're welcome to it." I was nicer this time, at least, but I still wasn't going to get it for her.

She sucked it up and shook her head. "No, I'm fine, but thank you."

"All right then." I glanced down at the six-page questionnaire in front of me. "Are you ready, Miss Henry?"

"...Yes."

I slid the questionnaire across the desk toward her.

"I want you to tear it up," I instructed, and nodded at the paper.

Reluctantly, she took the paper by the stapled corner, turned it horizontally, and then tore it in half.

I leaned forward, looked her in the eyes.

"First and foremost," I told her, "if you *really* want to change your life, to stop hating yourself, to feel good in your skin, then you'll do everything I tell you to do, and you won't look for excuses not to." I leaned in farther, folded my hands. "Make no mistake, Miss Henry, you *are* the way you are because you want it, because you've been in that skin for so long you're too comfortable, regardless of how much you hate it. Every sad moment, every negative thought, is because *you let it in.* You're in an abusive relationship with yourself, but you're afraid to leave, you're afraid of the unknown. And only one of three things will happen." I held up three fingers. "You'll stay in the relationship forever, as a punching bag"—I dropped one finger—"you'll end up dead"—I dropped another finger—"or, you'll tire of the abuse, find your strength, and leave it for a better life." I dropped my hand. "You will aim for the latter. I'm going to help you to help yourself, but if at any time you make an excuse, and you fall back, I will wash my hands clean of you because I don't have time to work with bullshitters—do you understand?"

She nodded reluctantly.

"I'm not here as your ear or your shoulder—stamp that on your brain right now. I don't care what happened to you when you were growing up. I don't care about your step-father, or your mother, or the kids in school who bullied you. And I don't care about the guilt you feel over the baby you aborted, or the boss who humiliated you, or the so-called best friend who stabbed you in the back. I don't care what happened to you yesterday or last week or last month or last year—say it: Allister Boone does not care."

"Allister Boone does not care."

"Because when you care you give it power."

"Because when I care I give it power."

I glanced at the torn paper.

"We will not spend your time here," I went on, "talking about all the things that happened to you; I will not tell you how 'terrible' those people were and how what they did doesn't define you today, or any of that—none of it matters, because reliving the past and looking for reasons for why any of it happened really has no bearing on the person you *want* to be right now. They mean nothing—say it."

"They mean nothing."

"Reliving the past is a waste of time—say it."

"Reliving the past is a waste of time."

"Dwelling on the past is an even bigger waste of time."

"Dwelling on the past is an even bigger waste of time."

"Because you're an intelligent woman," I told her. "With a perfectly healthy brain. And deep down, underneath all the layers of self-depreciation and self-doubt and self-pity you already know the answers to all of your questions; you've already learned from your mistakes and the mistakes of others; you already know how you *should* be, how you *should* think, how you *should* feel; you already know that what happened to you in your past doesn't define you, and you don't need me or anyone else to tell you these things or to explain them to you—You. Already. Know. Say it."

"I already know."

And lastly, you don't need me or anyone else to fix you—you can fix yourself. Say it."

"I can...fix myself." She didn't seem as convinced that time.

I stood up.

"You *will* fix yourself."

"I *will* fix myself."

"Do you want to know the one thing," I said, held up my finger, "the simplest answer to what will make you care about yourself?"

"Yes."

"To care about yourself, you have to stop caring about yourself."

"Huh?"

I sat on the end of the desk.

"I have an assignment for you," I told her, ignoring the question. "Starting tomorrow, when you wake up and begin to get ready for your day, skip the makeup and hair regimen."

She looked borderline mortified.

"B-But I have to go to work."

"Yes?" I asked, but my face read: Is there a problem?

"I-I can't go to work without…looking presentable." She blinked rapidly as she shook her head and glanced at her lap. "As if I don't get enough shit from those people—I can't let them see me like that."

"Is there anything in your work policy at a call center that states you have to wear makeup and wear your hair a certain way to sit in a cubicle for six hours? Or, anything that states that looking presentable requires makeup?"

She thought about it, her eyebrows crumpled in her forehead.

"I uh, well, I don't think so. But…it just…looks bad to show up one day out-of-the-blue like I just rolled out of bed."

"You're making excuses, Miss Henry." I stood. "Is this going to be our last session?"

Her fingers twiddled nervously on her bright-yellow lap; I would back the threat with action and she knew it.

"No," she promptly said. "I'll do it. But just so you know, this will probably make me feel even worse about how I look. It'll draw more negative attention to me than I already deal with on a daily basis."

"Like what?" I challenged.

"Like…well, the looks I get," she tried to explain, but wasn't so sure anymore. "And I know the Cigarette Break Girls are always talking shit about me outside."

"Wow, you must really think highly of the Cigarette Break Girls," I told her with sarcasm, "to give two-shits what they say about you, all huddled around the ashtray like hyenas around a carcass. They must be beautiful. And you must be in the seventh grade."

"Hell no I don't give—." She shut herself down, realizing. "Okay, but why *all* makeup? I'd feel better if I could at least wear mascara."

"The next thing I want you to do," I continued, ignoring her attempt to get me to loosen the rules, "is to smile at everyone you see."

"Smile? Everyone?" This seemed worse than the makeup and hair rule.

"Yes, that's what I said."

"Why?"

"Because it's what I want. Do you have a problem with smiling?" Yes, Margot Henry had a problem with smiling—she rarely did it; it made her feel violated; it made her feel like she was opening some secret door into her life and that the people around her would all come running in to take advantage of her. Margot Henry had spent half her life perfecting that sour face, and it would be difficult for her to change it.

"I guess not..." She sighed. "It's just that...I'm not really looking to make friends with these people."

"I don't want you to smile to make friends," I explained. "This is how you'll work on your confidence. Smile without fear."

Not convinced she could pull it off, she changed the subject. "What else?" she asked.

"When you're alone in your apartment tonight," I said, "or any night from here on out, and you hear that voice inside your head telling you to do what you want, eat that mint chip ice cream; the voice that'll try to convince you I'm a scam artist, and that there's nothing I can do to help you, etcetera; tell it to go get bent, and don't let it influence you even just a little."

"How'd you know I have mint chip in my freezer?"

"A friend told me."

She smirked and brushed it off as coincidence.

"Okay," she agreed. "So that's it? You're not gonna give me any worldly advice, or tell me that I'm a beautiful person on the inside and that the outside doesn't matter—anything like that?"

I smiled with sarcasm. "Only the innocent are beautiful on the inside, Miss Henry." I waved a hand at the wall to indicate the world. "All of you are wretched things, wickedness on two legs with an ego bigger than the universe." I stood. "But that doesn't mean I'm above helping you."

I glanced at the clock on the wall.

"Yeah, yeah, I know," she said. "My fifteen minutes are up." She stood and shouldered her purse. "Next week, same time?"

I nodded. "No excuses," I told her and approached the door. I opened it for her; the smell of lemon air freshener and melancholy crept into my office from the waiting room.

"You are a strange man," Margot Henry said standing in the doorway. She studied me for a moment, trying to figure out why she liked and hated me so much. "With an ego bigger than the universe." She smirked. "But that doesn't mean I'm above letting you help me."

"I'm glad we're finally on the same page," I said.

She nodded, smiled without fear, and then left, already a better Margot Henry than when she stepped into my office minutes ago.

Nancy, looking wary as always, watched Margot leave with her head a little higher; no stomping out the door, or a red face bloated with anger and humiliation; no combative words flinging like shit in a chimpanzee enclosure at the zoo.

She looked at me, confused, but with approval.

"Your two o'clock is here," Nancy announced in a quiet voice, and her eyes skirted the man apprehensively.

There was only one person sitting in the waiting room, surrounded by fifteen cushioned chairs, his head pressed against the eggshell-white wall just beneath an abstract painting.

This one, I knew the moment he walked into the building, was a lost cause.

13

His name was Joel. White male. Thirty-eight-years of age. Born and raised in a small town in the Midwest to a racist, homophobic, "Christian" family who, like all racist, homophobic "Christian" families, were the male nipples of an evolving world. Again, I was not religious, and I was on no one's side, not even my brother's, but I would be remiss not to point out the sheer stupidity and hypocrisy of mortals as I saw it. I was on the side of common sense.

Like most, Joel's beliefs and views altered his religion to suit his preferred lifestyle. Worse was that he believed his own lies and excuses with powerful conviction, and he was emotionally and mentally unstable, making him a danger not only to himself, but to those closest to him. He was violent; he abused his wife and terrified his children who, unfortunately, would probably grow up to be just like him—if they grew up. He worked hard and drank hard and even tried hard, but he was never happy; he could never be satisfied. He thought the world owed him something; everyone was beneath him—particularly women and people of color—and he was a murder-suicide in the making.

Joel did not have Actual Depression. Joel did not suffer from Post-Traumatic Stress Disorder, Bipolar Disorder, or any of the various mental disorders that *did* affect the chemical makeup of the brain. Joel suffered from irreversible brainwashing, and the growing, paranoid fear that his race and sex were on the brink of degradation and extinction. Not so very different from brutal terrorist organizations, people like Joel were born into hate, making it nearly impossible to change him. I doubted even I could change him. I had given up on him before he sat down in the chair in front of my desk.

So, then what was I even seeing him for? Well, I knew Morty had sent him, and I would continue to play The Game even if it was inevitable I lost a hand or two.

"Hello Joel," I said as I took my seat. "I'm Allister Boone."

"Good to meet you," he said.

He came empty-handed; the only things in his possession were his keys and wallet buried in different pockets of his paint-stained jeans. He didn't even have a cell phone.

"I see you chose not to fill out the questionnaire," I said. He never filled the one out online, but he could've printed one off like some of my distrusting-of-the-internet patients had.

"No need, really."

"And why is that?"

He shook his head, manipulated the inside of his bottom lip with his teeth, crumpled his nose. Then he shrugged and said, "Why write all that crap down when you can just ask me and I'll tell you?"

"Fair enough," I said. "Then why don't we begin with why you came here, Joel. I'm getting the impression it was not by choice."

He cocked his head curiously to one side, fiddled his calloused thumbs on his lap.

"Yeah?" he asked.

"Yeah," I answered.

He wanted me to explain how I knew that, what gave me that "impression", but I was the one in control here and I would not let him have it. Joel liked control, he thrived on it, but I wasn't his wife, or his kids, or the Black man who worked at the gas station he liked to intimidate, or the Brown woman he raped last year at the hotel she worked as a housekeeper, and he knew she wouldn't report him because she was "illegal".

When he realized I wasn't going to give in to him, he sighed, slouched in the chair to get comfortable and propped his right ankle on his left knee.

"My boss, Larry," he said. "He's a good friend of mine. I've worked for him for fifteen years."

"What do you do?"

"Construction. Company's based in Missouri where I live, but we travel all over; sometimes stay for weeks, even months on a job." He was a good liar and manipulator. Not that he was lying now, but people who offer more information than what is asked tend to be good liars and manipulators.

"So, that's what brought you here. Your job."

He nodded.

"We're working on a new residential area just outside the city," he explained. "One of those private gated communities."

"How long will that take?"

"Another two months," he said. "I get to go home, see my family, spend my birthday there, and then it's back here for another couple months."

"And why did your boss send you to me?"

(I didn't technically tell him my boss was who sent me.)

"I got into a fight," he answered. "With another guy who works for Larry. If I want to keep my job, I have to...get some help." He rolled his eyes at his boss's choice of words.

"So, then you've shown violent tendencies at work before."

(I don't like this suit-wearin', city-slicker already.)

He didn't answer.

"You mind telling me what the fight was about?"

His eyes flashed remembering the details.

"The guy disrespected me," he said. "So, I hit him in the fucking mouth."

"How did he disrespect you?"

He paused, gritted his teeth behind closed lips; his foot bounced up and down against his knee anxiously.

"Does that really matter?"

"Yes. It does. When a grown man assaults another man for any reason unrelated to self-defense or defense of another, he obviously has issues that need to be addressed."

He shot up from the chair.

I remained in mine, calm and silent as I studied the human grenade while he paced the floor with his hand on the pin.

"Look," he said, "can't you just give me a note or something saying I was here? This is ridiculous."

"I could. But I'm not going to."

"Why not?" He gritted his teeth again.

"Because this is my show, Joel, not yours. And I'm the one in control."

His nostrils flared, he clenched his fists; rarely had anyone ever had the gall to put him in his place like that. He wanted to assault me just like he did that co-worker who had a "big mouth" and deemed it necessary to admit proudly to Joel he didn't vote for the "clown" who won the election. Not my words—I wasn't political, either.

Instead of an assault charge, he calmed himself.

(Just let it go. This guy don't know shit about nothin'. Just let it go.)

"Did you want to kill your co-worker?" I asked; I was trying to get under his skin just to see how easy it was.

He froze, his eyes wide.

Slowly, he turned only his head to look at me.

"Why would you ask—"

"Just answer the question, Joel," I cut him off. "Did you want to kill your co-worker?"

(Yes.)

"No"—he shook his head—"I don't know why you'd even ask me something like that."

"Because you have that look in your eye," I told him. "I've seen it many times."

"You can't judge someone because you think you see something in their eyes." He crossed his arms and paced.

Switching gears, hoping to open him up some I said, "Tell me about your family," but I knew I'd get nowhere with him.

"Leave my family out of this," he warned. "I'm here for me, and only me."

"But your family is a part of you," I pointed out. "What do you enjoy doing together? How long have you been married? How many kids?"

He marched toward the door. "I knew I shouldn't have come here—a fuckin' waste of money."

The painting on the wall rattled when he slammed the door behind him.

And that was that. Gone as quickly as he'd come. And he wouldn't be like Margot Henry. He'd die before he paid the bill he'd get in a few days; he would not come back to tell me off; he didn't feel like he needed help, therefore he didn't want it, and I could shove my awards and certificates and certifications—albeit they weren't real—right up my anal cavity.

People like Joel, usually men, thought that people like me were "quacks", that we were just smug, nosey assholes that "don't know shit about nothin". But mostly, people like Joel were not too proud to admit they needed help—they just believed there was nothing wrong with them and that it was everybody else who needed to get their shit together. It wasn't often I got a *Joel* in my office, and almost always it was a forced situation: court order, threat-of-losing-one's-job, etcetera.

Before I even got out of the chair, Nancy barged into my office with a look on her face I wasn't used to seeing: panic.

"What happened?" she asked, one hand on the doorknob. "Is everything all right?" She wasn't speaking in a hushed voice, which meant we were alone as my three o'clock wouldn't arrive for nearly another hour.

"Everything's fine."

She glanced into the waiting room.

"That one is dangerous," she told me. "I got the worst feeling when he was out there." She came all the way into my office and let the door close behind her.

"Yes," I agreed, "he's dangerous. He'll probably kill his family and himself before the month is over."

Nancy just stared at me for a moment, unblinking.

"Let me guess," she finally said with sarcasm, "you have no proof and you're just going on another one of your hunches—which are always right, by the way—he didn't admit to anything; there's nothing for you to report."

She sighed and stepped up closer, traded sarcasm for determination. "But you *can* report your professional opinion, Mr. Boone; get him put on a list," she said. "And what about his kids? Any abuse? You can report *that*."

I shook my head and shuffled through a stack of folders on my desk. "You know they never do anything with 'professional opinions'—they never do anything when they have irrefutable proof that someone is dangerous. And no, Joel doesn't abuse his kids," I told her. "They're just afraid of him. He actually loves his kids more than anyone or anything, and he'll do anything to protect them."

"But you just said he'll kill them…"

I nodded. "Yes. I did say that."

She waited for me to explain.

"He'll kill them because—"

"Because he'll think he's protecting them," Nancy cut me off, figuring it out herself. She crossed her arms and paced a trench in the carpet.

Nancy had a big heart, and there wasn't a malevolent bone in her body. And when it came to women and children and minorities and animals and nursing home victims and the

105

handicapped and bullied kids—okay, when it came to anyone wronged or harmed who she considered innocent—she was not only an advocate to their cause, but a wannabe superhero waiting in the shadows to swoop down and save them from the evils in the world.

Unbeknownst to Nancy, she had a sixth-sense; she knew when someone was "evil", when someone posed a threat, when someone was sick, when someone was on the brink of ending their life. Nancy was an empath, like most people with Actual Depression are, often picking up on everybody else's emotions in addition to her own. And yes, Nancy suffered from Actual Depression herself. But she was stronger than most, and she was not suicidal—she was too determined to fix the world than to leave it—and she easily hid her disease from society.

"Well, what are you going to do?" she asked with desperation in her eyes.

"Nothing." I opened the drawer on my left and put away the files.

"Nothing?" Her eyebrows drew together stiffly in her forehead.

"Well, right now I'm going to have lunch, now that I have time to spare."

Her cheeks flushed with red-hot anger; she crossed her arms firmly over her breasts.

"How can you be so...you know what, never mind." She opened the door. "I'll report him myself."

"You can," I told her, "but you know as well I do that it won't change anything."

"At least my conscience will be clear," she argued. "At least I'll have tried to do *something* about it"—she gestured harshly at the window—"instead of brushing it off like it's nothing and dining over deaths I could've tried to prevent."

Then, just before the door closed behind her she said, "Even one death you don't try to stop, and you can lose everything."

The painting on the wall rattled for the second time that day when she made her exit.

Nancy had no clue about my deal with Morty Finch; her comment meant something else entirely, but she'd changed my mind where Joel was concerned. I had to try. I had to do something. But what? I'd already ruined the session, as I knew he would not be back.

Fuck.

14

It was Friday. I was on my way to meet Lucifer when I felt the familiar sensation of a life lost and a new soul I would need to reap. A detour was not an option. I couldn't reschedule my meeting or it could be another week or more before I could get in to see him again. And this particular soul was one I had to reap myself. I couldn't send the ravens to do it for me, but they were adamant as always.

"Let me do it!" one raven insisted, perched on my left shoulder. "I waaantit! *Caw!* Let meee! I'm begging you master! Pleeease!"

"I asked him first," said the raven perched on my right shoulder; he fluffed up his big black feathers. "And you whine too much, didja know that? *Caw!*"

"Neither of you will carry him," I said, walking along the sidewalk. "He's mine."

"But they all end up yours, boss," said the raven on my right shoulder.

"Yeah! *Caw!* What difference does it *really* make?" said the raven on my left shoulder, trying to manipulate me.

"Same difference it always makes," I told them both.

"But if yah leave it to wander too long, boss…"

"Yeah, master—*Caw! Caw!*—If you let it linger you could lose it! *Caw!*"

"I won't lose it," I said, confidently. "Now make yourselves useful and go find a soul to carry—just not that one."

"Fine! Fine! *Caw! Caw!*" cried the raven on my left.

"We'll find another soul!" said the raven on my right.

Their ruffled feathers tickled my ears before setting off.

I couldn't get to every soul that needed reaping at the time of death every moment of every day, so I employed assistants to carry the souls for me. Temporarily. Just long enough to keep them from floating around in Limbo. Eventually I'd get around to reaping them, but the longer my assistants carried them, the less the effects I'd feel when I finally got around to them myself. It was why the ravens wanted that soul I forbade them to touch, because, like me, they were addicted to certain kinds.

But they weren't getting that one—he was mine. I just hoped I was right about not losing him. It was a risk, I admitted, letting a soul wander freely for too long. Anything could happen. And anything often did.

I picked up the pace and made it to Lucifer's building two minutes before the scheduled time. I walked past his secretary—Lucifer's "job" at the time was real estate—and I let myself in.

"And there he is," Lucifer said dramatically, opening his hands. "My dear brother come to strike a deal with me."

"I'm not here to strike any deals, Lucifer."

"But you need my help."

"You could say that."

He smiled. "Well, you know, Azrael, that my help doesn't come free." He wore a black suit with a gray-and-red tie; his dark hair was slicked back with a thick layer of gel shiny underneath the fluorescent light running along the ceiling.

I made myself comfortable on the leather sofa near the window overlooking Downtown Los Angeles. I sighed.

"I'm already up to my eyeballs in bad deals," I told him, propping an ankle atop a knee. "Cut me some slack."

"Oh, come on now," Lucifer said, getting up from his chair. "If I start doing it for you, I'll have to do it for everybody."

"We both know you never do anything you don't want to do, so spare me the monologue."

Lucifer rolled his eyes exasperatedly and gave in.

"All right," he said, sitting on the other end of the sofa, "I'll do you a favor—"

"Favors come with returns," I cut in. "Besides, do I need to remind you about the favor I did for you not so long ago"—I cocked my head—"involving the soul of a certain...dictator?"

"Fine. I'll make it a freebie." He held up his index finger. "But only one. Now what's the problem?"

"The Someone Elses are helping Morty," I said. "I've got inevitable suicides practically lining up at my office, and more on the way. Not to mention, one who's bound to off his family before offing himself, and because of him I've got Nancy on my back."

Lucifer grinned.

"Nancy, huh? I like that one. And so do you." His grin deepened.

"This isn't about Nancy," I said, irritated. "Look, Luc, you have a valuable soul riding on this. If *I* lose *you* lose, you said so yourself. So, it's in your best interest to help me."

He opened his hands. "Why don't you just tweak the lives of your patients a little?" he suggested. "It's not gonna kill you to lie just a smidge." He put his index finger and thumb together in front of his face, his eyes squinted.

"Nothing will kill me," I said, "but I'll be touching doorknobs and cutting out my tongue for eternity if I do that, and you know it."

Lucifer shook his head. "I'm so glad I'm not you," he said with genuine pity. "I take a soul and drop it off at the intersection of You Might Get Lucky Street and You're

110

Fucked Boulevard, and I rarely ever see them again. But you"—he motioned at me—"poor fool gets stuck with them; you really did get the shit end of *that* stick, brother." He laughed.

"Yes, I suppose I did."

"Well, there *are* options," he suggested. "You don't have to keep the souls *all* to yourself."

I smirked. "Of course not," I said, "but you never take the ones I'd like to get rid of, only the ones I'd like to keep—the ones I *need.*"

"Yes, but you know how...particular I am." He motioned a hand, pointing at the wall as if pointing at the world. "Most of them are going to Hell eventually, Azrael, but right now, before the apocalypse, or whatever they like to call it nowadays, I have a reputation to maintain. I can't just let any wannabe in"—he laughed—"Hell is L.A.'s hottest fucking nightclub! If I start taking in those whiney, boring bastards that float around inside of you Azrael, Hell will start looking more like the kid's pizza joint over on Seventh Street."

"Perhaps," I said, and I leaned forward, "but what if I stopped sending them to you at all? What if I decided one day that I didn't need to do you anymore favors?"—(Lucifer flinched)—"What if I decided one day that I can break my vicious cycle of honesty, and unbiasedness, and start playing by my own rules?" I stood up, and looked down on my brother, my hands in my pockets. "What if I decided one day to keep all of the souls for myself and never give you another one until that day when the apocalypse comes and I have no choice?" I smiled. "How would your L.A. nightclub start looking then, *dear brother?*"

A grin spread across Lucifer's face, and he held it there for a moment. "You are definitely my brother," he said proudly, and stood up to join me. "I'll help you, like I said, but only once. Don't expect me to intervene in every life you're trying to save. You get to pick one, and only one."

He paced.

"But I know you, Azrael," he went on, "and if I thought there was any chance you'd lose to Morty Finch I never would've bargained for the pastor's soul."

I smiled slimly.

"He is dead, you know," I said. "John Macon."

Lucifer's head snapped around mid-stride. "Oh? And when did this happen? How?"

"I just found out about it on my way here," I said. "Unsure of the details, but I *am* sure it had everything to do with my meeting with him recently."

"Morty," Lucifer said, shaking his head and looking out ahead of him now. "I thought he'd let John Macon live until he was ninety."

"Apparently," I said, "revenge burns hotter in Morty Finch than his need to be entertained."

Lucifer shrugged. "Yeah, well, there's no shortage of up-and-comers to take John Macon's place, that's for sure."

I nodded in agreement.

He sighed. "Welp," he said, turning, "looks like he's playing hard. He intends to win this game. And you've got your hands full."

"Yes. I do. So, how do you intend to help me?"

He thought on it a moment.

"I don't think you'll need my help," he said. "But in the event that you do, you call me and I'll be there—I can change anyone's mind." He grinned a dark and mysterious grin. "You do remember Isabis Gyasi, don't you?"

"Of course I do. The murderous African warlord butcher-turned-Christian—you really did a number on that one."

"Yes, I did." Lucifer smiled. "He is to me as John Macon is to Morty Finch—my entertainment." He chuckled. "I get bored too, y'know."

"Don't we all," I said. "But what's Isabis got to do with anything?" And then I understood. "Ah," I said. "Not only were you the one who made him do all of those things,

112

but you were also the one who converted him to Christianity."

"Guilty as charged." He smiled.

"Why exactly?"

Lucifer chuckled. "The simple answer: because I could." He stepped over to the encompassing window and he gazed down at the thousands of ants moving back and forth from the home base and the resources. "The detailed answer: because I am the puppet master, Azrael, and pulling the strings is what I do. Mortals are so easy to manipulate, to control, and I enjoy it."

"No, I meant why Christianity?"

Lucifer shrugged. "First religion that came to mind. They're all pretty much the same."

I nodded. And then I asked, "So, then he never spoke to God as he believes."

"Not that I'm aware of," Lucifer said. "I would imagine forgiveness doesn't apply to someone like him; but it's fun to make him believe it does—there really is a special place in Hell for people like Isabis. But the point is, Azrael, that I can make anyone do anything I want. And your patients are no exception."

"So, that's it," I said. "I'll call and you'll come."

He smirked.

"No favors, remember?" I reminded him as I felt the looming sensation of one.

He shook his head. "No, I wouldn't call it a favor," he said, "but I'd feel better about it—and my reputation would stay in-tact—if we came to some sort of...fair agreement, rather than me just giving away my help."

Leery, I looked at him in a sideward glance.

"What kind of...fair agreement?"

He paced again, his hands buried in his pockets.

"Oh, I'm thinking maybe if you win against Morty," he began, "then I get John Macon's soul as I'd bargained."

"You knew I was going to keep it?" I said.

He nodded "I had a feeling."

"But I always give you the souls you make deals with," I pointed out. "What gave you the impression I'd intended to keep this one?"

Lucifer looked me up and down with the sweep of his eyes, a crooked, knowing smile set in one corner of his mouth.

"You're losing yourself again, Azrael," he said. "You *need* John Macon's soul. You stink of desperation. And impending insanity. And if Morty has anything to do with it, he'll make sure you don't get to reap another soul like it, at least until after The Game is over."

I had considered this, in my meeting with John Macon. I was beginning to consider it more.

"You think he would use my sanity against me to win?"

"Would, or *is?*" Lucifer suggested. "Morty is a dirty player—Time is the dirtiest of *all* players, Azrael; he'll do anything to win."

I thought about it. He was right.

"I will split the soul with you," I offered.

Lucifer looked surprised.

"Whether John wins or not," I went on, "we will split his soul—he won't be needing it if you have to grant him his request to become a demon and walk the earth forever. But either way, whether I win or lose, we'll go in fifty-fifty."

"Hmm," he pondered, and then said, "It's a deal."

He walked over to the wet bar and poured himself a drink, offered me one, but I shook my head.

"Why are you doing this, anyway?" he asked. "Playing this game with Morty? Is it really because your existence is so terribly monotonous, or is it something more personal?"

I sighed. "I want to know if it's true," I said. "If Death and Time are equals."

Lucifer smiled and sipped his drink, his eyes watched me from over the rim of the glass.

"Why?" he asked.

"Because I just do."

He nodded. "Ah," he said, and his eyes fell away from mine.

He set his empty glass on the bar, inhaled a deep breath, and slapped his hands together. "Well, if the Jehovah's Witnesses are right," he said, "Death won't exist when this is all over."

"Yeah...well, let's hope they're wrong."

Lucifer walked to the window. "Let's take a stroll," he said, and motioned for me to follow.

In a blink, we were seventy-two-stories below his office, walking along a busy sidewalk, side by side. The buildings rose up all around us like metal and concrete giants, but I still felt like the mortals moving past us were the ones who were so very small. The woman on the corner waiting for the bus so she could visit her dying mother in the hospital; the man with a tattoo of a famous actress' name peeking from the collar of his dress shirt, who was on his way home to masturbate to her pictures like he did every day at the same time; the pet groomer sitting on a bench thinking about the dog she choked to death yesterday because it wouldn't sit still so she could cut its hair: *(Fucking little shit!)*; the man crossing the street clutching the hand of a boy he kidnapped from the park forty-two minutes ago; the college student thinking about dropping out of school to do humanitarian work overseas; the man sitting on the bench next to her thinking about following her home so he could rape and murder her.

Mortals. To us they were as relevant as a bacterial infection. But could Death...could *I* be as relevant as them someday?

"I made a deal once," Lucifer said. "Didn't work out for me in the end—I know you must've heard about it."

I nodded. "Yes, we've all heard about it." I glanced over at him. "Seems you're as suicidal as I am, trying to end the world like that."

Lucifer chuckled.

"We're all a little suicidal, Azrael," he said. "You, me, Time, and everybody out there." He motioned at the passersby in the street. "They all know it," he went on, "that something about their existence is a little...off, that something's not right about the whole thing."

"But I thought you loved this place," I said. "The Devil's Playground. Earth. You're in control here, you do what you want when and how you want; you're the master of this domain. Why would you try to end it all? And so dramatically at that." I glanced over at him again, brow raised.

Lucifer smiled. "It *was* dramatic, wasn't it?" he admitted proudly. "Trying to reverse The Fall of Man. I mean, why *not* dramatically?"

He had a point. Why not?

"That still doesn't answer my question," I reminded him. "Why'd you do it?"

"I've *been* doing it," he said. "Norman Reeves wasn't the first—just the first one everybody talked about."

Surprised by his admission, I stopped on the sidewalk and looked at him, waiting for him to explain.

"That's not important," he said, waving it off, and we went into motion again. "The point is that I made a deal once too—more than once—and I've lost every time. And there's one reason why I keep losing: the part of me that wants to lose is stronger than the part of me that wants to win."

"You want the world to end, but you like it too much," I said.

"Yes. I have a love-hate relationship with this world. I *am* the master of this domain; I have everything I've ever wanted in the palms of my hands, power in my fingertips, but when it comes down to it, I'm just another John Macon."

I looked over.

"I'm tired, Azrael," he said. "Like you, and John, and Morty, and everybody else, human and immortal alike, who are beginning to feel the weight of The Lie too heavily on their shoulders. We're addicted to this world—it's our comfort zone—but we despise it as much as we suck its tit for nourishment."

"What are you trying to say?"

"Just that if you truly want to win, and prove that you're better, more important than Time, then you *will* win." He pointed his finger at me briefly. "But you need to be prepared for what that win will mean, how things will change, because things *will* change and you cannot change change— you following me?"

I nodded slowly. "Yeah."

Lucifer sighed. "I want you to win, Azrael," he said, "not because you're my brother, but because maybe if you win, and you change everything, I'll get what I want most without having to do it myself."

"Suicide by cop," I said.

He shrugged.

We rounded the corner, and we found ourselves at a busy intersection where a Vietnamese man spent his days crossing the street with crowds of tourists, a sign in-hand above his head that read: REPENT, a microphone in the other hand, his voice carrying loudly through the speaker on his back.

"Despite all that," Lucifer went on, his voice diminished by the speaker, "I want you to win because I want Morty to lose. He's a jackass. He's the fucking thorn in my side. Next to him, I'm no better than Vanity and her bitch sisters, only capable of influencing the death of humans—I'd like to take them out just like he does. The fact that he can choose when to end a life makes him higher on creation's pedestal than any of us. And, quite frankly, that pisses me off."

I've never really thought of it that way…

"But that's *all* he can do," I countered after I'd thought about it. "We have just as much power as he does."

"It still pisses me off," he argued.

Lucifer stepped off the curb and into the street as the tourists went into motion to cross. I remained on the sidewalk. "I should have that right!" Lucifer shouted at me, his hand raised above him and the heads of people. "It's the one thing I don't have! And I want it!" He laughed. "I want it, Azrael! Allister! Death! The Fourth Horseman! Because you're already here! Don't you see? Don't you see it?" And then he whispered something into a tourist's ear, and then he shouted at me: "You better win, Azrael!" And then the tourist barreled through the crowd, knife in-hand, and he stuck the blade deep in the Vietnamese man's back. The Vietnamese man's legs buckled, and the crowd screamed and cried and dispersed. He fell onto the asphalt, the microphone popping and screeching as it hit the ground and rolled. Everyone watched with horror, but no one rushed to the man's aide. No one went after the attacker who made a run for it down the middle of the busy street as cars swerved to avoid hitting him.

When I looked back at the intersection, Lucifer was gone.

But Morty was there. He winked at me from afar, knelt over the body of the Vietnamese man still alive and bleeding to death on the street.

And with one touch, the man was dead, and Morty left casually through the crowd of gasping onlookers, a cheap cigarette dangling from his lips.

The world turned gray. The bodies in the street were gone. Nothing moved or made a sound; time had stopped. It always did for this moment. I never knew why. I never thought to ask, because who would I ask? Morty? *Ha! Ha! Ha!*

"Am I dead?" I heard the soul say.

I looked up from my expensive dress shoes at the Vietnamese man standing next to me, his human form wispy and fading.

"Yes. You are dead," I told him.

"Who are you?" he asked.

"I am Death."

"Where are you taking me?"

Without answering, I opened my mouth and the soul was instantly swept into my being, swirling and hot and cold and violent. My eyes bled and my fingernails cut the skin of my palms and my palms bled, and my feet bled from the pressure of billions of souls pressing down on me from the inside.

I fell to my knees when the new soul showed its true colors. The pain the man felt when he was alive, the abuse he endured, the torture he was subjected to, the lives he was forced to take to save the lives of his family. I felt the sting of every lash inflicted upon him, the pressure and tear of every rape he'd survived, his sorrows and his happiness, but most of all his relief that it was now all over.

TORVI TACUSKI

THE
STRATEGY

15

Twenty-three days had passed since my meeting with Lucifer and little had changed. Except that Morty was catching up to me in points, and I was getting nervous. Of the many new patients Morty sent my way, I saved few. Jason Layne, Ann Singleton, Margot Henry, and Joel, were still among the living, too. Though, technically Joel was no longer my patient, but I'd been keeping tabs on him because since he was sent by Morty, he still counted—and I had been wrong about Joel's murder-suicide by the end of the month.

The one thing I noticed that had changed was my willingness to be Allister Boone, the psychiatrist. I was still the same brutally honest monster in a suit, but I realized how much I enjoyed my new job, and that The Game going on in the background was becoming less and less the reason for my new role. I looked forward to seeing my patients, to seeing the looks on their faces when they met me their first time and realized I was not what they expected. I *liked* it. I got off on it. But mostly it was relieving my boredom, the monotony of my existence. It gave me something to do. And it allowed me to get things off my chest, things about mortals that suffocated me: their stupidity, their blindness, their hypocrisy—did I mention their stupidity?

But not all of them were sheep. Jason Layne was as intelligent as they came. It was a shame that someone like him wouldn't be around much longer to set an example for the rest of the sheeple. Then again, I needed him—his soul—inside of me to balance the souls driving me mad. It only benefitted me to let Jason die. But I couldn't. He was a pawn in this game I intended to win. He would die soon, I kept telling myself. But, after twenty-three more days, I also thought: *The world needs more people like him. It's a shame he must die so soon.* But why? Since when did I care about what the world needed, or that it was unfair Jason Layne's life would be cut short? I shouldn't have cared, but I did. Maybe it was just the feelings of the people around me, I thought. No. It couldn't have been, because none, Nancy included, knew what kind of person Jason Layne was. Jason was a loner. He always kept to himself. He never spoke his mind. He simply accepted life the way it was—*his* life, anyway; everybody else's was another story, and I'll get to that soon enough. So, no one knew that the world needed more people like him. No one but me. Like Joel, I kept an eye on Jason. I knew what he was doing most of the time. I *had* to know, in case I needed to swoop in and save him from himself.

Other than the eye-keeping, I had seen little of Jason Layne as he'd skipped his weekly sessions. And I'd still charge him the fee for not giving the required forty-eight-hour notice. And Jason always paid his bill in-full, promptly, without ever once complaining.

He was ten minutes late today. He sat in the chair across from me. His health was failing at a fast rate; he was frail and pasty and I could hear his brittle bones crackling underneath his skin when he walked, his unsteady breathing, the heavy beating of his overworked heart. The cancer had spread to his lungs but he didn't know it yet. He'd refused to see any more doctors. And the doctors didn't mind he was done with them, because he was dying and they were pretty much done with him, too.

But his loving sister minded, and she was terrified Jason would die alone somewhere, maybe in a dark alley surrounded by homeless drug addicts waiting to pick his pockets after he breathed his last breath, and that they'd leave him there to rot next to a dumpster.

"Are you still avoiding your sister?" I asked him.

"Yes." He licked the dryness from his lips. "I can't let her see me like this."

"Where have you been staying?"

"In a hotel."

"That'd cost a lot of money in this city," I said. "But then what do you need money for anymore, really?"

"Exactly." He nodded, paused, and switched gears. "I've been doing what you told me. But not five. I couldn't think of five things."

"How many?" I asked.

"Three."

I waited.

"I started going to church," he said, licking his lips again. "But not for the reason you probably think."

"Tell me about your reason." I got up and retrieved a bottle of water from the mini fridge, opened it and set it in front of him.

"Thanks." He took a small drink with a shaky hand.

"I'm agnostic," he began, and tightened the cap on the bottle. "I wasn't raised this way—my mom was an every-now-and-then church-goer—but I never really believed in any of that stuff. It just doesn't make any sense. But even if it were true, people tend to twist the stories to suit them. It's so obvious. To everyone but the ones doing it, of course."

"Yes. I agree."

"You're agnostic?" he presumed.

No, Jason Layne, I know that God exists. I'm just not on His side. I'm on nobody's side.

"This isn't about me," I told him. "Let's spend your time talking about you."

"All right."

He adjusted in the seat, grimacing with the effort.

"Even though I've been agnostic all my life," he went on, "I've always been drawn to church. Not because of God,

123

but...well, it's hard to explain because I don't fully understand it myself."

"You've always been drawn to *the truth*," I answered for him. "Because even though you don't really believe in God, deep down you can't shake the feeling that there's *something* out there."

"Yes," he said. "I can't commit to believing that all of this—the world, the universe, everything—was created by accident, that some particles smashed together in space and here we are talking about it billions of years later—what created the particles, huh?" He scoffed, shook his head. "Hey, I'm a firm believer in science, but it really ticks me off when scientists go on record stating this or that *definitely* happened, that their findings are taken so seriously that kids are taught this stuff in school as fact, and not just theory."

"What don't you believe?" I asked.

"The Big Bang for one," he answered. "Most scientists don't believe in God, or any sort of higher power, so to explain these kinds of unexplainable things, they put together a complex theory that may or may not be true, and they claim it to be true." He motioned his hands. "I don't care how much science you used in your quest to 'prove' it— it *can't* be proven. Not *that*. It's impossible. Humans are so self-absorbed they think they're smart enough to know how we were all created. They don't know—they *can't* know. Nobody knows if it was God, or if it was science, or if it was both." He caught his breath, looked off at the wall.

"And the age of the universe," he continued the topic from before, "scientists don't know that for sure, either—it's impossible to know that unless you know how it was created, and since that's impossible to know, they *can't* know it!"

I had never seen Jason Layne so riled up, so confident in his beliefs. And angry.

"And the *size* of the universe—there's no possible way to know that!"

He took a breath and calmed himself.

"We don't even know most of what there is to know about the ocean, or the nearby planets—how can anyone claim to know how the universe was created and how long ago it happened and how freakin' big it is? It's ridiculous."

I nodded.

"On the other side," he continued, "people who believe in God but not in science, well they're just as delusional. Worse actually."

He stopped to take another drink.

"The Earth is flat. The Earth is only two thousand years old. Dinosaurs never existed." He rolled his eyes and sighed exasperatedly. "Just saying it out loud I feel like my IQ dropped fifteen points." He looked me in the eyes. "These things have been proven—they *can* be proven because we live here on Earth, because scientists can study the bones of dinosaurs and the Earth itself to determine age—it's right there in our backyard, not out there"—his hand jutted out—"trillions of miles away. And we've left the planet many times, so we know the Earth isn't flat." He rolled his eyes again, shook his head with disappointment. "People who believe this stuff are just like the scientists who believe in the Big Bang: they refuse to believe the other, so they make something up to explain it. Only the religious ones just flat-out refuse to believe what's in front of their faces. And the scientists refuse to believe that science can't prove or *dis*prove everything. It baffles me."

"So, where do you fit in all of this?" I asked. "As an agnostic, you don't necessarily believe in God, yet you don't fully trust there isn't one, either. And you believe in science, yet not fully."

"I don't know, but it seems to me that maybe they both exist, and that God *created* science; that He created...."

I waited impatiently—I wanted to know what Jason Layne believed so desperately and organically that I refused to listen to his thoughts so he could tell me himself.

But he backtracked at the last second, not trusting his own gut instinct—like most mortals do.

"It's all very complicated," he said. "I thought maybe if I finally started going to church that my mind could be opened up. Y'know, get both sides, and not just the side of Science."

"And has it? Opened up?"

He scoffed. "Not by a long-shot," he said. "I mean, I still feel drawn to knowing the truth, but sitting in those churches listening to people preach crazy stories from a book that was written by men, *human* men, well, let's just say I feel ashamed to be sitting there at all. I look around at the people sitting in the pews, clapping their hands and raising them in the air during song, nodding with devotion at the preacher's words, and I feel like I'm in danger of catching whatever sickness they're all infected with."

"But you don't," I said. "And you continue to go. Why?"

"Because, in a roundabout way, you told me to."

I paused, smiled.

"I'm getting nothing from it," he said. "I'm sorry, I know you meant well, but it's just not working. But...I guess I am glad I tried, at least. I do feel a sense of satisfaction having tried, even if my views haven't changed."

"So, then you did get something from it," I said.

He looked into his lap.

Then he raised his head. "Yeah, I uh...guess maybe I did."

I nodded once and moved the session along.

"And the second?" I said. "You said there were three."

"Yes. The second is something small."

"What is it?"

"I started a blog."

"A blog?"

Overcome with conviction, he wanted to stand up and explain this thing that was so important to him, and he started to, but decided against it once he realized that pacing would only hurt and make him short of breath.

126

Frustrated, he repositioned himself in the chair again.

(I wish I'd die already...I...I don't want to live my last days like this...)

"Jason?" I said, and he looked up, snapped out of his dark thoughts. "Tell me about your blog."

He swallowed, rested his hands in his lap.

"Well, technically it's called a 'vlog', a video blog. Instead of text, I record videos of myself. It's nothing major," he said, "just something I've wanted to do for a long time. Even before blogs, I'd always wanted to...speak my mind. But I was too afraid. I avoided conflict and controversary all my life. I'd just sit at the lunch table in Jr. High School and fume quietly while students were bullied. In High School I wanted to join Debate Team but never did. And as I got older, and the world got shittier, all I wanted to do was fling open the fucking window of my apartment and shout from it all the things I'd always wanted to say about the cruelty and injustices in the world."

Like anger, I'd never heard Jason Layne curse before. Seemed death was bringing him out of his shell. It always does.

"So, I started the vlog," he said. "I figured I'm going to be dead soon, so why not do what I want, say what I want? Conflict and controversary can't really touch me now, right?" He shrugged. "But my vlog isn't really reaching anyone yet—takes a lot of time that I just don't have—I don't imagine I'll have much of a following by the time I'm dead, but at least I'll have done it. I've been making sure to say my piece on everything that's important to me. No one sees it, but that's all right. I'm voicing my opinions, and that's what matters."

"That's bullshit," I said. "You *want* people to hear you, Jason, otherwise you wouldn't waste your time doing it."

He glanced at his hands in his lap.

"But you are right about one thing," I added. "You'll probably be dead before anything like that happens. Your lonely little 'vlog' will deteriorate like an un-watered garden after you're not there to tend to it anymore; it'll be lost in the millions of other untended vlogs out there, and no one will ever know about your opinions that never would've mattered much even if they *had* known."

He stared at me, his tired eyes set in surprise amid the sickly pallor of his skin.

Then he sighed and his shoulders fell into a slump.

"I think that's why I keep coming here, Mr. Boone— you say what you feel; you're not afraid to speak your mind. I admire that about you. I...envy you." He lowered his head. "I wish I'd met you sooner."

I waited for him to elaborate, but he didn't.

A moment later I asked, "And the third?"

He glanced at the window behind me, and then his eyes fell on mine. "Jillian Bowden," he said, very serious, as if hers was the last face he wanted to see before he died. "I've thought about that girl since seventh grade."

My skin crawled along my muscles like maggots on a carcass. Love. Relationships. Sex. Human bonds that involve sharing bodily fluids, and the self-inflicted torture of emotions. It was the part about being human I despised most. Not that I was human, but wearing the skin of one and reaping the souls of billions made it difficult to separate myself from them entirely.

Unfortunately, part of my job as a psychiatrist was listening to *all* of the problems my patients faced, and not just the ones I chose.

"Tell me about Jillian Bowden."

Jason interlaced his fingers on his lap.

"I was the guy in Jr. High too afraid to ask out his crush. *She* was my crush." He lowered his head, twiddled his fingers. "I don't know why I still think about her after all this time. I mean, we hardly ever spoke in school unless it was about an assignment, and once she said 'excuse me' when she'd accidentally bumped into me in the hallway. We never even had a friendship, much less a relationship, so why I've not been able to get her out of my head since seventh grade is beyond me."

"Do you think it's love?"

He shrugged.

"Honestly, I don't know," he said.

"Then it's not love," I told him, and he stopped twiddling. "If you don't know, then it's not love. It's something else."

"Maybe you're right," he said, "but I don't know what that something else could be. I'm not a weirdo—I don't stalk her or anything. I mean, I think she's pretty, and I'd be lyin' if I said I'd never dreamed of being with her—a crush is a crush—but…well, I just don't know."

"And that's precisely why Jillian Bowden is one of those things I want you to pursue," I said. "Because, like Crater Lake, something about Jillian Bowden has followed you around most of your life, and now here you are, trying desperately to figure out why before your time runs out. Where is she now?"

"She lives in Brooklyn."

"I see." I leaned back in my chair, crossed my arms. "And what have you done to pursue her? Have you reached out to her yet?"

He shook his head. "Oh no, I don't think I could do that."

"Why not?"

"Because she's married."

"Your goal isn't to sleep with her."

"No, but…it just isn't right." He shook his head. "I don't want to start anything."

"Conflict and controversary can't really touch you now, can it, Jason?" I leaned forward again, rested my folded hands on the top of my desk.

"But what am I supposed to say?"

"Speaking your mind doesn't always mean you know in advance what you need to say—just that you need to say *something*. If you don't pursue Jillian Bowden before you're dead, you'll never know what it meant, why she was so important to your life that she never left it since the seventh grade. You will die…incomplete."

Jason stared intensely into his lap; his twiddling fingers went into motion again.

"Okay. I'll reach out to her. Maybe online or something."

"You'll reach out to her in person," I instructed. "Go to her house. Knock on her door. Tell her who you are and—"

"And *what?*" He looked apprehensive suddenly. "That I'm on a mission to find out why I haven't been able to stop thinking about her since Jr. High School?" He shook his head. "That *will* make me a weirdo, Mr. Boone. She'll probably call the cops on me."

"So?" I said.

He opened his hands in front of him.

"Live a little, Jason Layne," I told him, "before you die."

When his session was over, Jason Layne left my office with a level of boldness and determination he didn't have before he'd arrived. I read his thoughts as he stood in the elevator on his way down to the ground floor; he was thinking about what he would say to Jillian Bowden, because he was determined to visit her, despite the fear.

How it would all turn out was as interesting to me as it was to Jason. I looked forward to our next session when he could fill me in.

16

I was equally interested in being filled-in by Ann Singleton. Apparently, her small brush with death was enough to save her more than one more day, because there she was, still alive after twenty-three. She was still very much suicidal; her brush with me didn't open her eyes to any new possibilities or give her ambitions or make her feel grateful to be alive. She still wanted to die, and she still wished every day that a bus would hit her as she crossed the street, or a brain aneurysm would shut off her lights, or that dark mole on her back would turn to melanoma and spread like a California wildfire. Ann Singleton was alive for one reason: she was curious about me.

"Who are you, really, Mr. Boone?"

It should've made me nervous, but instead, the idea of telling her the truth about who—*what*—I was felt liberating.

But I did not forget Lucifer's warning.

"What exactly do you mean, Ann?"

"You're an enigma, Mr. Boone," she said. *(And I think...)* She'd started to add to her comment, but instead, she leaned back again and decided on another approach. "Have you ever met someone who right away you didn't trust? Or, someone who just generally gave you a bad vibe?"

"I give you bad vibes?"

She shook her head.

"No, it's not that. It's the opposite, actually."

"So, then I give you *good* vibes?"

"Well no…it's…" She leaned forward in the chair, her face hardened with concentration. "You give me 'different' vibes, Mr. Boone. I feel like I can trust you fully. But most of all I just…well, I just feel like"—she leaned back again, crossed her arms—"Never mind."

"I won't think you're crazy, Ann," I told her. "If you feel like you can trust me fully, then you should be able to tell me anything without fear or concern."

(Why do I trust him? I've trusted no one like this before. Not even Michael!)

She stood up and paced my office.

"Maybe I *am* a little nuts," she said, not looking at me. "All the time I feel like I'm wearing someone else's skin, or like I'm…just not in the right body. I fantasize about the apocalypse. So yeah, I might be a bit on the abnormal side if you're out there looking in at me. But personally, I think I'm more in tune to reality than most people, and that's *why* I am the way I am." She stopped and gestured her hands. "There's nothing wrong with me"—her hand jutted out, indicating the rest of the world—"*they're* the ones that are sick, Mr. Boone. And you"—she looked me right in the eyes—"I get the feeling you're not one of them. I think in a lot of ways, you're…just like me."

In some ways, yes, I was like Ann Singleton. Suicidal. Not comfortable in the skin we wore. Feeling out-of-place in the world. Knowing—although I knew for certain and Ann had only her hunches—that reality isn't reality, and that everything they see and touch and smell and taste and hear is just another Blue Pill scenario.

But the one thing that made us very different, that overshadowed all the things in which made us the same: I was Death and she was mortal.

"You're right, Ann," I said, and I stood up from my chair, touched my fingertips to the desk. "I'm not one of them. But I'm not one of you, either."

Intrigue and surprise swam in her eyes.

She waited.

I contemplated.

"I am...neutral," I finally said. I had started to tell her the truth, but at the last second, decided against it.

It wasn't a lie, but it bothered me how easy it had become for me to dance around the truth rather than just stating it. I wasn't comfortable with that; it was on the cusp of being a lie, and for me, that was walking a too-thin line.

The surprise and intrigue in Ann's face faded into her slumped shoulders. She sighed and sank into the chair, disappointed. And I knew then, in that pivotal moment, that Ann's life hung in the balance of that too-thin line between my almost-lies and the truth. She knew there was something different about me because people like her could sense it. But the gift was also a curse, because the not knowing was torture. She needed something more to keep her tethered to this world, something that her fragile shell could use to contain her powerful soul. She needed knowledge, proof she had a purpose and that her existence was not meaningless. She needed to know that she was the way she was because she was not the one who was "sick", and that everyone else was delusional.

Ann Singleton needed something...impossible.

I couldn't tell her she wasn't the one who was sick. I couldn't tell her—with any more honesty and detail than I already had—that the Someone Elses targeted her because they were threatened by her, and that she was the way she was because she had a better grasp of reality than "happy" or "normal" people had.

I couldn't tell her...because it was all true.

That kind of truth is dangerous. That kind of truth opens a soul up to Darkness like bacteria to an open wound. That kind of truth creates men like Pastor John Macon. And it damns souls, like his would certainly be damned. I did not want that for Ann. I—Again, why did I even care?

I needed time to myself, a chance to sort out my own problems instead of sorting out everyone else's. I needed to balance the souls inside of me, and I needed to do it soon, before I basically handed Morty the win over, wrapped with a golden bow and everything.

But I needed to fix Ann Singleton first. Because with my one almost-lie, I'd taken her right back to where she was when I'd first met her.

"Ann," I said, and she looked up at me standing over her. "I will tell you what I believe, right here, right now"—I pointed at the floor—"and then in one hundred ninety days, I will tell you what I know to be true." I pointed the same finger upward. "But only under one condition."

The surprise and intrigue found their way to the surface of Ann's face again. After a moment, she nodded slowly, unsure of what she was agreeing to, but sure she wanted to know.

"Okay."

I looked right at her and allowed her to see the dark depths of my eyes; I gave her the inch more she needed to know in her heart I was that enigma she'd believed me to be. I could feel her soul slipping around inside of me until it could hold itself up in such an unstable environment; I could feel its powerful fingers clutching my organs, its sharp teeth piercing and shredding my veins. Dear God, her soul was one of the strongest I'd ever encountered. *She won't be like John Macon. She won't be like John Macon...* Her heart beat furiously behind her ribs, and her hands trembled, and the moisture evaporated from her mouth. She wanted to close her eyes, but she couldn't; the harder she tried the further she slipped into the abyss of the truth.

"Swear on your soul," I said, and she snapped back into the only reality she'd ever known, "that you will not, under any circumstances, harm yourself before the one hundred ninety days are up."

She thought about it, staring off into space, wondering what had happened to her seconds ago.

"Okay," she finally said. "I swear on my soul..."

And with those words, Ann Singleton's soul, even if she took her own life, could only ever belong to me. I had secured it. It would be mine.

There was a method to my madness, and it was much more than saving Ann and securing her as my win. Like Morty, with suicides, he cannot choose the time in which to end their lives, and I cannot choose where to send their souls after I reap them. I cannot keep their souls for myself. At least, not without their permission. And she had just given me hers.

Reaping a suicide soul differs from every other soul. It's like lifting a feather as opposed to a bag of stones. Suicide souls aren't as deeply rooted in this world as everybody else. And the only other difference is that I have no idea where they go after I reap them. I never see them again. And I couldn't let that happen with Ann Singleton. I needed her soul—I *wanted* it.

I took a moment to myself to prepare her for the things I would say, the things I believed were true but I did not know for sure. They would change her, all right. But in what way? Would they help her, or make things worse?

I was soon to find out.

"I believe that mortals such as yourself are the most important pieces in the Grand Design that is Life."

With my hands in the pockets of my dress pants, I walked to the giant window and then gestured for her to join me.

Together we gazed out at the industrious concrete jungle that was New York City under a cloudless blue sky, the bustle and flow of yellow-roofed cabs and food trucks and cars and ants, thousands of ants of all shapes and sizes and colors and religions and languages moving back and forth in a pressurized line of monotony and obedience.

Ann never looked at me, but her mind was open only to me.

"Only one-percent of the world's population, past, present, and future, will make it past this phase. The ones who are oblivious and 'happy', the ones who live as they are told, who conform to familial and societal and religious norms rather than thinking for themselves, will one day wither into the nothingness from where they were born, never knowing their purpose for being here, and never allowed into that divine place you people call the Afterlife." I glanced at Ann. "One-percent." I looked back out at the city. "Those who believe they know where they're going when they die, the ones who think they have it all figured out, they're the ones who'll be in for a nasty surprise when it's all over. But this isn't about them."

I stopped, turned to face Ann, my hands folded down in front of me.

"This is about you," I said. "And those like you. You're a rare breed of human being, Ann Singleton. One thing I do know as fact—so this is a freebie—is that you truly are the way you are because you're more in tune with reality than everybody else. And because of your gift, your soul is wide open to the outside forces that will continue to attack you every single day for the rest of your life until you can't take it anymore and you *end* your life. They *want* you to fail. They want to take you out before you reach the finish line. They will use every weapon in their arsenal. And they will. Not. Stop. Because suicides go…somewhere else. Somewhere they're no longer a threat, somewhere they no longer matter."

Her eyes grew wide with wonder, and then shortly after, fell under wrinkles of incomprehension.

"In short," I said, "if you take your life, they will win, and you will eternally regret it."

After a moment, she asked, "Who are *they*?"

"You know who they are," I told her. "Not so far beneath the surface of that extraordinary mind of yours, you already know the answers to all of your questions. All of them save the ones about how you were created, or what will happen to you after you die, or what's the meaning of life. But right here"—I pointed at the floor—"right now, questions about this world and the people in it, the struggles you face every day just being human, the questions you ask yourself about right or wrong, which path to take, is this or that real or is it just your imagination—you already know. But they don't want you to realize you already know, and the closer you get to the truth, the harder they'll hit you with lies. And suffering. So, until you either step out of that human skin and use the gifts you were given to fight back, then they've already won. And your death will be…unfortunate."

Silence. The room was thick with it. And then…

(I don't know why I believe him, but I do. Part of me wants to tell him he's the one who needs help, but…I can't. I can't believe that because…he's telling the truth. This is unreal…Am I dreaming?)

"How do you know?" she asked after a moment.

I gazed out at the city again; the sun reflected blindingly off the windows of nearby buildings. I wasn't sure which part of all that I'd said she was referring to, but I answered, nonetheless.

"It's not something I know, but something I feel every time someone takes their own life."

I stepped away from the window and paced the room. She remained, looking down at the city, my words blending perfectly in the background of the silent, slow-motion scene in front of her.

"That is what I believe," I told her at last. "But if you still want to know what I *know* to be true after what I've told you, then you hold on for one hundred ninety more days, and I will hold up my end of the deal. If you'll believe me. Something tells me that you will."

"Is it worth it?" she asked, turning from the window. "Whatever it is you're gonna tell me—is it worth it?"

What her question really meant was: Is it going to change my life? Is it going to change everything I've ever known? Is it going to be The Truth? The Impossible? Is it going to make me want to live?

A smile slipped across my face like a shot of whiskey blooming in my chest.

"Yes, Mrs. Singleton. It will be worth it."

Ann Singleton would live. For at least one hundred ninety more days. But after I told her the truth, would she still choose to live?

I believed she would.

What she would do with the information, I looked forward to witnessing almost as much as I looked forward to witnessing—and participating in—The End of Everything.

17

"What a load of crap." Morty Finch's laughter preceded him as he came around the corner and entered my office.

Ann Singleton had just left.

For the briefest of moments, I sensed his almost-decision to take her life right then as she passed him in the waiting room. He'd nearly touched her, but he let her go.

"If anything I told her was a load of crap," I said, "you wouldn't have thought for a second to kill her just now."

Morty smiled, and then plucked a cigarette from his shirt pocket.

"No smoking in the building."

His eyes rolled upward and he sighed with irritation, slipped the cigarette back into the pack, giving the filter a tap with the tip of his finger.

"What does Ann have then?" I asked, knowing she must have something—bad heart, blood clot, anything that could drop her unexpectedly—that would allow Morty to pull her plug.

"She asked for it," he said, and plopped down on the chair in front of my desk. "But it doesn't matter, Allister. You're not gonna save her no matter what cockamamie stories you put in her head. I gotta hand it to yah though"—he laughed—"you get an *A* for creativity, that's for sure!"

"You know I don't lie," I said. "Besides, you believe what I told her as much as I do, Morty."

"Nah." He shook his head, pursed his rough lips. "That's your problem"—he pointed at me with a crooked, arthritic finger—"you think too much. Should just leave that one alone."

"Ah"—I grinned—"then you *do* believe it."

Morty wasn't smiling anymore; he chewed on the inside of his cheek.

"And it looks to me like the Great Morty Finch is almost as susceptible to the Someone Elses' influence as the mortals are."

He snarled.

"Not true," he said.

"No? Then what was that out there? Felt to me like a life was about to end right there in the waiting room. Did you forget I can sense those things?"

He refused to look me in the eye, a sure sign I was right and he knew I couldn't be convinced otherwise.

I sat on the end of my desk.

"Sure, they're working with you, Morty," I said with a sigh, "but you and I both know everything they do is only to benefit themselves. Because all they care about is their agenda." I leaned toward him and added in a lowered voice: "And their agenda is to end lives and damn souls—especially ones like Ann Singleton's. You were going to kill her, even though she's off-limits when it comes to our game. They're *using* you, Morty. They always have been."

I leaned away and sat upright.

"Bah! So what if they are—as long as they help me win, I couldn't care less what their agenda is. I'm using them, they're using me—sounds like a fair arrangement."

I smirked. "But it bothers you. It bothers you that you have no idea what all their agenda entails, that you—like me—are just another pawn on their chess board. It bothers you that they know more than we do about"—I opened my hands, my eyes moved around the room—"what all this means. It bothers you they are the real players and you and I are just the pieces. Like all of them out there; every single life you've ended with the stroke of a finger—it bothers you we're not as superior to them as we thought we were."

"Oh, stop it, Allister! You're screwing with my head again. You know I don't like it."

I nodded once, mouth pinched on one side. "Yeah, I know you don't like it, but you know I'm right."

He crossed his arms and mumbled something under his breath.

"Why are you here?" I asked.

The angry look on his face existed for about three seconds more, and then he shrugged it off.

"Hey, I just wanted to drop in," he said, all-smiles again, "see how you work."

There was a knock.

"Seems you're just in time," I said as I went toward the door. "You're always around when Margot Henry is here. I wonder why that is?"

Morty looked faux-shocked—as if I didn't know about his spying.

"What are you implying, Mr. Boone?"

"You've been working extra hard on her since we started this thing," I said, and placed my hand on the doorknob. "Did you bring a half-gallon of ice cream? A supersized order of burger and fries with a side order of self-loathing and razorblades? Or, maybe your little sidekick, Gluttony?"

He shook his head. "Nah, I don't need her for this one. Thought I did before, but your girl, Miss Henry, is too easy a target."

"Are you sure about that?" I grinned, and opened the door.

Nancy led Margot Henry inside, and gave me a peculiar look before showing herself out. She'd probably overheard me talking to "myself" again, as she'd heard it often when I'd get a visitor like Morty.

Margot walked with her head high; she wore indigo today, from head-to-toe like always, but it looked decent on her. She knew it. Everybody in the building who saw her on her way up to my floor knew it. And, as a result, I knew it too.

And she was not wearing makeup.

"You look nice today," I told her and motioned at the chair.

"Thank you." She sat down, unknowingly, on top of Morty.

His old, weathered face scrunched up with revulsion, and he disappeared and then reappeared on the other side of the room, stood by the wall.

"You've made a lot of progress in such a short time," I told Margot.

"I guess so," she said. "I've done everything you've told me to do. I've smiled at everybody"—she gestured at her face with all ten fingers—"and no makeup. How long will I have to do this, by the way? I happen to like wearing makeup."

"Why do you like wearing makeup, Miss Henry? Explain it to me."

She thought about it.

"I like the way it makes me look."

"What's wrong with the way you look now?"

Stumped, she said nothing for a second; she got the feeling it was a trick question.

"I uh, I guess I just think it makes me..." She hesitated. "...Look better?"

"Was that a question or an answer? You don't seem sure of yourself."

She shifted uncomfortably.

"Fine." She gritted her teeth. "I like it because it makes me look better."

"Better as opposed to what? The real Margot Henry?"

"How am I not the real Margot Henry just because I choose to put makeup on?"

"Because you choose to put it on to look as everybody else expects you to look. There is nothing about painting your face that you do for yourself, but for everyone else who sees you. You've made yourself believe you choose to do it because *you* like it, because it's what *you* want, because it makes *you* feel good. But the truth is, Miss Henry, makeup and styled hair and nice clothes are just costumes that everybody is expected to wear for everybody else. Am I wrong?"

"Yes. I think you're wrong. Just because a woman chooses to wear makeup doesn't mean she does it so people will look at her."

"Actually, it does," I said. "Especially in your case. The same way a woman will go to drastic measures to get breast implants, or a nose job. Nobody goes through that because it's what *they* want for themselves—they do it to feel better about themselves by how others will *perceive* them. Makeup is simply the cheaper, less painful nose job. She wears it so people will look at her in a way that makes her feel good about herself. Which, in turn, Miss Henry, means she wears it not because *she* likes it, or that it's an independent decision, but because she wants *everybody* else to like it, which makes it *their* decision. The fact that you are uncomfortable without makeup proves you wear it to impress and please others more-so than yourself."

"So, the key is to not give a shit what others think."

"No, the key is to not give a shit *at all.*"

She huffed and bit down on her bottom lip.

"So, you're saying I should never wear makeup, or style my hair, or wear nice clothes?" She looked me up and down with a snarl. "Why do you wear that suit, Mr. Boone? Why do you style your hair that way?" She smirked.

"Which side of the desk are you on, Miss Henry?" I leaned forward, seizing her perplexed gaze. "Which one of us sought the help of a psychiatrist? Which one of us cares so much about what society thinks of her that she's become a slave to it? Weak. Vulnerable. A blubbering mess of a human being when she gets her feelings hurt." I leaned back again, relaxed against the chair, gestured my hand. "And no, I'm not saying you should never wear makeup, or style your hair, or wear nice clothes—I couldn't give a shit less—I'm saying you shouldn't until you can go without it and not give a damn what anybody else thinks."

"I'm not wearing it now," she pointed out. "I haven't worn it since the day you told me not to."

"You're lying," I said, and her lips snapped shut; her fingers tangled nervously on her lap. "You've worn it to work every single day. The only time you've gone without it has been when you've come here to see me."

Her head shot up. "How'd you know? Have you been *following* me?" Her face shifted from disbelief to discomfort.

"No, Miss Henry. I didn't have to. You admitted it just now."

Morty laughed.

Margot's shoulders fell into a slump and she looked off at the wall. "All right, I lied," she said, making eye contact with me again. "But what was I *supposed* to do"—she gestured her hands animatedly—"get myself fired? I start going to work without makeup and I feel so self-conscious and shitty about myself that it affects my performance; my boss looks at that and adds in my suddenly looking like hell every day and he thinks I'm too much of a risk to keep on the payroll." She slammed her hand down on the top of her thigh. "I'm all about helping myself—that's why I'm *here*—but I can't lose my job in the process."

"You're here, Miss Henry, because you want someone to feel sorry for you, to tell you all the clichéd things your poor little heart begs to hear about being confident in your own skin, only so you can be motivated and empowered by the advice long enough for you to rush off to the gym to buy the membership you'll use once, then to the grocery store to buy the diet foods you'll force-feed yourself for about a week, and in less than a month you'll be the same fucking Margot Henry, unmotivated, desperate, stuffing your face with Self-

Loathing Chocolate Chip, wearing makeup to work to hide the ugliness behind it that no one *truly* sees but you." I cocked my head. "People still think you're an ugly, fat nuisance *with* makeup, so what does that tell you?"

No answer.

"It has nothing to do with the makeup," I answered for her. "They see only what you see in yourself. You create your own reality, Miss Henry—all of you do. And if you were here for help," I continued, "you would've done what I told you, and not made up excuses to get out around it."

Morty's eyes bounced between Margot and me—all he lacked was a tub of popcorn.

"You're right," Margot said, and it surprised me. "I-I know, you're absolutely right. Everything you said is true. And I'm an idiot for not listening." She looked me right in the eyes. "So, how do I fix it?"

I stood up.

"You had your chance, Miss Henry," I said, and a look of panic spread across her face. "I warned you that if you ever made excuses, that I'd wash my hands clean of you."

She couldn't speak for a moment, all the things she'd wanted to say were a jumbled mess of letter tiles behind her teeth.

"But..." she finally managed. "Mr. Boone please give me another chance. I screwed up, I know, but...please. I-I know you can help me—I *want* you to help me. Just tell me what you want me to do. No more makeup to work—done. I won't wear it *anywhere*."

Despite knowing she was telling the truth this time, I walked to the door, placed my hand on the knob and held it there.

"You're on your own, Miss Henry."

She shot up from the chair, left her indigo purse—and her begging—on it, and she marched over to me, fists clenched down at her sides.

"My hour isn't up," she said (she'd used up her free fifteen-minute days a long time ago). "And I'm not leaving this room until I get every last second." She stepped right up into my space, crossed her arms. "I don't care if you call the police to have me escorted out of the building, I'm getting my"—she glanced at the clock on the wall—"forty-one minutes"—she pointed her finger in my face—"and there's nothing you can do about it, or I will be here every single day for the next forty-one *months*, making your life a living hell; you got that, Mr. Boone?"

Morty's eyes were wide with excitement.

And deep down on the inside, so were mine.

18

My hand fell away from the doorknob.

"How did you feel when you came into my office today?" I asked her.

She stood there, confused by my reaction, but still very much with both feet firmly grounded in her political stand.

"I'm—what do you mean?"

I moved away from the door, paced the room with my hands folded on my backside.

"A part of you felt...confident," I explained. "You came to my office today without makeup, your hair fixed in a simple, yet efficient bun on top of your head, and you dressed your usual. But the first thing I noticed when you walked through that door was how you carried yourself. You held your head high, and you didn't shy away from me when I looked at your unpainted face. So, tell me what made you the way you were when you came here today."

She thought on it, her brows drawn in concentration, but she still didn't understand.

"Let me ask another question then," I said. "How are you able to come here without makeup, and with confidence, but you can't bring yourself to do it when you go to work or anywhere else?"

She thought on it more.

"Probably because it's what you told me to do?" she finally said.

"Sure," I said, "but I didn't tell you to come here with confidence. I can't assign confidence, Miss Henry, you have to develop that all on your own, so it had to have come from somewhere. Think about it."

She thought about it. Five long seconds. Seven. Nine. Then she looked at me.

"Maybe because I knew you didn't care what I looked like without makeup." She paused, rethinking her answer. "Or...maybe it was because *I* didn't care what *you* thought about how I looked without makeup." It was becoming clearer to her then, but she still needed help.

"Which is it?" I asked. "Think about it really hard."

She had made it back to the chair without realizing, but she did not sit down. She stood behind it, her hands rested on the back; Morty remained by the wall, getting the most out of his visit as suggested by that wide-eyed look of amusement on his face.

"To be honest," Margot began as she slowly lifted her head, "it was both. I knew you didn't care how I looked with or without it, so it was easier not to stress on it. But at the same time, and *more-so* now that I think about it, you had pissed me off enough I really didn't care what you thought." Feeling even more confident now, Margot's eyes swept over me with a repelled look. "And you're not exactly my type, so wanting to impress you wasn't even on my radar."

Morty snorted, and I snarled at him. Margot glanced over, wondering what I was looking at.

"So, then you confidently came to my office without makeup not giving a damn what I thought," I restated what I'd told her before. "Why is it so difficult for you to accomplish this outside of my office? Are you sexually attracted to your boss or your co-workers?"

She made a face. "No way."

"Do you secretly worship any of them on a makeshift shrine at your apartment? (She looked aghast.) Do you want to be like them? Live in their shoes? Fuck who they fuck? (She looked *aghast*-aghast.) If any of them were to come up to you and demand you strip naked, or lick their toes, would you do it?"

"NO! God no! What's your point, Mr. Boone?" She looked appalled.

"Then why do you care for one second what they think of you? Why do you let the words and thoughts of others dictate how you feel about yourself? They are human, just like you; they hate themselves just like you do; each and every one of them has something to hide, has something about themselves they're ashamed of, just like you have. It might not be obvious, but it's there; if you look close enough you might see it. They shit like you and they stink like you do when you sweat. Even the famous ones, there's nothing special about them—they're as pathetic as you are, crave attention as much as you crave it, make the same idiotic mistakes, have the same regrets, and will grow old the same as you will one day when your tits will sag to your knees and your teeth sit in a glass beside your bed. The point is, Miss Henry, you're *all* disgusting, flawed creatures, and are the only creatures on this planet that *de*volve as they grow, so why in *hell* would you want to bow down to any of them?"

"Wow, you're makin' my head hurt," Morty said.

Shut up, Morty.

"All right," Margot said after a moment of deep contemplation. "So, then you're saying I should be confident in my own skin, ready to take on the world without letting anyone get in my way. That I should love myself and never let what other people think of me, dictate how I feel about myself, or how I treat myself?"

Not…exactly.

"Is that the message you're taking from what I've said?"

She nodded. "Yes. I-I mean, that's what I got out of it. I think." Finally, she sat back down.

"Then do with the information what you will."

149

Morty threw his head back and roared with laughter. "Why do they *do* that?" he said. "Ask questions they already have their own answers for?" He laughed again, smacked the wall behind him.

"You mean how you just asked a question you already knew the answer to?" I said out loud, though Margot couldn't hear us.

Morty made a face.

"You know what I mean, Allister."

"They see and hear and believe only what they want to," I told him. "Nothing more. Nothing less."

He pushed away from the wall and strutted over to Miss Henry, circled her, and then stopped on her left side and leaned toward her ear.

"What kind of clichéd message was that, anyway?" he taunted her. "That's what everybody says, the same old advice you can get for free on any street corner, or printed on some fancy self-motivation cards in the nearest gas station. But it can't help *you*, Margot; your problems are different; your problems stem from sexual abuse and your bitch of a mother who fed you until you were fat and then blamed *you* for it. Your problems aren't anything like everybody else's in the world, and this guy, this so-called psychiatrist doesn't know how to help you anymore than he knows how to help himself." He leaned in closer, his sing-song voice became a whisper. "Your time is running out, *Mar-got*. You'll be *bar-ren* soon. But you're too fat for any man to find your sweet spot, much less love you after he falls in. You should just kill yourself."

I shook my head at Morty's attempt. And, I admitted, I kinda wanted to hit him for being so cruel.

What's happening to me?!

Margot looked up from her lap, and right at me.

"There was something else you told me to do," she said, "and I'm doing it now."

"And what was that?" I asked.

"Ignoring that annoying voice in my head trying to tell me you're a scam artist."

I smirked at Morty.

He grimaced.

"I'm going to tell you something," I said after a moment, "because I think you deserve another chance—you're persistent, mouthy, you stand up for yourself with me, and I believe you have more than enough potential to do the same thing out there in the world. So, I'm going to give you my straightforward advice, without fat-shaming or sarcasm or threats. You can do what you want with that information, too, it's all up to you."

"Um…okay?" She pressed her purse against her stomach with both arms.

I walked over and took a cigarette from the pack in Morty's shirt pocket, popped it between my lips, and then lit the end aflame with Morty's lighter.

"What in Samhain are you doing?" Morty said, a big flabbergasted smile twisting his features.

"Where'd that cigarette come from?" Margot asked.

"Time's pocket," I said.

With her mouth agape, Margot slowly nodded, doing what all mortals do: dismissing what they don't understand.

"It's not what I was telling you," I began, "the stuff about being confident in your own skin, and loving yourself and never letting what other people think of you, dictate how you feel about yourself. It's what you assumed because that's what everybody tells everybody. But you were wrong—*everybody's* wrong."

She waited for me to correct her, but a part of her wasn't sure she was ready to know the truth. She was human, after all, and if anything I had to say meant she had to lift her finger too high to achieve her goal, or if she had to give up something she loved too much, she would find excuses. She would become the gym-membership-buyin', diet-food-wastin' Margot Henry and be that person for the rest of her short and unfulfilled life.

"The truth is, Miss Henry, it's not about being confident, or loving yourself—that just creates high-n-mighty rebels so full of themselves they trade self-degradation for flaming narcissism. The truth is…it's not about you at all."

There were those confused blinking eyes again—from Margot *and* Morty.

"Remember when I told you that to care about yourself you have to stop caring about yourself?"

She nodded.

"Well, that's precisely what's wrong with this world," I began. "Humans fall out of the womb onto an ever-turning wheel of lies. They grow up believing that life is all about them; they're trained, *groomed*, from birth to be self-loving, to view the world as a competition with everybody around them, they are taught to see that to be beautiful and to fit into society—or even to be loved by their own families—they must look and act and speak a certain way. They go to school to better themselves, they eat cake and ice cream once a year to celebrate the day they were born, they graduate and get jobs to pay for all the things they need, the things they *want*. They have goals and dreams: Allen wants to be an internet star, Jennifer wants to be dancer, Marissa wants to be a model, Jack wants to be an actor, Elliot wants to be a soccer player, Leon wants to be an FBI agent, Leslie wants to own her own business. Why do they want these things? Because they want success, fame, money, power, respect, and recognition. They want to be viewed as thriving, prosperous individuals, they want to be envied, looked up to for what they have whether it's wealth, beauty, or intelligence, or all of the above. Many just want to be comfortable. Others want to be remembered. But it's all the same thing: selfishness."

I paused to make sure Margot was listening. She was. I took a drag of my cigarette and held the smoke deep in my human lungs for a moment.

"I know what you're thinking," I went on, pointing skyward. "But what's wrong with wanting to be successful? Let me tell you." I blew the last of the smoke through my lips. "Because they're doing it for *themselves*. They're doing it because their parents instilled in them the drive to be successful, to work hard and to be financially independent—for *themselves*. But it's not about them"—I motioned my cigarette hand—"and only a handful of souls, past, present, and future, ever figure that out. It's. Not. About. Them. It's not about *you*."

Morty's bushy old-man brows were knotted together in his forehead. "You have seriously lost it, Allister," he said.

Margot looked lost, her eyes as blank as the thoughts in her head—I checked, there were literally no decipherable thoughts I could pick up for about four long seconds. She just sat there, gazing up at me, probably expecting me to continue. And I had intended to, until:

"So, what you're saying is I should think about others first. Not the ones who don't respect me, but like give to charities or something? That it'll make me feel better about myself by caring about others in addition to myself." She didn't seem sold on the idea—that was entirely *her* idea, by the way—but the gears in her mind were working hard to make the whole thing fit into a mold she could be onboard with.

Morty's eyes rolled over into New Jersey.

Margot stared off at the window, contemplating, on the verge of "figuring it all out".

"There are so many overweight young girls out there that need help feeling better about themselves," she said, though more to herself than to me. "Maybe I could help them somehow." She looked up at me, her face full of hope and anticipation. "What do you think, Mr. Boone?"

You should probably sort yourself out first, before trying to sort out anybody else.

I nodded with a quiet sigh. "I think it's an admirable idea," I answered truthfully.

Margot shouldered her purse again and went to leave, this time with a generous smile on her face and a lot of pep in her step. She looked great, I admitted—wonderful, actually.

But I also couldn't deny that I was disappointed that she, once again, did not truly understand what I was trying to tell her. Though to be fair, it wasn't her fault. Margot Henry was an intelligent woman. But she was human, and like all humans, she didn't understand the root of my message because her human mind didn't *want* to understand it. The same way people who encounter something preternatural but refuse to believe anything but the "logical" explanation.

And I was equally disappointed that I gave even the smallest fuck she didn't understand. I knew I was slipping further and further into insanity every day. I was supposed to be unbiased to, well, *everything*. But there I was trying to steer her in a particular direction. And it was much more than giving advice for the sake of the win—I was giving advice with some hidden agenda; I was becoming passionate about making them hear me and understand me.

I was becoming…*human.*

Margot Henry left.

Morty looked impressed.

"I have to say, Allister, you're not half bad at this."

"Are you worried?" I asked, though *I* was the one who was worried. For other reasons than he thought, of course.

"Nah," he said. "But when this is all over, you should think about continuing your little façade. I could send broken souls your way all day long."

I scoffed. "And what would you get out of that, Morty Finch?"

"Amusement, my friend. Amusement."

19

There was another knock at the door.

"Welp, I'm outta here!" Morty said.

He came over and took the half-smoked cigarette from my fingers.

"You shouldn't smoke, y'know." He popped it between his lips. "You might get cancer."

"Only humans get cancer," I told him.

"Yeah. I know." He raised an enlightened brow and vanished from my office just as Nancy entered.

"Smoking now?" She made a face as she waved a hand in front of her. "This ain't the seventies. You know it's illegal to smoke inside public buildings now, right?"

"What do you need, Nancy?"

She stepped over to the cabinet above the mini fridge and retrieved a can of air freshener. "I have to talk to you about something," she said as she pressed her finger against the nozzle. "Your two o'clock called and cancelled. But she rescheduled."

"Okay?"

Pshht! Pshht! Psshhtt!

"All right, that's more than enough," I said, waving my hand in the air; I coughed a little for added effect.

Nancy set the can on my desk.

"The cancellation isn't what I wanted to talk to you about," she said. "It's about your session with Margot Henry."

"What about it?"

"The things you were telling her," she said, "I was surprised I heard those words coming out of your mouth, but...well, I was glad to hear them."

"You were listening in on the session?"

"Yes. I knew there was something I liked about you. When I first started working here, it took everything I had in me to hang around after seeing how crude you were. But I'm starting to realize *why* I hung around—you're not as atrocious as I thought. Deep down you really care about these people."

Umm, no, actually I don't...

She crossed her arms.

"What part of my session with Miss Henry did you hear?"

"All of it," she said. "But the part about it not being about her, about *any* of us, was what stopped me in my tracks." She paced. "It felt like you were reading my mind, Mr. Boone. You said things to her, word-for-word things, that I've said to myself more times than I can count."

It was all becoming clear then; I shook my head at myself knowing then that it was Nancy saying those things, and not me.

"I really was starting to think I was the only one."

"The only one what?" I asked.

"Who believes that we've got it all wrong"—she gestured a hand—"that even those of us who are genuinely good people, who volunteer at homeless shelters and animal shelters and hospice centers, who send monthly donations to charities, who care about the environment, who protest the injustices in this world—even they have it all wrong. I mean, they're definitely on a better path than all those people out there who don't give a damn about anything but themselves, but they still have it all wrong."

I sat down on the edge of my desk while Nancy paced in front of the window; I couldn't deny that I was a little awed by her blooming speech. And my grasp on how it was my connection to her that had made me say such things to Margot Henry—relief washed over me.

Nancy continued.

"You said: 'Humans fall out of the womb onto an ever-turning bed of lies. They grow up believing that life is all about them; they're trained, groomed, from birth to be self-loving, to view the world as a competition with everybody around them...' Those were my words, Mr. Boone. I'm gonna ignore the fact that you pulled a one-in-a-billion coincidence out of your hat like that, because I don't want to waste time trying to understand how that could have possibly happened, and I'm going to stay on the point." She pointed at me. "Maybe if people started to understand what they've been getting wrong all this time, then the world would change. Maybe if people like you and me stood up and waved our hands in front of all their faces, we could *make* them see what they're doing wrong."

Even though I wasn't entirely sure what she was talking about, I still said, "You can't force a child back into the womb, Nancy. All of these people have already been born, and despite what some of them believe, there is no such thing as being born-again. At least not in the metaphorical sense. Besides, you use words and phrases like that and you alienate yourself by default over at the bible-thumpers table."

"I don't even believe in God," Nancy said. "So, all that born-again nonsense doesn't apply to me anyway."

"What is your point, Nancy?"

She paused, looked at the floor in thought. "I'm..."—she raised her head—"...not sure exactly what my point is. I guess I just wanted you to know that I agree with you, that I believe you, that I believe *in* you, and that despite the way you treat people, I also believe there's some kind of method to your madness."

Hmm. Was she the one reading *my* mind now?

"And…maybe you're onto something." She said this as if she wasn't entirely sure she should, like she was admitting something she didn't want to.

"And what would that be?" I asked suspiciously.

She went toward the door and gestured for me to follow.

I stepped out into the waiting area where all of the seats were empty save one. But Nancy couldn't see the woman sitting there, only I could. The woman gazed at me, her face serene, unblemished by humanity. She sat with her legs crossed, her hands folded on her lap. I had seen her many times before, nearly every day. Monday thru Friday, there in the waiting room, always sitting in the same chair— she went wherever Nancy went.

Nancy took me around to the reception desk and pulled her spiral appointment book from a three-tiered desk organizer. She laid it upon the desk and flipped through the pages, pointing here and there as if it was supposed to immediately mean something to me. She waved her hand at the names and numbers she had jotted down. "Every page is full," she said, flipping more pages. "Every single day and time available from today until the middle of next year." Her eyes kept looking for mine, but the contents of the appointment book held most of her attention. "You're doing something right, Mr. Boone. I'm not sure what it is, but I've been flooded with calls from people wanting to reserve a session with you. And I feel awful that I'm having to tell some of these people they can't get in for many months. Do you have any idea how hard it is for someone to admit they need help, then to talk themselves into seeking it? It's all a very delicate process that should be handled with the utmost care, and telling someone they have to wait six months is like throwing a stick in a bike's spokes."

"There are other psychiatrists out there," I reminded her.

She shook her head with a dismayed expression.

"Yes, but the good ones are a hit-or-miss, Mr. Boone. *I* know. I went through my fair share before I finally gave up and realized that I personally didn't need one—I was my own psychiatrist." She waved a hand in front of her face. "But this isn't about me—*look* at this"—she tapped the paper—"*Every* slot filled. I couldn't believe it. *Why?* I asked myself why anybody would want to sit in that chair and be told they're basically the scum of the earth, by a hypocritical, poison-tongued, self-absorbed pig like you."

"Well, I thank you for that…honest observation."

Wait…hypocritical?

She waved off my faked offense.

"Anyway, that's why I listened in on your session with Margot Henry—I just needed to know what you were saying to these people behind closed doors."

I shrugged.

"Look, the point is," she said, "I just wanted to say that whatever you're doing, keep it up. Even though I don't particularly agree with your methods, I'm not so close-minded that I won't recognize another viewpoint."

She closed the calendar and put it away.

"I'm curious," I said. "How are they getting it all wrong?"

Nancy opened a desk drawer and pulled her purse from it, set it on the desk next to her keyboard, and then sifted through it. "You don't have to be religious, or believe in any God at all, to be a good person," she said, and glanced up from her purse at me. "You don't have to believe in the stories of the bible to agree with their messages. Me, personally, I would never put my trust in anything written by a man, and that includes the bible—*especially* the bible—but that doesn't give me, or anyone else, a reason to be a piece of shit."

Seemed Jason Layne and Nancy had a lot in common. Too bad that whole dying thing would keep the two from ever forming any kind of bond.

"They're getting it all wrong," Nancy finally said, "because I believe the way we should all be is a lot like that famous carpenter in that story who was crucified for being genuinely good."

She pulled her hand from her purse and held a stick of gum out to me.

I took it.

"You can't just give to a few charities, or attend a few churches, or stand on few street corners and picket injustice, and expect that's enough." She shouldered her purse and came around the desk, stood in front of me. "You have to give up everything, Mr. Boone: your money, your big fancy house, your greed and your vanity and all your nicely wrapped excuses for why you do the things you do, and stop caring about making a comfortable life for yourself, so that you can help others. Full-time. Not this once-a-week or only-when-the-need-arises bullshit. The need is *always* there. It's always there, Mr. Boone. You really need that gum for your cigarette breath."

Without taking my eyes off her, I unwrapped the gum and put it in my mouth.

Nancy's explanation had been the real message I had tried to convey to Margot Henry. I felt better about it now that I knew it wasn't *my* explanation. Even though I agreed with the logic.

"I'm taking my lunch late today," Nancy said. "I worked through my usual time trying to sort out all those new clients. Since no one will be here for another hour…well, I'll be back by three."

And then she left; I watched her distorted figure through the frosted glass door until she turned the corner at the end of the hall. Then I spit the gum back into the wrapper and tossed it in a nearby waste basket.

"Now I understand," I said to the woman sitting in the chair. "Why you're always hanging around Nancy. Aren't you going to follow her?"

The woman nodded slowly.

"I will. In due time. You are *here*, so she is safe."

"There are other threats out there," I reminded her.

I sat beside her, propped my right ankle on my left knee, my arms draped across the arms of the chair.

"You know they never work out," I said. "Two thousand years and not one."

"One will. One day," she said in her gentle voice. "The woman has all of the qualities."

"The woman, is a *woman*," I pointed out. "A human. A mortal."

"So was He."

"But He was not a woman."

"No. He was not."

After a moment I said, "I won't interfere in Nancy's death."

"You will try. You always do."

"I like Nancy."

"You liked all of them."

"Yes. I suppose I did."

"This shall be no different," she said.

"The scenario? Or the outcome?"

"That you will try to be the death of her."

"I'm the death of everybody, lady."

She nodded.

"That, you are, Azrael."

I got up, and I went back to my office, but I stopped, and turned to face her still sitting in the chair.

"What about Ann Singleton?" I suggested. "She seems like a good candidate."

The woman shook her head slowly.

"You already have plans for Ann Singleton," she said. "We would never interfere in your plans as you interfere in ours. Besides, she lacks one of the most important qualities."

"And that would be?"

"The ambition to live."

"Ah, I see." I smirked, and casually slid my hand in my pants pocket. Then I pointed at her with the other. "You need someone who wants to live so they can be tortured to death just to prove a point." I chewed on the inside of my cheek, slid the other hand into the other pocket. "You're more barbaric than I or my brother have ever been."

"Only a human would think as so," she said.

"I am as human as I'll ever be," I assured her. "I have never let it go too far, and I never will."

"It is no secret," she said, "that you are becoming unstable again. You are beginning to care for these mortals. You are becoming submissive to their emotions."

"Hey, if you're talking about the stuff I said to Margot Henry, that wasn't even me. Those were Nancy's words, you heard her say so yourself."

"But it was not her emotion that angered you when Time was shaming Margot Henry," she revealed. "No one heard him but you, Azrael."

The relief I'd found before vanished in an instant. I looked off at the wall.

"And the feelings you feel for your patient, Jason Layne. *The world needs more people like him. It really is a shame he has to die so soon.* Those were your thoughts. No one else's."

I tried to shrug it off as inconsequential, but it was hard to do with any level of sincerity and I knew it looked as believable as it felt. "Emotions are not unusual when I've gone this long without a proper balance," I said. "It's a necessary side-effect of the job. A fight I've fought at least once a millennium since the beginning of time."

"You are losing that fight, Azrael. And that is why you *will* interfere," she pointed out. "And why I will stop you. I will not fail as the rest of us have."

"Perhaps," I said. "But you seem to be overlooking one very important detail."

"And that would be?"

"Nancy is an atheist."

She smiled gently. "For now."

I blinked and the Angel was gone.

20

Nancy had been right: I was booked up for the next seven months, and people were still calling daily trying to get in "as soon as possible". She had to start a cancellation fill-in list, and it was already two pages deep. "Why don't you start offering sessions every other Saturday?" she had suggested hopefully. But, to the dismay of my Jesus-II-in-training secretary, I quickly rejected that idea. "I need my weekends," I had told her. And my refusal was enough for Nancy to lose any hope she'd had in me joining her in her ambition to wave our hands at the world to try and change it. Nothing would ever change the world. Except an apocalypse, and I was all for that.

Initially, I had thought the unexpected surge of new patients was all Morty's doing, that besides sending me the most difficult-to-cure patients, he and the Someone Elses were trying to overwhelm me with a never-ending workload.

Apparently, and to my surprise, that was not the case.

Sure, Morty had sent some of them, but the majority had come from, of all things, referrals. Yeah, I couldn't believe it either.

"I've heard a lot about you from a co-worker," Joanne Emerson had said at her first session. "She recommended you. Said you were brutally honest, nothing like the bots who all say the same thing and shove pills down people's throats. She says you're different and worth spending my hard-earned money on." There was a we-shall-see-about-that twinkle in her eye.

"So, Joanne, I want you to name one thing—only one—that you dislike about yourself." I just wanted to get to the point, as small-talk was never my forte.

Joanne Emerson was the typical, run-of-the-mill, self-pitying, selfish human, the kind of souls I was full of, bloated by, disgusted by. She was far from being suicidal, and that told me she hadn't been sent by Morty Finch.

She used suicide as sarcasm.

"I feel like I just want to drive off a bridge sometimes," she said. "I do so much for people, and it makes me *so* mad and *so* hurt"—(she was good at dramatic expressions of misery)—"that nobody ever appreciates it. Can you believe I invited my son's girlfriend over for dinner—I was trying to be nice, start a relationship with her even though I don't like her—and she never even sent me a thank-you note. So rude and unappreciative. See if I ever try again with *her*."

And she went on and on about all the things she had done for people: the elaborate meals she'd slave over for people who did not "properly" thank her; the time and effort she'd put in to caring for a "so-called" friend's ailing mother; the errands she'd run for her "ungrateful" sister who lived on Social Security Disability and could not afford to buy a new car to run the errands herself; the gardening she'd helped her elderly neighbor with; the sixty-dollars she'd loaned her brother; and the other things she'd so graciously offered to do for people out of the "goodness of her heart".

I disliked this woman. I wasn't supposed to be biased, or hate or love anybody, so maybe it was all just due to my deteriorating condition, but I *really disliked* this woman.

"Was your son's girlfriend kind to you at the dinner?"

"Well, yes, I suppose so…"

"Did she thank you before she left?"

"Yes."

"And your friend's mother," I went on, "did you offer to care for her?"

"Well, yes, I—"

"I'm speaking," I cut her off and her mouth shut like a mousetrap; frustration filled the lines in her face. "And has your friend thanked you for helping?"

She hesitated. She didn't want to answer anymore because she knew exactly where this was heading: me pointing out her blaring errors. But I didn't need her answers to know the truth about everything:

"This is delicious," her son's girlfriend had complimented with a genuine smile. "I feel like I'm at a restaurant."

And before the son's girlfriend left that evening:

"Thank you for inviting me to dinner," she had said. "It was nice meeting you."

The Ailing Mother:

"I don't know how to repay you for helping with my mom," the so-called friend had said.

"Oh, you don't have to pay me anything," Joanne Emerson had said, brushing the "ridiculous" comment off. "I'm just glad I could help; I know you're going through tough times."

The Ungrateful Sister:

"Joanne, really, you don't have to do that," she had said as Joanne insisted she go down herself to the utility company and pay her sister's bills for her. "Jeff said he was going to do it."

Joanne made a disapproving face.

"I'm your family," she argued, "and I should be the one you trust to handle your finances." She put up her hand to silence her sister. "I said I'd do it."

Her sister sighed, gave in, and thanked her.

The Elderly Neighbor:

"Would you mind giving me some pointers on where to plant my flowers?" she had asked. "I see how beautiful your yard is—it's like right out of a landscaping magazine."

"Oh, well thank you, Mrs. Lyons," Joanne Emerson had said, feeling *so* proud. "I'll do more than give you pointers, if you'll let me."

"Really? Are you sure? I-I mean, I can't pay you, but maybe I could sew you a blanket."

Joanne Emerson waved the offer off.

"No payment needed," she had said. "Now, let me show you what I think will look wonderful…"

The Brother:

"Thanks for the loan," her brother had said as he handed over the amount in-full in repayment. "It really got me out of a bind last week. I'm starting a new job Monday morning, so I'll be back on my feet in no time. I'm really sorry I had to ask you."

"Hey, don't worry about it," Joanne Emerson had said. "Anytime you need help, you know I'm here for you."

Instead of answering my question, she got defensive, as I knew she would, because her kind always do.

"I've helped Janice with her mother for the past two months," Joanne argued about her friend whose mother she helped care for, "and not once has she ever done anything for me in return. I called her up one day and asked if she'd go with me to Branson for the weekend so I wouldn't have to go by myself, but she told me she couldn't." She chewed on the inside of her cheek. "And then there's my sister. She was always wanting everybody to feel sorry for her when we were growing up"—she smirked, crossed her arms—"I guess she got what she wanted after that warehouse accident that messed up her back. I bet she's faking it. Anyway, she never appreciates anything I do for her. I'm always helping her, and sometimes she hides inside her house when I show up so I won't catch her and 'ruin her day'"—she made sarcastic quotes with her fingers—"with that good-for-nothing boyfriend of hers who shows up over there more than I do. And then there's Mrs. Lyons across the street; I was so nice to do her whole flower garden myself, and when I sent my young niece over there to sell Mrs. Lyons some chocolates from her school fundraiser, that woman had the gall to decline. The least she could've done for my helping her was buy a bar of chocolate." She threw her hands up in the air. "I think I'm done—I'm done helping *every*body."

"It's probably for the best," I said, and she perked up for a millisecond, thinking I was going to agree with her, until I added: "None of those people need you in their life. You're a classic case of self-victimization, an attention-seeker. You're in constant need of praise and recognition, you wouldn't be happy even if someone applauded you or gave you medals for your 'good deeds' that are really just traps you set for people so you'll always have someone else to blame for the way you feel about yourself." I leaned forward, folded my hands on the desk. "Your sister hides from you because you're overbearing, obstinate, and, quite frankly, you drive her bat-shit crazy. She doesn't *want* your help because with it she's required to kiss your rosy ass for the rest of her life. (Joanne Emerson's head drew back, shock plagued her face.) Your brother respects you, and he loves you probably more than your sister ever will, or else he never would've braved the hippo-infested waters of your territory to ask for that loan. But despite him probably always at your beck and call, you still find room and reason to call him selfish—and you don't even know why. Probably because it's just so natural to you."

I leaned in even farther; Joanne Emerson was infuriated, humiliated, and too stunned to find her voice.

"You *want* to hate your son's girlfriend," I said, focusing on her wide eyes, "because she's a threat to you, because you know deep-down that boy you raised won't be around for you to control forever, and she's essentially taking your place. The girlfriend could shout from a rooftop praises about how kind you were to her at that dinner and you'd still find reasons to hate her. And that friend of yours who couldn't go with you to Branson—perhaps, I mean in the off-chance she had an ailing mother and was having 'tough times' in her life, it's safe to assume she had more important things to do than going on a vacation." I pointed at her briefly. "Have you ever thought that maybe Mrs. Lyons is diabetic? Or that she's allergic to chocolate? Or that maybe, just maybe, she scrapes the leftovers from her monthly government check and the meager sales from sewing blankets just to buy groceries, and she can't afford luxuries like chocolate and landscapers?" I waved my hand between us. "Ms. Emerson, you don't do anything for anyone unless you expect to get something out of it. You're not the kind, compassionate, giving person you believe yourself to be—and you *do* believe it, that is the sad part—but you're just the opposite: you're full hate, for yourself and everyone around you; you're angry at how your life turned out, and you make it your mission to piss on everybody else as often as you can if they even remotely show the tiniest ounce of happiness that you know you'll never experience. And if you stay on this path, you're going to die a sad, lonely, pathetic death, and when you die the birds will still chirp in the trees, the wind will still blow, the flowers in your neighbors garden will still bloom, and the people in your life, all those you were unkind to and made life difficult for, all those you blamed and criticized will quietly sing their praises that you're gone, because you did nothing to make them miss you."

Joanne Emerson looked as though I'd just slapped her.

I moved the questionnaire she'd filled out about herself, over in front of me, but I didn't look down at it.

"You wanted the truth when you came here," I told her, "and I'm giving it to you." I tapped the paper with my fingertip, and my eyes never left hers. "I do not like you. I am not your friend. I am not here to side with you or to tell you only the things you want to hear just because you pay me. I'm not here to stroke your fragile ego, or to listen to you cry your heart out as you tell me your sob story. But what I will admit, what I will side with you on, is something you wrote in your questionnaire." I tapped the paper again.

She glanced down at it.

"You don't owe the world, or the people in it, anything," I said. "People are terrible, and cancerous, and you really are a fucked-up human being because of your upbringing, because you were abandoned by everyone in your life who was supposed to love you, all the while you did whatever you could to make those same people see something in you that they might've found worthy, or that could make them love you as much as you loved them. But they never did."

The anger and humiliation in her eyes failed to something more grasping. She still couldn't find her voice, but she was getting closer to crafting a worthy argument inside that one-dimensional head of hers.

"As you grew older," I went on, "your heart turned bitter, and eventually you became the very people who hurt you. And today, you blame everyone around you for your own weakness, you push away those who care for you, all because they, for some reason you cannot fathom, never appreciate you, they never give you credit for all the wonderful and kind things you do for them, for going out of your way to make them comfortable and fix all their problems—that's what you see. But the real problem is *you*, Ms. Emerson. If you genuinely cared for your friend and wanted to help her mother out of the kindness of your heart, you would've done it with an honest smile, and not only would you have never expected a thank-you card, but you never would've even *thought* of needing one. Genuinely good people who go out of their way to help others, do so because the act is what makes them feel good *about* themselves, in an entirely selfless way. But you, Ms. Emerson, do not. You are the epitome of sel*fish*, and you deserve no appreciation for all the things you've only *pretended* to do for others."

If I didn't know better, I could hear the footsteps of the people on the sidewalk twenty stories below it was so quiet in my office.

What happened to that argument she had been stirring in that big black pot of hers the whole time she had been sitting there? I couldn't even read her thoughts anymore. Joanne Emerson, for the first time in her fifty-nine-years of life had no words, verbal or otherwise.

"Do you like dogs?" I asked her.

She blinked confusedly, and all she could look at was the questionnaire on the desk for a moment, though she wasn't seeing it.

"Huh?" She finally said, looking up.

"Do. You. Like. Dogs?"

Another confused moment, this time looking at her aging hands, but not seeing them, either.

"S-Sure I do," she said.

"Well then, I have an assignment for you."

"Umm…"

I jotted down an address on a green sticky note, then pulled it from the block.

"I want you to go to this address," I told her, handing the note off to her stuck to the tip of my finger, "and find a dog, the first dog you see, to take home with you. More than one if you'd like, it's up to you how many."

"You want me to…*what*…?"

"Dogs are the most loving, loyal, and affectionate creatures on this earth," I said. "Because I agree with you about how terrible humans are, and that you don't owe them anything, I want you to focus on creatures that are the exact opposite of humans."

I stepped around to the side of my desk.

"Not only will these dogs give you the attention, appreciation, and recognition that you were denied in your younger years and later denied yourself, but more importantly, they will give you the unconditional love you never had. They will never willingly leave you, or hurt you, or even reject you. And then maybe, somewhere down the road, you'll learn what kindness and generosity and compassion really are, and how they truly feel when gained by selfless acts rather than selfish ones."

Joanne Emerson reluctantly took the sticky note, her eyes darting to and from it and my unwavering gaze, her mouth slightly agape.

Without another word, she left with the address, and I never spoke to her again.

21

Joanne Emerson was one of many not sent by Morty Finch. One of many who didn't need a psychiatrist—just somebody to talk to—but were willing to pay the hefty price tag it had cost to get into my office, nonetheless. It was the strangest thing—yet, also entirely believable—so many people *wanting* to be verbally abused, *wanting* to hear the truth about themselves because they had lived their entire lives being lied to and pampered and consoled and coddled by the bosom of propaganda. The truth was a dangerous and exciting new endeavor, and humans thrive on danger and excitement and self-torment.

Penelope Winters. Twenty-five-years-old. Upper-class family. Daddy's girl. Falsely independent.

"I'm getting married in six months," she had said, tears tumbling down her porcelain-and-pink cheeks, a tissue crushed in her dainty hand. "I don't want much, just my dream dress, and a beautiful wedding cake, and for all my friends and family to show up. But my fiancé doesn't want a big wedding. Or the cake I picked out. A-And"—she sobbed into her hands—"he's mad about the dress I picked out, too!"

I passed her another tissue, not because I felt bad for her, but because the snot glistening in her nostrils was making me uncomfortable.

"Why is he mad about the dress?"

She wiped her nose with the tissue, sniffled back more tears.

"Because it costs eight-thousand-dollars," she said with a hint of uneasiness, and then she went into a defensive rant. "I saved for a year and a half to buy that dress. Not to mention, my dad is paying for half of it." She dragged the tissue underneath both eyes; black mascara came off in a perfect line. Then her face turned darker, her mood shifted from upset to resentment. "But Anthony, he thinks it's too much—it's not even his money I'm using to pay for it." She gritted her teeth.

"I take it this has been an ongoing problem between you and your fiancé, the cost of the wedding."

"Yes." She gave one hard nod. "The day I showed him the dress online and told him it was the one, when he saw the price, he became a totally different guy, like he wasn't the same Anthony I'd met jogging in that park. He was some weird, cheap guy lecturing me about how kids in some countries eat from landfills and whatnot and that I shouldn't be wasting money on a wedding dress—it's not my fault there are poor people in the world. And I'm not exactly rich, so it's not like I can do anything to help them." She crossed her arms and huffed her irritation. Then she looked at her engagement ring. *(Makes me wonder how much he spent on this…)*

"It's a one-time moment in my life," she said aloud, "one of the most important days, and everybody I know will be there, and I should be able to wear the dress that makes me feel like a princess. I'm not a bad person—I'm a *good* person, Mr. Boone. I love kids and animals and I didn't vote for You-Know-Who, so don't I deserve to have the perfect wedding day? Is that really too much to ask?"

"You deserve any wedding day you want," I told her.

"Thank you."

"I think if you want an eight-thousand-dollar wedding dress and a twelve-hundred-dollar cake and a five-thousand-dollar flower budget, then that's exactly what you should get."

She nodded, seemed a little surprised that I had agreed with her so easily, but she was pleased.

"But I also think Anthony should find another woman to marry."

Penelope Winters' eyes sprang wide open and stuck there like that, unmoving; her bottom lip quivered.

"Apparently, Anthony needs a life partner who thinks that children eating from landfills and whatnot are a more important issue than an expensive wedding." I put up my hand. "Don't get me wrong, I'm not siding with him, I'm just stating my opinion based on observation. The truth is, Miss Winters, that certain types of people simply do not belong together, as it would never work out in the long, or even the short-run. Your type tends to lean heavily on material things to make you happy: cars, and kitchens with granite countertops, and walk-in closets chock-full of clothes you might never get around to wearing, big Christmases with the best tree and the shiniest wrapping paper, family vacations, monthly self-pampering sessions at the spa. Whereas, your fiancé's type tends to lean more toward making others who are less fortunate more a priority than material things. My suggestion is that you call off the wedding now and go your separate ways, find a man who would jump at the opportunity to spend eight-thousand-dollars on a wedding dress, and let Anthony find a woman who would jump at the opportunity to travel the world with him to help feed proper meals to children eating from landfills." I shook my head. "Save yourself the time, heartache, and money now, because if you go through with it, your marriage *will* end in a nasty divorce, that I can assure you."

Tears streamed down Penelope's face; her fingers were like claws of stone gripping the armrests of the chair. She wasn't angry, she didn't want to tear my eyes out, she was just hurt.

"There will never be any room for Anthony to love you, Miss Winters," I said at last, "because you love yourself enough for the both of you."

Again, I wasn't being biased—it was simply the truth. I never spoke to her again, either.

But many of my patients didn't come for ongoing treatment. For most, it only took one session to get what they needed. They came for the truth, or just the abuse that would make them feel alive for a change. Secretly, I called it Truth Whiskey, and I was Frank the bartender filling the shot glasses of the weary, all those living The Great Lie for far too long. I cared little what any of them did once they left my office, but I wondered, although briefly, if the things I had said made any difference. Did they hate me? Did they believe me, but still hate me? Did they want to kill me, but still believe me? Did they respect me? Did they change their life, or keep on keepin' on? It was an equal mixture of everything, it seemed.

Daniel Dolan drove up from New Jersey for a session with me. He had heard from his best friend's girlfriend's aunt, or something like that, all about the "Notorious Mr. Boone in New York City" who could "make a tough man cry like a little bitch"—interesting choice of words, I thought—and so like any tire-squealing, risk-taking, sex-addicted twenty-something-year-old, Daniel Dolan wanted to challenge me. He wanted to "secretly" live-stream our session, so all his friends could see him flex his metaphorical muscles online and get his fifteen-minutes of internet fame.

I pretended not to know anything about the video recording on his phone, even though he often held it at odd and obvious angles while trying hard to pretend it was just the way he held his phone in general. Clearly, he was stupid in more ways than one, and I knew I'd enjoy pointing that out to him. And his hundreds of followers snickering on the other side of that thousand-dollar glass screen he had broken the same day he bought it, after falling, drunk, from a one-story balcony at a frat party.

I had asked him the typical first-question I'd always asked, but he just shrugged it off and asked *me* questions instead.

I played along.

"What makes you so qualified to be telling me how I should and shouldn't live, Mr. Boone?" He sat sprawled out in the chair, his back slouched, his elbows propped on the chair arms, one hand holding that cell phone any way he could to "discreetly" get me in the video without me noticing. He smirked at me, and I remained my calm, seemingly unemotional self, because even with billions of souls trapped inside of me, literally making me crazy, I still had more self-control than this rich-boy living off his parents' money and who had no idea about the shitty slope his life would soon take a slide down.

I simply pointed at the fake certification framed and mounted on the wall.

He did not look impressed.

"*Tch.* A piece of paper," he said. "Let me tell you what I think." He propped an ankle on a knee, shook his suspended foot. "I think you're a control freak, and a shock-value con artist. My girlfriend's step-sister's aunt told me—told the whole family—the shit you said to her. Now, that just wasn't very nice, Mr. Boone, was it?"

"Who is your girlfriend's step-sister's aunt?"

"Margaret Anaheim."

"Ah, yes, I might remember a Mrs. Anaheim."

"So, then you admit it?" He looked at me sidelong, waiting impatiently for me to confirm or deny.

"Anything that was said in my session with a Mrs. Anaheim is between her and me. But why don't we get to the real reason you're here, Mr. Dolan? Because we both know you don't care the slightest bit about your sister's girlfriend's aunt."

His eyes flashed, and his hand tightened around the cell phone.

"*Girlfriend's step-sister's aunt,*" he corrected me icily. "Are you calling my sister a lesbian?"

"I don't know your sister," I casually told him, "but I'm sure she would make a fine lesbian, nonetheless."

He slammed his free fist down on the flat surface of the chair arm.

Even I had to admit I was blindsided by how quickly and violently Daniel Dolan's mood had changed.

"There are no fucking lesbians in *my* family," he spat. "Or any of that fag shit, so do yourself a favor and keep my sister's name out of your mouth."

I sighed, getting irritated. Not at his roller-coaster personality, but at his dodging my questions and jumping off the topic cliff.

"Mr. Dolan," I said with a little edge in my tone, "it's obvious you came here for something, to make a point, perhaps, but"—I glanced at my watch—"you're running out of time in which to do it. So, let's start over, and why don't you tell me why you're here. To defend the honor of an aunt of a girlfriend you only pretend to love so she'll keep spreading her legs for you? Probably not. So, then what is it?"

Daniel Dolan looked shell-shocked. He glanced at the phone in his hand, hoping the people listening—especially the girlfriend—didn't hear my comment.

Because it was true.

"You don't know a thing about me or my girlfriend," he finally said, and he looked remarkably uncomfortable. "You don't know anything about me at all—you notice I didn't fill out that paperwork, right? So, bold accusations like that only make you look exactly like the con-artist I said you were."

Then the rollercoaster took another deep dive, and Daniel Dolan dropped the aggressive act and traded it for one he hoped would make me less inclined to say anything else that might incriminate or humiliate him. In short: he realized his error in coming here.

"All right," he said, "the reason I'm here is to..." he thought it over, pulling something random out of the air, "...I guess to get help with my...drinking problem."

He certainly had a drinking problem—him and almost every other guy his age who lived off their parents' money—but he didn't for a second think it was a problem, and even less so was he here to get help for it.

It was all just part of the show, his YouTube debut to garner hits in the hundreds of thousands and make him temporarily famous.

We talked for a few minutes about alcoholism; I was feeding his feed, per se, and only telling him the boring pamphlet basics. I was just a bot reading from that universal script, because anything more, even shaming him in classic Allister Boone fashion, wouldn't have made a bit of difference. Daniel Dolan was the type who could never be convinced that his actions could have severe consequences— he just didn't care. If I'd told him how drinking was "bad", or if I'd shown him gruesome images of bodies pulled from drunk-driving accidents, he would say something like: "Those idiots probably couldn't drive when they were sober", and then he'd chug a case of beer the following Friday night, and the one after that, and the one after *that* until he killed someone—but not himself, because the drunk drivers rarely ever die in the crashes they cause—in an alcohol-fueled accident of his own.

Getting frustrated with me that I wasn't giving him the push needed to make our session internet-famous-worthy, Daniel took a desperate dive on that roller-coaster to get things moving.

"Look at you," he said with the condescending sweep of his eyes, "you're a fraud in a suit."

Well, technically that was true.

"I bet you were molested or something," he went on, trying to get under my skin—oh, if he only knew what was under my skin. "You get off on talkin' shit to everybody else, but you're just a hypocrite. I bet you never get laid. What is it? Can't get it up anymore? Or maybe you like guys." Proud of himself, I caught him adjusting the phone below the desk, so he could smile into the camera. "That's it, isn't it? You probably wanna suck my dick right now, don't you?" He laughed at himself and glanced into the camera again.

"I—"

"Oh now, wait a minute," Daniel cut me off, feeling bolder, majestic, "let me finish what I was saying before you go into some bullshit spiel about how I'm—"

"About how you talk an awful lot about homosexuality," I cut *him* off. "Hate and hostility toward homosexuality is often a defense mechanism, Mr. Dolan. It's okay that you think about homosexuality more than you want to. There is nothing wrong with it."

Panic asphyxiated him; his body went rigid on the chair.

"If you'd like to talk to me about any closeted secrets you might have…"

He swiftly ran his thumb over the broken screen to end the live feed.

"I'm not gay," he hissed. "My parents are very Christian. So, you're going down the wrong path, Mr. Psychiatrist."

"*Very* Christian?" I asked, because I just couldn't help myself. "As opposed to what? A *little* Christian? Christian only on Sundays? Christian as in condemning lesbians except the ones you have threesomes with?" I shifted back to the topic. "I don't believe you're gay, Mr. Dolan—masturbating a few times to gay porn doesn't make you gay—but I do believe you're on a collision course that'll put you in an early grave. You're not an alcoholic, either, but you're a reckless drinker, you don't give two-shits about anybody but yourself, you're too busy trying to impress others by doing stupid things and acting like a spoiled man-baby who the world can't touch, who death can't touch." I cocked my head to one side. "You should never taunt Death, Mr. Dolan. Death often comes for people like you, so swiftly on your heels and with a great rush of satisfaction in his chest." My eyes flashed preternaturally; I didn't intend for them to, as I was too gripped by my desire to end him, to notice.

179

But Daniel Dolan didn't see it. He was so blinded by his own thoughtless and wild version of reality that he couldn't see me in front him, *showing* him who I was.

Daniel Dolan left the session early. After haughtily berating me with a few choice words and giving me the finger on his way out the door, video recording again, and in plain view so I and all those watching could see how "awesome" he was.

"You called?" I heard a voice say moments later.

Gazing out the window at an always-bustling New York City, I kept my back to the demon in the room. He was once a human man with a conscience, a man who came so very close to ending the world, but, in that pivotal moment, he chose not to. I had despised him ever since, because he had the power in the palms of his hands to end *everything*, to give me peace, but he *chose* not to use it.

He had once worked for Lucifer, but now he worked for me. Because I owned his soul. Because he knew if he ever refused to do my bidding, he would find himself in a jar on The Hermit's shelf awaiting judgment in his very own personal Hell.

"Daniel Dolan," I said, still with my back to the demon. "I want you to watch him. No need to influence him to do anything because he'll do it all on his own. But the next time he gets drunk"—I turned only my head to see the demon—"I want you to spin me a bloody, terrific story."

"Sure thing," the demon said.

Perhaps I *was* a bit sadistic. And vindictive. But I was always a lot of things I wasn't supposed to be when I wasn't so much myself.

Two days later, Daniel Dolan was in a fatal drunk-driving crash on the highway, his body unrecognizable when they pulled it from the warped metal.

And following the incident, the rush of new patients calling in for appointments, particularly between the ages of eighteen and twenty-six, had grown staggeringly. The thing was, when Daniel Dolan swiftly shut the video recording down on his phone that day, I had covertly turned it back on and his hundreds of viewers had heard everything. They heard me warning him about taunting death, and when he died so soon after, I was dubbed by that group of very imaginative kids, of all things: The Reaper. Of course, they believed it only as imaginative kids would, but the last thing I wanted or needed was a bunch of audacious children using my office as the scary house on the hill they dared one another to enter by themselves.

But that was the least of my concerns.

I had a game to win. And when Morty Finch discovered my new and overflowing patient list, he did…well, what I probably would've done, and started using the ones already there instead of working that much harder to find new ones to send my way.

22

I was busy, busy, busy, and because of Morty Finch, I ended up working on Saturdays, after all. *Every* Saturday. Just to keep up with the barrage of emotionally damaged people who would die before their time if I didn't do whatever I could to help them.

Lindsey Reyes. Married for fifteen years to a man who abused her. And she felt trapped with no way out, she was Level One suicidal, which could easily become Level Three with Morty at her ear.

I gave Lindsey the mouthful of nasty truth I gave everyone, though I admitted I was a bit more delicate with her considering she was afraid for her life, but I still told her what she needed to hear.

"But that's why I'm afraid to leave him, Mr. Boone," she defended. "There's no telling what he'll do to me if I leave."

"If you stay," I told her, "he will kill you eventually."

"So, then you're saying I die either way?"

"No—one way you die for sure. The other at least gives you a chance."

Lindsey Reyes did leave her husband. But instead of him finding her and killing her, he had killed himself. Thankfully, he wasn't one of my patients, because I didn't see that one coming.

And with his death—after a short week of blaming herself—Lindsey Reyes came to her senses, basically told Morty to fuck off without knowing it, by finding her strength and moving on with her life.

Then there was Jacqueline Perry. Actually, there were so many Jacqueline Perry's that I vetted Nancy's patient list, instructing her to call and inform them that their sessions had been cancelled, that I had read their questionnaires—most filled them out online before their sessions—and I didn't find them in any particular need of my services.

"How can you do that to these people?" Nancy scolded, her eyebrows drawn together in her forehead.

"They bore me," I told her honestly. And then I sighed and gave in to her like I always did when her face darkened like that. "Don't you want me to help the people who really need it?" I asked as I attempted to reason with her. "You know how long it's going to be before most of these people can get in. Weed out the casual cases and make room for the more serious ones."

She was hesitant, but satisfied by my reasoning and did what I'd asked.

And there were *a lot* of casual cases:

"My husband wants the bungalow-style house and I want the colonial—I just don't know what to do anymore! Why does life have to be so difficult?"

"I'm not sure," I said. "Maybe you should ask those who live in the cardboard-style homes."

"My grandma died recently, and my aunt won't give us any of the money from her estate. That greedy bitch is keeping everything—"

"...away from another greedy bitch," I said.

"My wife is starting to gain weight; I love her and all, but I don't think I can keep loving her if she gets fat."

"You never loved her to begin with."

"My sister was always the favorite when we were growing up. I hate her, and it's her fault I'm so depressed all the time."

"I believe I know why she was the favorite."

"I was without a car for a week. I had to walk six blocks to work one day because nobody would give me a ride. It was *so* hot, I almost died! Really, death would be better than having to do that ever again."

I could arrange that for you.

"I have suffered all my life, Mr. Boone. We didn't have a dishwasher when I was a teenager, can you believe that? No internet. Microwave only cooked our food halfway through. I didn't even have a cell phone—it was so embarrassing. And now here I am, as an adult continuing the cycle, working for minimum wage, and I can't afford internet. My life sucks. It can't get any worse than this."

"Oh, sure it can," I said. "Let me show you how…"

"But we're having our first baby in three months. We need out of our tiny apartment and into something bigger. I have my eye on a five-bedroom in the country on fourteen acres. That would be perfect for our family of three, but Rick thinks it's too big and expensive. I guess he just doesn't care about his family."

"And neither do I."

"*Pfft!* I don't care if my bills pile up, I'm not taking a job cleaning toilets. That's slave work, and I'm nobody's slave. So, what should I do? I can't find work *anywhere*—I feel worthless."

"That's because you *are* worthless."

"My dad cut me off. I couldn't believe it, that he'd ever really go that far, but he did. He closed all my credit cards, took the money out of my savings, and now I have nothing. *Nothing!* How could he be so cruel? I could end up on the streets, homeless—or dead!

"The world would be better off."

"I just can't afford to chip in for my cousin's cancer treatment. I have so many bills: car payment, mortgage, electricity and gas and water, cell phones, internet, cable, my daughter's piano lessons, my son's karate lessons; I'm getting the house painted next month and was supposed to trade in my two-year-old car for a brand new one in a few weeks—I just can't afford to give money away like that. But the family makes *me* out to be the 'bad guy'. I'm just so hurt, Mr. Boone. Why can't they see my side of things?"

And so, I arranged for her to have a terminal illness of her very own so they could see her side of things.

"I think I'm just gonna kill myself. Every time I try to do nice things for others, my good deed gets thrown back in my face somehow. I should probably just step in front of a bus or something."

"Oh—were you talking to me?"

I had had enough of the "casual cases" of the world, and the only thing worse than having to deal with the one's I'd already accepted, were the millions I knew I'd have to deal with someday after their deaths. I was only putting off the inevitable.

But I continued to break all the rules of modern-day psychiatry, finding it particularly annoying that some people were so offended when I would use the big no-no technique and point out how much worse other people's lives were than theirs.

But in many cases, pointing out these truths was essential in making them understand that their problems, no matter how significant or petty, were just distractions to keep them from realizing the key to everything: that life wasn't about them at all.

Humans have become so incredibly fragile, that simply telling them the truth is so offensive and hurtful that it is essentially forbidden in society. Humans *want* to feel sorry for themselves, they *want* the attention and the pity and the advice, they *want* someone to walk with them down their sad, lonely little paths because they're too afraid to walk it alone; they want others to agree with them even when they're blatantly wrong. It is the Comfort Zone, the tit they suck long after they've learned to walk and talk. Adults. They're the biggest fucking babies in the world. And every single one of them that came into my office, I made sure to tell them that.

However, I was more careful with those like Ann Singleton who had Actual Depression, and I knew better than to shame them in any way. The difference between the Ann Singletons and the Jacqueline Perrys was that one couldn't care about themselves enough, while the other cared far too much.

Though, a Casual or not, I never turned away anyone who was potentially suicidal, those who had been infected by Time's taint. But there were a lot who said things like: *I think I'm just gonna kill myself,* and *I should probably just step in front of a bus,* or try to be cryptic about it by dropping ominous, but obvious hints like: *It'll all be over soon,* or *They will all feel the earth shake when I'm gone,* that they thought somehow made them seem dark and mysterious and on the verge of transforming into some two-headed monster only the gods could control, when really they just sounded silly.

But none were suicidal, at least none of the ones who came to me for help. Not that there weren't people out there who said those things and wouldn't later follow through. That was why it was good to be me—I knew the truth; I could easily separate the pity-partiers from the real-deals.

I had saved many and lost many over the months the game raged on. By day three-hundred-forty-nine, the score was 79 Allister, 21 Morty. And with just sixteen days left on the timer, Morty was getting worried.

But I let him stew. I knew I was home-free, and there was no way he could catch up to me, much less surpass me, in just sixteen days.

I was going to win. And I was going to win because my patients were going to live.

It had always been in the nature of humans to survive at any cost. Humans stranded and lost in inhospitable environments would kill and eat one another to raise their chances of survival. Humans had endured incredible pain, torture, and suffering just to stay alive; a great majority of humans, if faced with the choice, would give up their offspring to save themselves. Because for all of their faults, humans were created with one extraordinary asset: their determination to live. Many had even dedicated their entire lives to finding a way to live "forever".

Sixteen more days.

Could it be true? That Morty was right about Death and Time not being equals? What would it mean if we proved it? I was both eager and nervous; there could be grave consequences, but there could also be great rewards, and I was prepared to accept both.

Perhaps my readiness was only due to the confidence I'd gained by how easily I was winning. But I knew I shouldn't be *over*confident, as that always ends in disappointment. And so, just to make sure I wasn't letting anyone slip through the cracks, I decided I should check in on my patients, make a few house-calls, both to those who seemed like they had gotten their lives together, and those with a long way to go.

And then there was Jason Layne, with the luxury of neither. He hadn't been showing up to his appointments, and I still kept sending the bills. He'd also made it past June without dying, naturally or by his own hand.

I took a taxi to the apartment he shared with his sister.

"Can I help you?" his sister said as she peeked through the crack in the door, the chain still locked.

"I'm looking for Jason Layne."

"Who are you?"

"I'm his…psychiatrist." I wasn't supposed to tell her that, but, well, she had asked. "My name is Allister Boone."

She paused, stared at me for a moment, and then opened the door the rest of the way.

"I didn't know he was seeing a psychiatrist," she said, a little hopeful.

"Do you know where I can find him?"

She shook her head.

"I haven't seen him in days," she answered, hoping maybe I'd be the one to change that and find him for her. "He calls every now and then, just to let me know he's okay, but he won't tell me where he is. I don't understand why he's shutting me out. Especially now…"

"When was the last time you heard from him?"

"Yesterday. He called around two o'clock."

"Thank you," I said, and walked away.

"Hey, wait a minute," she called out.

I stopped, turned.

She looked me in the eyes, wanting to say one thing I could not make out, but she sighed and said instead: "If you find him, could you tell him I miss him and I…well, just tell him that he needs to come home."

I nodded, turned on my heels, and left.

I knew where to at least look for Jason Layne. He wasn't dead yet, or almost dead, so I couldn't just pop in uninvited wherever he was in the world and find him. Only angels could do that with the living.

Jillian Bowden was easy to find. A little internet investigating and I not only found her house, but I found Jason Layne having lunch with her in a nearby diner. It was an entirely innocent lunch. In fact, Jillian's husband had

188

joined them. I sat unseen in the booth across from their table and I listened to the energetic conversation between them about activism and charity work and other such things that made Jason Layne the rare human that he was. And he did something I had never seen him do when he talked to Mr. and Mrs. Bowden about these things he was so passionate about—he smiled. Underneath all the pain, and the pallid, dehydrated skin, and the weakness that had settled so deeply into his muscles and bones it was difficult for him to hold his fork for too long, Jason Layne was happy. In an I'm-going-to-die-but-at least-not-unfulfilled sort of happy.

And later, I followed him discreetly to the hotel he had been staying in. Or rather, a motel, in a shady part of town where drugs were sold in alleys and sex workers walked the streets.

I sat on the chair in Jason's dark, musty room with cigarette-stained walls and grossly-stained carpet while Jason sat on the small bed, his weak legs hung over the side, his bony arms holding up his light weight that felt so heavy, his hands pressed into the mattress.

He vomited on the floor.

Then he rolled over, curled up on the bed, and went to sleep.

Jason Layne was happy. But he was also suffering.

I read his thoughts, and there were none that indicated he'd still intended to take his own life, but I knew I had to keep checking in on him. At least for another fourteen days. After that, I would let him do whatever he wanted.

A part of me felt…guilty. A part of me wanted to let him do what he wanted *now*.

But that was just the human part, the part I despised, and so I ignored it.

23

I had grown to enjoy Margot Henry's company. Did it have anything to do with the fact that the people around her had started to enjoy her, and I was only picking up on their feelings as I'd always done? Perhaps. But I think it was a little bit of me, too.

Margot Henry, in a rather short time, had completely turned her life around. She still weighed "fat" on society's scale, but that was the point of our sessions—mostly, anyway—that the message really was the clichéd mumbo-jumbo everybody says when they don't know what else to say. But I knew the pats on the back, and the cooing, and the motivational refrigerator magnets were useless in a world hell-bent on shunning positivity and only reacting to the negative. Tell a human a lie and they will appreciate you for it, but tell a human the truth and they will hate you just enough that they'll appreciate themselves.

Humans are masochists by nature.

Humans thrive on drama and witch hunts and public executions—of the metaphorical *and* the literal kind.

Humans are virtually deaf and blind to the easy fixes (even though they claim to prefer them), they get off on breaking a few fingers and bleeding a few veins—of their own *and* everybody else's—just to find out something they already knew. It is the way they were wired, so, a motivational speech would've helped about as much as telling a child not to stick a metal barrette into a light socket—the second you turn your back, they'd have to go and do it anyway to find out for themselves.

I skipped all that and just stuck Margot Henry into the light socket head-first, stunned her, woke her the hell up, shocked the blindness out of her eyes and forced her into a restart.

I had intended to make a house-call to visit her, too, but today was her day at my office. And when she walked in, the confidence emanating from her urged me into a gentlemanly stand. The color for today was teal. She wore makeup and her hair was styled nicely and I thought she was stunning, but the makeup and hair had absolutely nothing to do with my thoughts. She liked herself, therefore I liked her; she respected herself, therefore I respected her as well; because she didn't care about how much she weighed, neither did I. She had power over herself now, instead of giving it away to everybody else.

"Good afternoon, Miss Henry." I gestured my hand at the chair in front of my desk. "How have you been?"

She took the seat, set her black-and-teal purse down on the floor beside it.

"Great," she said. "A lot has been going on."

"Oh?" I sat down.

"Yeah," she said, "I've started my own sort of business. Well, I guess a better way to describe it is self-employment."

"Really? Do tell. Would you like some water?"

She paused. I expected her to question her confidence, even if only for a millisecond, but she didn't. I was impressed.

"No thank you, Mr. Boone. I'm not thirsty."

I paused for a moment, too, giving her a chance to reconsider. She was telling the truth about not being thirsty, but a part of her was curious.

(I wonder if he'd get it for me if I said yes.)

I got up anyway, walked over to the mini fridge, retrieved a bottle of water, cracked the seal for her and set it on the desk in her reach.

"Now, tell me about this business of yours." I sat back down casually.

She was surprised, but did well to hide it from her face. Nothing was ever said again about the water. Nothing needed to be said.

Margot Henry put her lifelong hobby to work for her, and she started writing, self-publishing, and selling children's books: *Big & Skinny, Josie & Penny*, a series about two best friends navigating the world together on opposite sides of the acceptance spectrum. A friend at work—yes, Margot had made friends at work, with the Cigarette Break Girls, of all people—after hearing her idea, referred her to a children's artist, and another friend told her all about the new world of self-publishing, and then Margot took it from there.

"I still hope to land a traditional publishing deal one day," she explained. "It's almost impossible to get your book in bookstores if you self-publish. But I've already sold nine thousand copies of the first two books online—in one month. I've been invited to a few book signings, my ratings are excellent, and a literary agent contacted me yesterday. I really like her, and I think I'm going to accept her offer for representation."

"That sounds nice."

"Yes. It really is." In a moment of self-reflection, Margot glanced at her hands folded on her lap, then back up at me, and a small smile had brightened around her eyes. "I've been taking my books to elementary schools and reading to the children in the libraries. It's really special, I think, Mr. Boone. I dunno, but I feel like these kids are connecting with me, and that they really understand the book's messages." Her smile grew. "That's the most important part about this whole thing. I mean, sure, I love the extra income, and I can't deny the attention is nice, but what I love most is working with the kids. It's a good feeling." She waved her hand. "Anyway, I didn't come here today to talk about this stuff."

"Oh?" I looked at her inquisitively.

"No, I came to tell you it'll be my last day."

"I see."

"Yeah, I don't think I need you anymore—no offense."

"None taken."

"It's just that, I...well"—she raised her back from the seat—"I know I have a long way to go, but I guess I just needed the proper kick in the ass. Don't get me wrong, I still think you're a jerk, but I can't deny that you really did help me."

I nodded.

"You were right about one thing in particular," she went on. "At first, I thought it was the worst thing you could've said to me, or anyone else, about how my past means nothing, that I shouldn't waste a fucking minute even giving it any thought. But you were right—at least for *me* you were right." She took a breath, repositioned her hands on her lap, and then straightened her back. "I spent half my life feeling sorry for myself, blaming my past for how shitty my life turned out and never doing anything about it, or taking any responsibility for it. But when I look back on that now, I'm just disappointed that I let it have so much control over me, for so long." She waved it off. "Anyway, it's not important. It never really was. I'm doing great now, and I really think I've got an even greater life ahead of me."

"I believe that you do, Miss Henry."

She chuckled suddenly.

"You wanna know what I did?" she asked.

I nodded.

"When I first decided I wanted to finally start living my life—shortly after I stopped wanting to strangle you—my goal was to start dieting and lose a bunch of weight, y'know, do what just about everybody like me tries to do." She shook her head. "But that first day, when I had my meals planned out and all that, I realized that's not what I wanted, that by torturing myself to lose weight I'd be doing pretty much the same thing I did every day when I couldn't leave the house without makeup: trying to please society. I mean, sure, a part of me still wants to be skinny so I'll fit *into* society, because, unfortunately, that's just how humans are. But screw that! I don't care what they think of me anymore, Mr. Boone. I care about being healthy, so I choose now to eat good food and not overeat for health reasons—for *me*, not for them. The same with exercise. You couldn't pay me to go to a gym, but I never knew how much I'd love walking in the park everyday—I get a lot of great story ideas there—and just generally getting outdoors more. If I happen to lose weight in the process of all this, then great, but that's not *why* I do it."

I sighed heavily and rubbed my fingertips in a circular motion against my temples.

"Is something wrong?" she asked.

"You talk too damn much," I told her. "It's good that you've turned your life around, and I'll always be here if you find yourself slipping, but I really couldn't care less about the glittery details."

She crossed her arms and bit down on the inside of her cheek.

"Well, guess what?" she said.

I waited.

She pointed at the clock on the wall.

"I've got forty-four more minutes, and you can bet your ass I'm going to use every single one of them making you miserable."

I grinned.

And she did. For the next forty-four minutes, Margot Henry told me all about how things were going "so great" for her, and how she'd even caught the eye of a man at the restaurant where she'd had lunch every day, and that she was sure he'd have her "on all fours" soon. By the time she finally left, I wanted to set fire to my eyes and pour acid into my ears.

Margot Henry never was suicidal, and Morty had given up on her shortly after seeing her in my office that day, but I still followed through with helping her. I didn't know why. I didn't care what happened to Miss Henry outside of The Game, and I could've cancelled her remaining sessions with the rest of the Casuals, but for some reason I kept her around.

The same was true for a few of the other Casuals: Miss. Death-Would-Be-Better-Than-Having-To-Walk-Six-Blocks-In-The-Heat, the "Greedy Bitch", and my Casual-Turned-Terminal. Each was interesting in some way or another.

But none could compare to Ann Singleton. And the Angel had been right about Ann: I had plans for her.

Unfortunately, Ann had plans of her own, too.

24

When I found her, she was on the bathroom floor of her little house, white tile beneath her glistening with the deep crimson color of her human shell as it spilled from her wrists, her glassy, lifeless eyes fixed in a haunting, motionless gaze at the wall.

But she wasn't dead. Almost. But not yet.

The tub had been filled with hot water, droplets fell from the faucet into the steam wafting from the surface like fog lifting on a lake. On the side of the tub was a photo of Ann when she was just three-years-old; she wore white sandals and a big nearly-toothless smile. A large dog, a German Shepherd, sat on its haunches beside her, ears perked, tongue cradled between its teeth. It was a summer day in the country on her family's land. There was a lake nearby, a small store on the corner that sold Ann's favorite orange push-up ice cream; a watermelon patch and a grapevine and a garden and a giant walnut tree. At night Ann would lie in the field and look up at the stars and listen to the Whippoorwills sing to each other. And in the day, she would run off—alone, or sometimes with her cousin as adventurous as she was—to the creek behind the house and stay there for hours hunting crawfish under rocks and living the carefree, innocent life she was always meant to live.

"I remember the soap," Ann said. "My great-grandmother always used Dial soap. There was always a shriveled bar on the tub in the bathroom in the back of the house. I never forgot the smell of it. Throughout my life, whenever I'd smell that soap somewhere, it transported me back to this place."

"Tell me about this place," I said. We were standing there together in the bathroom where a window overlooked the backyard. "Tell me why you're here, Ann."

"Because this is where it began," she whispered.

Then we were standing outside suddenly. It was a warm summer day. Cloudless. Humid like it always was in the summer in the South. The smell of honeysuckle and pine was thick in the air.

"It's not time for that," she whispered. "I'm not ready to relive that moment yet."

I placed my hand on her shoulder from behind—and I flinched, felt the heat—she stood motionless, gazing off at a wooden building where cages were made of chicken wire, and a tree, and a wooded path nearby that led to the creek where she had lived that carefree, innocent life until…she didn't anymore.

I knew why we were here, but it was Ann's job to tell me. Not as her psychiatrist this time, but as the one who would carry her soul away from the world she couldn't wait to leave.

"When you get close to death, even if death isn't for several more years," Ann said, "you start to remember the happiest moments of your life more vividly, you start to mourn them. It's like they're coming back to haunt you, to remind you how much you miss them, how you'll never feel the way they made you feel again, and you'll never be the person you were then, and that no matter what you do in your life, no matter how hard you try, you'll never even come close to recreating them. We're never as happy as we *used* to be, because we're never truly happy in the *moment*, except when we are children. As adults, only after the moment is gone, do we miss it. And by then it's too late. So, just as fate does not exist, neither does happiness. More illusions."

I was not Allister Boone then, so it wasn't my place to argue with her. I wouldn't have anyway. Because she was right. There is only a small window in a mortal's life where they experience true and unquestionable "happiness", when they are oblivious to the horrors of Reality—*their* reality—and they're able to live without fear or worry: as children.

"I remember when my grandparents lived in the city," she went on. "The blue nightgown my grandmother always let me wear when I'd sleep over; the room that was off-limits because my uncle slept during the day and worked nights; the big bible in the spare room that I liked to look at the pictures. I remember peanut-butter-and-jelly sandwiches and grilled-cheese and "The Young & The Restless" and fireworks in the street and dressing up for Halloween. I remember playing in the backyard, and eating dog treats and popsicles and chocolate gravy. I remember elementary school—I loved elementary school *so* much—and the trailer park I lived in where I played with my childhood friends whose memory was as much a part of my later life as that soap was. Madonna and Michael Jackson and jelly-shoes and rubber bracelets and Monopoly and "Ghostbusters" and Saturday morning cartoons and tree forts in the woods with my brothers. I remember swimming in the pool with my dad and him taking me to see "Superman" in the theatre. I remember eating chili dogs and watching "The Dukes of Hazzard" with my family. I remember riding with my mom and my brothers to my grandparents' house in the country—*that* house—before it was built, and then after it was finished."

Ann turned and looked across the dirt road.

It was the house with the field in the front and the walnut tree and the garden and the grapevine and the watermelon patch in the back. A man and a woman—her grandparents—sat on the porch with an ashtray on a little table between them. The protective German Shephard from the photograph was running alongside a young Ann through the field as her grandparents looked on.

She smiled thoughtfully and a tear tracked down her face. I moved my hand from her shoulder. It burned too much to touch her anymore.

"My grandmother made me a Mississippi Mud cake every year for my birthday," she said. "I remember fishing and swimming at the lake, taking a ride to visit other family members down the road, sitting outside by an uncle's pond swatting mosquitoes and being careful of snakes. I remember my grandparents and my aunts and uncles playing cards and drinking coffee and smoking cigarettes and talking about life. I was loved. I was happy. I didn't have any fears in the world. I didn't know anything about the all the terrible things that went on around me. I was blind to most of it, not seeing enough to open my mind to any of it long enough to damage me. My life was wonderful. I had everything: a loving family who gathered every year, festive Christmases and sweet-smelling Thanksgivings and colorful Easter-egg hunts and warm family reunions that few ever missed." She paused, and the reminiscent smile faded. "That was childhood. *My* childhood. How every childhood should be, all over the world."

She turned to face the other house on the other side of the road where we were standing before in the backyard. The sky was no longer clear, but full of dark gray clouds that rolled in an angry pattern and blotted out the sunlight. It was still hot and humid, and uncomfortably so.

The moment I thought that, we were transported back inside the house where the bathroom window overlooked the backyard. I could smell the soap just as she'd described it—unforgettable, triggering. A little girl, a little Ann, stood in the window peeking through the thin yellow curtain that covered it.

"They had told me not to look," she said, "that I should stay inside and not come out until I was told I could."

Little Ann's hands shook as she grasped the curtain in her small fingers. We watched her quietly, but little Ann never knew that we were there. "It" hadn't happened yet, therefore little Ann didn't know what being an adult was, she didn't know what death was, so she could not see us, her adult self and Death, standing there watching as her time came, the moment in which she would be forever scarred, when her mind would be touched for the first time by the cruel face of her Reality.

Little Ann gasped and clutched the curtain *so* tight, the shaking spread from her hands and into the rest of her body.

"I could hear the rabbits screaming," she said, now standing in the window next to little Ann. "I saw them beating the rabbits in their heads with hammers. I was frozen in that spot, the smell of soap burning my eyes and nostrils. And when the rabbits were dead, they hung them from that tree and skinned them."

Ann turned and looked at me.

Little Ann turned and looked at me—and she *saw* me.

"That was the moment I saw the horrors of humankind. The cruelty. That was the moment I saw Death," Ann said. "I ran out of the bathroom and out of the house and I don't remember anything innocent after that as vividly as everything before it. Because I never forgot it. Because it was the moment I lost my innocence, the moment when the veil had been lifted from my child eyes and I saw The Truth of this frightening, horrific world."

And once you see The Truth, you can never go back.

Little Ann ran out of the bathroom and out of the house and we were standing outside in the yard when we saw her vanish. Little Ann was gone, replaced by the one standing in front of me, the damaged one who grew up never forgetting the smell of that soap that had been the backdrop of the scene that would change her forever.

"It wasn't their fault," she said of those who'd killed the rabbits. "It had to happen sometime because inevitably it happens to everybody, losing one's innocence. But that's how it happened for me."

I nodded respectfully, remained silent.

"After that," she went on, "I only ever remembered the terrible things. I remember my great-grandmother dying inside that house, right there in that bedroom." She pointed at the room on the front of the house closest to the dirt road. "I remember the family gathered there, all whispering, pretending that everything was going to be okay when I knew it wouldn't be because you can't hide that much darkness from a child no matter how hard you try." She sighed. "I remember seeing my great-grandmother for the last time, lying in the bed, frail and tired and brittle and incredibly old, and I remember being so sad and hurt and afraid that she was going to die, that I pretended not to care. I had tried to block it all out, and I remember smiling and rushing off into the woods to play with my adventurous cousin. But I *did* care. I cared more than my family probably thought I did. But I pretended not to. I *had* to. Because I was afraid of the hammers."

We walked together toward the dirt road slowly.

"I refused to go to the funeral," she said. "In fact, I didn't go to a lot of funerals after that. I wanted to remember those I'd loved and lost, the way they were when they were alive. Not dead in a casket. Fake-looking. *People* that once breathed and spoke and walked and loved and hugged me with their arms, but were reduced to stiff, frightening shells, mannequins that were no longer the people that I loved and never would be again."

We made it to the dirt road and walked down it and away from the houses.

"But death followed me everywhere," she went on, "because it tends to do that." She glanced at me, that look in her eye letting me know for the first time she knew what I was, why I was there. "And like I said, I only ever remembered the terrible things: the death of the dog in that photograph who followed me everywhere to protect me, my grannie and grampa, whom I loved with all my heart, dying just a few years apart; my adventurous cousin dying in front of me when they pulled the plug on him in the hospital after he'd shot himself in the head; the death of my pets, and later my friends, and more family as the years went on. I learned early-on that death would eventually come for us all, with a hammer and the screams, and so I became terrified of it. I hid from it, pushed it away, ignored it, despised it for taking away the people I loved, who loved me."

She stopped, but she didn't look at me this time. She couldn't. Because she was hiding from me, pushing me away, ignoring me, despising me—*(I fucking hate you!)*—and then, ultimately, she accepted me. *(Take me away...please just take me away.)*

"Why didn't you wait?" I asked her.

We were now in the bathroom of Ann's house, standing over the body of her former self on the white-tile floor, her sweat pants and tank-top soaked with blood, her body heavy and limp and lifeless, fake-looking, a *person* who once breathed and spoke and walked and loved and hugged, reduced to a shell of the person she would never be again.

Ann Singleton was dead.

"I decided I didn't want to know anymore," she answered. "I didn't know what you were then, but I knew you weren't right upstairs, that you were just as damaged as I was and I didn't want to know why. I didn't want to believe you, because then I *would* have been crazy."

"But I had plans for you, Ann. I had an extraordinary offer."

I was at a loss—I was *devastated*. What was I going to do now?

"What's done is done," she told me. "I just want to be at peace."

"But that's just it," I said. "You can never be at peace for what you have done."

Ann's husband knocked on the bathroom door.

"Ann?" he called. "Show's starting."

"How can that be true?" Ann asked me. "Death is the end, the finality, the Darkness, the Nothingness. How can there be no peace in the Nothingness?"

"Ann, hon, you all right in there? Didja fall in?" Her husband chuckled, but then it faded into an uneasy, uncertain clearing of the throat.

"Because the Nothingness only comes in The End," I said. "Not *your* end, but *The* End. Death is not truly final until Death itself has died—if Death ever dies. There is another phase between your mortal death and the End of Everything. And in it, for most, there is no such thing as peace."

Knock-Knock-Knock-Knock.

"Ann...? Honey...?"

Ann's blank, shattered stare penetrated me, the heaviness of her heart burned me—I wasn't even touching her and it was too painful to be standing so close to her. How could I have misjudged her soul? I had wanted it for myself, its powerful prose and heartache and the understanding of the world and the one beyond Reality that most souls inside of me did not have. I had made a deal with her, securing her soul as mine even if she had taken her own life. We had made a deal! And now I regretted it. I regretted it because her soul was too much for me; I thought it would balance me, but never did I imagine it would capsize me, make my existence that much more difficult to bear. I regretted it because I was stuck with it! A deal was a deal and I couldn't take it back!

Knock-Knock-Knock-Pound-Pound-Pound-Pound-

Pound! "Ann!" The door rattled in its frame, the knob shook violently. "ANN! Open the door! Say something! Open the goddamned door!" *Bang-Bang-BANG!*

"Please take me away," Ann whispered, trembling, tears streaming down her face—my God, I was burning from the inside-out!

She reached out to touch me, looking for consolation, hoping I would take her into my arms and press her head against my chest before taking her away from the scene of her own murderous crime.

But I refused.

If I was going to suffer, she would suffer with me. She would face the consequences of her crime, an eternal sentence I would make sure she served for as long as I existed.

There was a sharp *crack!* and the door came off its hinges as her husband forced the weight of his body through it. "Ann! No! God no!" With both hands he ripped the door the rest of the way from the frame and tossed it behind him. "No-No-No-No-ANN!" He slipped in her blood on his way to her body, fell beside her and grabbed her, with difficulty, into his bloodied, shaking arms.

"Take me away from here, Mr. Boone...*please*, take me away from here. I can't see him like this!"

"No," I said resolutely, trying with all my power to ease the pain inside of me that her soul inflicted. "You will watch. And you will feel. And you will suffer. And you will take it all with you, Ann Singleton, like a boulder on your back, the pain you felt in life, the emptiness, the torture of your existence. And the pain you have caused others, you will carry it all, forever, long after your back is broken and your legs have splintered from the weight of it all. You will carry it and I will carry it with you—but not *for* you."

"No, Mr. Boone! I can't see this! Please!" She lunged at me, her hands on my shoulders, her fingers like blades of fire digging into me.

"*Annnnn!*" her husband cried out as he rocked her limp and heavy body in his arms. "Why did you do this? Ann! Why? Why-Why-Why-Why?" His pain was so great I felt it, too, like the banging of a great bell that could be heard from miles in every direction, echoing, penetrating, piercing my skull with tremendous power.

Ann fell to her knees in front of me, she rested her head on my shoes. "Oh, Mr. Boone...I'm sorry, can't I take it back? Why must I suffer in death as I suffered in life? Let me take it back. I can't bear to feel this pain I've caused him, for all of eternity. I can't *bear* it!"

"My name is Azrael," I corrected her. "I am the Angel of Death. And you are hereby sentenced to an eternity of suffering."

I opened my mouth and the room spun with a great dark wind, blustery and blistering and biting, the colors and shapes that surrounded us swept up into a whirlwind of red and black and gray, the cries of Ann's husband intensifying, deafening in the chaos.

"Please! What was your offer? Tell me what the offer was! Please don't do this! Please…I take it back…I regret what I've done…give me another chance…please…"

Ann's soul disappeared into my being, and my mouth snapped closed, and the room stopped spinning, and all was calm and silent again save for Michael, Ann's husband, who sat on the bloody floor with Ann in his arms. He cried into her hair, and he rocked her, and he too wanted to die a thousand deaths just to make the pain of her loss go away. He would never forgive himself. He would never be the same. Ann's mother would never be the same when she discovered what Ann had done. Ann's brothers would never be the same. Ann's friends and neighbors would never be the same. Because suicide is a different kind of death, a death that never had to happen, and it was still a crime. A crime against humanity, a crime that caused the suffering of other human beings, and for that Ann would suffer.

It was true that I didn't know where suicide souls went after death, those that did not belong to me. But it was also still true that wherever they went, they were no longer a threat, they no longer mattered, because I could *feel* it.

No, I never knew where they went, but in this moment, with Ann Singleton's soul trapped inside of me, I finally knew *why*.

It was my Creator's only gift to me, because He knew I couldn't carry souls like Ann's around as they were far too heavy. My back would've broken, my legs would've splintered from the weight of it all and I wouldn't have been able to walk.

25

I wandered the streets of New York City under the lights and the scaling buildings and a heavy layer of exhaust and diesel fuel and cigarette smoke and dumpster stench. I sat in the subway, rode the subway, walked through the subway, stood silently in the subway. Then I walked the streets some more, past the big humming lights and into the enveloping darkness, my hands buried in the pockets of my slacks, my head hung low because it felt like the human thing to do. I passed nine wandering souls—two homeless men, three patients who had died in two hospitals, one woman who had died in her apartment, one man stabbed behind a hotel, and a husband and wife crushed in a car accident six miles away— without stopping to reap any of them. And then I passed nineteen more.

I left them all for the rats to carry until I was ready.

But would I ever be ready?

No, I didn't think I would be.

I had reaped and retained suicide souls before; only a few in my existence who'd sold themselves to me before they died, and like Ann Singleton, they carried the weight of their crimes on their backs. And although they were like turbulent winds inside my chest, in their own ways they helped to balance me.

But none were as harrowing as that of Ann Singleton.

What *have* I *done?*
What have I *done?*
What have I done?

I walked longer, farther, circling block after block after block with no direction or destination, inattentive to the things around me.

I was stabbed in an alley, but I didn't fall or even flinch. Though, I bled.

Why am I bleeding? My preternatural eyes flashed in response to the realization, and my attacker saw it.

"What the fu—?" The man dropped the knife on the concrete, a clinking sound echoing between the buildings. "What the fuck?" he finally managed.

I just kept walking.

I was harassed for money, cigarettes, drugs, but without a word I kept on walking.

A woman wanted me to pay her for sex, but I kept on walking.

A man wanted to give me a blowjob for "anything" I could give him, but I kept on walking.

The soul of a child sat lost and alone on the sidewalk, asking for nothing, expecting nothing, understanding nothing, but no longer afraid of anything—I kept on walking.

And then I stopped.

And I turned around. And I went back for the child.

"Hi there." I crouched in front of her on the street.

"Hi."

"What's your name, sweetheart?"

Sweetheart?

"Ruby," she said in her frail little girl voice.

I sat beside her on the curb, arms propped atop bent knees, hands dangled between my legs.

"Why are you sitting out here all alone, Ruby?"

"I'm waiting for my mom."

"Where do you think your mom is?"

She turned her head and looked up at me for the first time, big brown eyes framed by disheveled brown hair. Her face was dirty, and she was missing her two front teeth. "I don't know," she said as if she'd only just now realized it. "Do *you* know where she is?"

I nodded.

"Yes, Ruby," I said carefully. "I know where your mom is."

"Can you take me to her?"

I shook my head.

"No, Ruby," I said carefully. "But I can take you somewhere even better."

I stood and held out my hand to the little girl, and with my last ounce of emotional strength, I took her to where I take most children, before I collapsed unconscious on the sidewalk, the soul of Ann Singleton far too heavy to carry anymore.

I awoke hours later to empty pockets, shoeless feet, beltless waist, watch-less wrist, and I stumbled into a stand.

A taxi took me to my office building where I got out without paying.

"Hey!" the driver called sharply, and held out his hand with expectation. "Ride's not free, asshole."

From outside his window, I reached out my hand and touched his shoulder. He burst into tears, and he screamed something indecipherable through gritted teeth, and he banged his forehead against the steering wheel one, two, three times before just leaving it there where he cried long after I left him and slipped into the building.

It was 11:42 p.m.

A security guard sat behind a desk in the lobby.

"Hello, Mr. Boone." He waved two fingers. "Guess you aren't the only one from your office working late tonight. Hey, are you okay? Look like you got mugged. Hello? Mr. Boone? Would you like me to call—" The elevator door cut off his voice.

The elevator took me up very slowly it seemed, and on the way, I stood with my back against the wall, out of breath, waves of sorrow and anger and anguish crashed through me like a derailed train moving eighty-miles-per-hour on a sharp curve. I barely made it to the waiting room before I couldn't go on anymore, and I collapsed again, this time still conscious, onto a chair across from the Angel.

"You are bleeding," the Angel said, though not to make me aware of the obvious, but instead to make me aware of the other obvious. "You are almost human."

I ignored her. I was too weak and uncomfortable to respond.

"Many will die, Azrael, if you do not find your balance. It is your duty," she said, "to choose another body before you go too far. How long have you been in that one? Past the expiration date, it would appear. You did not choose one before The Black Death, or before the China floods of 1931 or the Soviet Famine—have you not learned from your mistakes?"

"I did choose one," I told her, and it even hurt to speak; my lips quivered and my eyes burned as I held back the offensive, salty, mortal tears. *Oh, Ann, what you could've been...*

"And was it not willing?" she asked.

"*She* would've been," I answered, offended by the Angel's informality.

Offended?

The Angel nodded; there was no emotion in her face, just the calm, stoic cadence of light that never fears darkness *because* it is light. She sat like she always did, with her back straight and her dainty hands folded on her lap, her knees pressed together modestly, even though there was literally nothing between them—if anyone was an "it", it was the Angel.

"Do you feel it, Azrael?" the Angel pointed out. "I feel it. The earth rumbles in the deepest depths of Cumbre Vieja; the waters are churning, disturbed by the earth's anger, and soon La Palma will break off and collapse into the ocean and a great wave will form on the surface. Millions will die as far as *right here*, along the East Coast, more than in the Indian

209

Ocean tsunamis in 2004. Is that what you want? A repeat of one of your most devastating emotional failures?"

"No!" I shouted through gritted teeth.

"Are you ready for a barrage of new souls to tear you apart when you cannot even tame the ones already inside of you?"

"*No...*" I was too weak to shout anymore.

"That body cannot hold itself together at the seams for much longer, Azrael," she warned. "You cannot continue sewing the busted seams with rare souls—the seams have tattered beyond repairing."

"I will have to find another body," I said weakly.

"One that is willing," she reminded me, clarifying that no matter how desperately I needed a new body instead of just another "patch job", that her project, Nancy, was not willing and that she was off-limits. *Oh Ann, why did you do it? What you could have been!*

Nancy entered the waiting room from the office next to mine, once occupied by a *real* psychiatrist who, after getting to know me and my "uncivilized" methods, cleaned out her desk and left to rent in another building.

"Mr. Boone," Nancy said, surprised to see me. But then she was surprised to see me in the condition I was in. "Goodness, what happened to you? Did you get mugged?" She went over quickly to the water-cooler near her desk and filled a Styrofoam cup, brought it over to me.

I waved it off.

She set the cup aside and then sat down beside me.

"Is that blood?"

"Yes."

"Oh my God. I'm calling an ambulance." She started to get up to fetch her phone from her purse, but I grabbed her wrist, stopping her mid-stride.

Her body went rigid, and she turned to look down at me, mouth parted, eyes wide and watering. I felt her trembling beneath my hand, not with fear but with emotion, her own and mine.

The Angel eyed me from across the room.

"Let this world go," she told me with a soft pat of sympathy in her voice. "You have longed for it, Azrael, and you will continue to long for it for all of eternity. Just let it go."

"I can't," I said, but only the Angel could hear me. "I'm tethered. Addicted."

"And for that, you are no less human than they are," she said. "So much so that you can't bring yourself to ride with your companions, to spread the End of Everything. Let Us do our job—let me do my job—and *I* can set in motion the end of your suffering. Let this world go and I can set in motion the end of *everyone's* suffering. You are tired, Azrael. But you do not have to be. You can be at rest. In the Darkness. In the Nothingness. In The End. You *long* for it."

"Yes, I long for it." I shut my eyes as stinging tears streamed down my face. "I can't go on like...I want to let it all go."

"Then let it *go*," she whispered. "Your regrets will be aplenty, your suffering will grow, and your pain will destroy you, if you do not."

I could not end the world alone; I could only participate. But if I gave in to my torment and stopped fighting the Angels, they could set in motion the beginning of The End. I could be free from all of this. I could, at last, be at peace. Knowing nothing, seeing nothing, hearing nothing, tasting nothing, feeling nothing, *being* nothing. Ah, the sweet lure of the Nothing...

It took all of Us: Death, Time, the Angels; we each had our places, our assignments, but all of us had to agree, each of us had to be willing to play our part. Like Lucifer, I wasn't quite ready, although I wanted to be. If I could just let the Angels do their part, maybe it would inspire me, motivate me to do mine.

Unable to find her voice, Nancy slowly sat back down beside me, and, heeding the Angel's warnings, I let go of her wrist. I could have driven her to kill herself, especially in my condition. The same way the taxi driver did moments ago sitting outside in his car on the street. He sat there now, slumped against the bloodied window, a small handgun still in his hand lying awkwardly on his lap.

"You're crying," Nancy said peering in at me, her face twisted with disbelief and concern. "Mr. Boone—"

"Why do you do it?" I asked her.

She flinched.

"Why do you choose to fight this world?"

"I...what do you—?"

I pushed myself into a weak stand, swallowed trying to work moisture into my mouth but to no avail. I wanted that cup of water now, but I didn't ask for it.

"Look at it, Nancy—look at *them*!" My voice was strident in the small space. "They destroy everything they touch; they're depraved, disgusting fiends who prey on all that would make their world a peaceful place. They're a mob of vicious creatures with gnashing teeth dripping with the blood of goodness and innocence!"

Goodness and innocence? Why did I care? Oh, I was so fucking tired...

Nancy's face had frozen, stunned, the creases in her forehead cavernous. Cumbre Vieja was waking up, and it would be because of me it erupted.

"I hate them. All of them save ten or fifteen!" I roared, my arms motioning wildly in the air. "If I could kill them all myself, I would!" I could kill many, but never all of them.

"Mr. Boone," Nancy said carefully to calm me; slowly she stood, but she didn't approach me. Not yet. "Are you talking about...*people*?"

"Yes." I couldn't look at her; tears still streamed down my cheeks.

"Tell me about them," she said, still carefully, still trying to calm me. "Tell me what they did to you." She thought I was referring to whoever took my shoes and belt and watch.

I turned a sharp eye on her. "What *haven't* they done?" I countered. "I have been raped and murdered and mutilated and humiliated and sodomized and cannibalized and molested and shamed and shunned. (She no longer thought I was talking about whoever took my shoes and shirt and watch.) All they do is piss and shit and eat and shit some more and fuck and breed more cancerous creatures like them to carry on their useless, destructive legacies. They're greedy bastards, hoarding money, stealing money, killing for money—for what? Their cruelty knows no bounds, their greed knows no bounds, their egocentric personalities know no bounds. They feel sorry for themselves, whine about everyfuckingthing, they think they're owed happiness and fairness, but they don't realize they're not worthy of it!" I clenched my fists in front of me. "Why can't they see that to be happy they must not *give a fuck* about being happy? Why can't they understand that to be worthy they must *give up* the self-absorbed belief that they should be worthy of *anything*? Why can't they understand that it's NOT ABOUT THEM?" I roared and punched the air with my fist. "WHY ARE THEY SO INCREDIBLY FLAWED? THE END! I LONG FOR THE END!" The windows shook.

I fell to my knees in the center of the room.

I was losing it—literally. Ann Singleton's soul was the final straw dropped onto the tip of billions of other straws, and it would topple and obliterate me. Again. Because it had happened before. Often throughout human history.

Suddenly, my anger turned to a sadness so great and devastating that I couldn't lift my body into an upright position. I lay on my knees with my forehead pressed to the floor, my body wracked with sobs.

"It hurts, Nancy," I cried. "It hurts so much."

"What hurts?" I heard her say in a comforting voice. She was close, crouched beside me. "Tell me what hurts, Allister."

"I...I don't know how to describe it. I...I think it's..." I fell onto my side and drew my knees toward my chest. I faintly knew of how ridiculous, how pathetic I must've looked, but I didn't care. I just wanted the pain to go away.

"Tell me what hurts, Allister," Nancy repeated, and this time I felt her hand briefly touch my shoulder. She was hesitant to touch me for longer, but I began to understand why as I sensed the Angel now standing nearby.

"I feel...empty, hollow, but at the same time I'm filled with a terrible sadness." I choked back my tears. "I just want to...die."

"Oh, Allister," Nancy consoled, and against the Angel's influence she laid her hand on my back and left it there. "You don't have to feel that way forever. I was that way for a long time. I know how it feels to want to die—I *know*. But it's all just an illusion, Mr. Boone. A drug. It's a trick They play on us to distract us from realizing how *important* we are."

Yes, Nancy, I know...but how did you know that?

They? Did Nancy believe in or know who "They" were? No, that wasn't it, I realized. It was something else.

"I may not believe in God," she went on, "but I do believe in forces out there that control all of this—all of *us*. I don't know what they are, but I feel them, so close all the time, Mr. Boone, smothering me, trying their damnedest to extinguish me, just like they're doing to you right now." Her hands squeezed my shoulders.

For Nancy, maybe that's what had happened, but that wasn't what was going on here. No one was preying upon me. This was all Azrael, this was all Allister Boone, the Angel of Death who wore the meat suit of a human to fit in with and interact with humans. I was Azrael, the Angel of Death who had done this before, and was doomed to do it again and again and again. Because I was tethered, addicted, and no less human than the rest.

But this time was different. This time I felt out-of-control of myself, and of the billions of souls trapped inside of me. This time I felt...like I was losing against them. Had I really waited too long? Was losing Ann Singleton the proverbial nail in my coffin?

"But you can't let them win," Nancy said with conviction. "You have to fight them!"

Them? Yes, Them. The souls. *They* were the ones I was fighting, not the Someone Elses.

"It's impossible," I told her between nauseating sobs. "This emptiness, it consumes me. I've never felt anything so…it's like an eternal ache, constantly stretching and pulling me in every direction, exhausting me—I just want to give in to it; I'm *so* tired that I can't keep them from pulling me apart any longer."

"Yes. You can."

Everything went silent—the raging in my brain, the aching in my heart, my pathetic sobs—and I looked up from the confines of my hands at Nancy now standing over me. *She* was who silenced the chaos and deadened the pain. She. Not he. Not He. A woman this time.

"Yes," she repeated, her voice was so soft, yet so powerful. "But you have to fight it, Mr. Boone, just like I did. I was at my lowest five years ago. Every day it was a chore just to get out of bed—or the closet. My closet had become the womb I wanted to crawl back into. I had been severely depressed for nine years before I had The Breakdown, the moment that would decide everything: my fate, how I would live or die, *if* I would live or die, how I would come out on the other side if I lived. I slept in my closet for six days, lying on the floor staring at the orange suitcase I'd stuffed in the corner. I cried so much and for so long that the headaches never went away. The only comfort I found was in my dog. He never left my side. But not even he was enough to make me not want to swallow the two bottles of prescription anti-depressants that sat beside me, waiting for me. I lost nineteen pounds in six days. I couldn't eat, I couldn't sleep undisturbed; nightmares and heart palpations and anxiety attacks woke me in the night. On the seventh day I crawled out of the closet, and I spent the next several days—I'd lost

215

count—in the bed, staring at the wall, unable to move. And then one day, I realized that I was the one in control, and that I wanted to live, but not like that anymore: not in control of the precious life I was given to *do* something meaningful with. And so, I got up. And then I began to think differently, to *know* that I was the one in control, that the course of my life depended solely on me. But more importantly, I realized I not only wanted to live, but that I wanted to live for *something*. I didn't want to go back to doing nothing, existing in a world where everybody else did the same: merely existed. I wanted to be a part of something greater than that."

Nancy reached out her hand. Hesitantly, I took it, and I went into a stand. I didn't know how I could be standing; I didn't know how I felt so…calm. Oh yes, because of Nancy. Because of Her.

"I had no idea what I could do," she went on, "what I could possibly put my heart and efforts into that would fulfill that desire, that need to be a part of something greater, but it didn't matter that I didn't know—I just knew I had to do *something*. Maybe I had divine help, someone or something that pointed me in the right direction—I don't know—but I filtered every part of me that hated this world into wanting to change it. One person at a time. One mental illness at a time. One life hanging in the balance at a time." She pointed at me. "And that's how I ended up here."

Nancy stepped up to me, and she placed both hands on my shoulders, and she looked into my eyes.

"I was meant for something, Mr. Boone. And I know this because I choose to believe it. And that's all it takes to beat Them off your back—*believe* you were meant for something more, and you absolutely *will* be."

Then she wrapped her arms around me, and as she touched me, a sensation unlike I'd ever felt before intoxicated me. My eyes shut softly and I breathed in her human scent, and I breathed in the same light that the Angel had been attracted to, and then I knew what Nancy's purpose was.

"If I die tomorrow," she said, squeezing me gently, "I know in my heart it will be because I was *meant* to, and that I'd fulfilled some critical purpose. Because I chose to live that day when I was at my weakest. I chose to fight and live rather than end my life early. I chose to live, and you will too."

The silence was short, just long enough to become a decision.

"Yes," I whispered, "I choose to live..."

"NOOO!" the Angel cried.

26

Now, I could lie and say Nancy went on to fulfill her dreams of helping people, one person at a time, one mental illness at a time, one life hanging in the balance at a time. But I do not lie. And although the truth is often the most bitter pill to swallow, it's always better than a lie that tastes sweet, but becomes poison as it goes down.

Nancy's guardian angel knew I always played by the rules, she knew there were things I would never do even if in my power to do them. Lying was one. Performing "miracles" or "magic tricks" to alter a person's life was another. But even angels can be blinded by their own naiveté, forgetting the simplest of things while focusing on the most complex: never say never.

She knew I would *never* take a life on my own, that I would *never* break the rules in such a manner.

But that was precisely what I did. I'd reached into Nancy's chest and squeezed the life out of her heart. And then her soul became mine. Her soul alone was powerful enough to balance me for at least another century, powerful enough to calm the torment of Ann Singleton's soul raging inside of me.

"You are a monster, Azrael," the Angel told me. "Many suitable souls out there, and you choose one of ours. You always do. I wonder why that is, hmm?" Her words were laced with sarcasm.

She came toward me, her movements graceful and unhurried.

"I was desperate," I told her. "I did what I *had* to do."

"You did what you *wanted* to do." She circled me slowly. "You always do what you want to do. You claim to hate this world, but you are too comfortable in it to let it go."

(...you are the way you are because you want it, because you've been in that skin for so long you're too comfortable, regardless of how much you hate it.)

(You get off on talkin' shit to everybody else, but you're just a hypocrite.)

(...a hypocritical, poison-tongued, self-absorbed pig...)

"Like your brother, Lucifer, you are. You knew that Nancy had the potential, you felt it when she touched you, you felt it when just by being in her presence she quieted the chaos inside of you, brightened the sad darkness that was consuming you. You *knew*."

"Yes. I knew. But I was also desperate," I repeated. "You saw it yourself, how quickly I was losing control. Another hour and the world would've run rampant with death. And your little project would've been sidelined. I *am* The End. I am, essentially, the Hand of God when it all comes down to it."

She stopped in front of me, shook her head.

"You are a fool, Azrael," she said with disappointment. "A narcissistic fool. (I blinked with offense.) You do not get to decide when that time comes. You cannot kill the world with the stroke of your finger, all you can do is throw it into chaos."

She was correct: during my temporary times of failure, the world would be thrown into chaos, and death would run rampant, cleansing the Earth of humans. It had happened often before: The Taiping Rebellion, World War I, World War II, The Black Death. And it will happen again before The End finally comes.

But it would not happen on this day. Because Nancy fulfilled her purpose. She didn't fulfill her dreams of helping people one person at a time, one mental illness at a time, one life hanging in the balance at a time—she did so much more than that. Because of her, the earth beneath Cumbre Vieja calmed and went back into a slumber, and La Palma did not break off into the ocean.

Nancy did not fulfill the Angel's hopes of becoming the new Savior, but she saved people, nonetheless. She saved millions of people with her sacrifice. And while it wasn't the kind of sacrifice the Angel had wanted for Nancy, she still served her purpose, her *grand* purpose.

"Consequences, Azrael," the Angel warned. "You know there will be consequences for breaking the rules."

"Yes," I said. "And I'll deal with whatever they are."

The Angel smiled eerily, and then she was gone.

THE
OUTCOME

27

I felt like myself again, if I could even claim I knew what it actually felt like to be me. Was it the time humans first crawled out of the primordial soup that I was the real me? Or a thousand years after they had evolved out of their caves, and they learned language, and fire, and tools, and weapons? Or maybe it was after humans had already mastered these things and they began to *de*volve, to understand that they could have more, be more, destroy more, thus destroying themselves.

I supposed I may never remember what it felt like to be the real me. And I cared little, either. It did nothing for me to care about something I couldn't change.

The Game was almost over. I was going to win. There was no way Morty Finch would ever catch up to me now. In thirty-two hours, I would know that Death was superior to Time. And in thirty-two hours, I would be prepared for what that win would mean, how things would change, because things *would* change and I could not change change, just like Lucifer had warned me.

But I was ready.

I was *ready*.

Before I could rub my victory in Morty's face, however, there were a few loose ends I needed to tie up.

It had been days since I'd spoken with or seen Jason Layne. Apparently, his sister had seen about as much of him as I had, and so she began calling my office daily to find out if I'd heard from him.

"No, Miss Layne," I told her, standing at Nancy's old desk in the waiting room. "I'm sorry."

It was, lacking a more fitting word, annoying having to hear that damn phone ring every few minutes. I didn't even know why I was answering it; The Game was almost over and I would not have to play this role anymore, yet I still kept answering the phone when I wasn't in a session with a patient. I didn't know how Nancy did it every day, every minute. I missed Nancy, I couldn't deny that, but not only because she kept the phone lepers off my back, but because, like Pastor John Macon, I enjoyed her company.

Admittedly, I left John Macon's soul to wander longer than I had ever intended. I just had a lot going on with losing my sanity and all, and I wanted to be of sound mind when I saw him again. Because John Macon was intelligent and influential and manipulative. And you don't want to be even a little bit off your game when in the presence of someone like him. One could end up a mindless "Christian" riding his heels and kissing his feet because he promised you the world, but would give you Hell eternal instead. Or, in my case, he could make me believe that splitting his soul with Lucifer was a "bad idea", or he could somehow use my own tricks against me to strike a new deal, and I might not've realized it until it was too late. Even Death can be tricked by the craftiest of humans. I'm not proud of it, but it's true.

But I, Allister Boone, was, in fact, of sound mind, and I was one step ahead of him before I later went in search of his wandering soul.

"Well, I'll be damned if it isn't Allister Boone. In the flesh," John said, and then he pointed at me with his thumb and added with a stiff brow: "And I use 'flesh' loosely in your case. Where have you *been*, my old friend?"

I'd found him roaming the Arts District of Downtown Dallas, just blocks from his former mega-church, a murder of crows perched on the powerlines and rooftops above him, all bickering, and waiting.

"Here and there," I answered.

"How's that game of yours coming along?"

"It's coming along nicely."

John grinned. "Ah, so I take it you're winning then."

"You could say that."

"And that means I lose." The smile on his face didn't suggest that him losing would be anything to worry about. That was John Macon: confident enough that just about anything he believed he could do, he certainly would.

John leaned against a red-brick building, crossed his arms.

"So, what took you so long?" he asked. "I heard you weren't quite yourself the past several months."

"I suppose you heard right."

"But you're feeling better now?"

"Yes. You could say that."

John smiled.

"But The Game isn't over yet," he said. "How much time is left?"

I glanced at the nighttime sky.

"Less than twenty-four hours."

He nodded. "I see."

He pushed himself away from the brick wall, and his crossed arms came apart. "I guess we should skip the small-talk and get to the reaping, huh?"

I smiled, close-lipped.

"But I enjoy our small-talk, John," I told him. "Why skip it?"

"Because it's *small-talk*," he said. "The pointless stuff used to fill pages, or awkward silence—nobody ever really gets anything out of it. Except more pages, and more awkward silence."

"Yeah, you're right," I agreed, "but humor me, why don't you?"

John studied me suspiciously, and then a grin appeared as he caught on. He pointed at me and said with laughter in his voice: "You're waiting for me to try weaseling my way into a better deal." He looked at me sidelong. "You *want* me to. But what for?"

We stood next to a bench.

"You made a deal with Lucifer," he said, realizing.

"Haven't we all?"

He smirked.

"And you're hoping I can find you a way out of it."

I shrugged. "Hoping is a strong word," I said. "Expecting is more appropriate."

"And what kind of deal was it?"

"That he and I would split your soul. No matter who wins."

"Oh, but that's a bad idea, Allister," John said, just as I knew he would.

"Do you even know why it's a bad idea?" I asked.

"Well, no, I don't, but it just *seems* like a bad idea. Ever split a soul before?"

"No. I can't say that I have. It never came up."

John sucked on a tooth, slid his hands in his pockets, and we strolled down the sidewalk in the darkness, passing beneath the glow of streetlights.

"Think about it," he said. "Part of my soul eternally tortured in Lucifer's Hell, and the other part trapped inside of you." He glanced over at me. "I'm not an expert on the subject, but it only seems logical that a soul, even if split apart, will always be whole, connected." (I glanced over at him then.) "If you think you were pushing the edge of insanity before because of the weight of the souls you carry, imagine the insanity with a soul inside of you directly connected to its other half in Hell."

Damn.

"Yeah?" John said with wide eyes, one brow hitching up higher than the other. "Can't deny my theory, can you? Maybe I'm putting my foot in my mouth by saying this, but wouldn't it be safer you just gave up your half—you know Lucifer won't ever give up his."

"No, he won't."

"But you want my soul all for yourself," John assumed.

And why *wouldn't* he assume? If that wasn't my intention somehow, we wouldn't be having the conversation.

"Well," John said, "I know how you are about lying and cheating, Allister. But like I told you before: Death gets cheated all the time, so maybe it's the hour Death fought back."

"Maybe." Simply considering it, like I had just done, was enough to make me uncomfortable in my skin.

But what other option was there?

"Maybe you could make another deal with Lucifer," John suggested. "Or just plead your case."

"Plead my case?" Nothing about "pleading" was even remotely interesting.

"Sure," John said as if it were that easy. "Explain to old Luc how the splitting of my soul would likely turn you into a madman, or something. Hell, you could become the next Hitler or Stalin or Mao Zedong; the new and improved John Wayne Gacy, or…maybe something worse. Think about it, Allister. What you could become, the chaos you could create, the death toll, all those tortured souls…"

"You're right…" I said absently. "That would be a…terrible thing to endure."

A terrible, beautiful *thing to endure…*

After a moment, I noticed John's hand waving in front of my face.

"Are you still in there?' he asked.

I blinked back into the present, reached up with both hands and straightened my suit.

"I have somewhere I need to be," I told him suddenly.

"Hey! Wait!" John called out behind me. "Where are you going? Don't leave me here like this, Allister! Hey! Ah, screw it."

I glanced back long enough to see John plop down on the concrete steps of a building to await my return.

28

I could understand any mortal's attraction to Crater Lake, its deep, piercing blue waters, the clean air, the distance one could see looking out from its peaks. It was a peaceful place of encompassing scope and beauty, far away from light pollution, and, more important, human pollution. It reminded me of the era before humans...Ah, yes, the time before their plagues and destructions and atrocities...Yes, I remembered *then* what it felt like to be the real me. And I could already feel my pale companion stirring beneath my legs. *Snap out of it, Azrael...*

Though, none of these things—clean air and beauty—were what attracted Jason Layne to Crater Lake. Death—not me, personally, but the idea of me—brought him here, and his lifelong journey to find meaning in whatever he could.

I stood behind him as he sat on a ledge of rock overhanging more rocks many feet below; light breezes coming off the water combed through my hair and clothes, dusted me with the smell of Jason's final moments and the disease that had devoured him.

"Did she send you?"

"Who?"

"My sister."

"No. She didn't send me."

"Good." He kept his back to me and continued looking out at the vastness of the lake.

"I'd ask how you found me," Jason said, "but I guess you knew this would be the only place I'd go."

"Yes. I knew."

After a moment, he said, "You were right. About Jillian Bowden. I wanted to thank you for talking me into going to see her."

"And what became of it?" I slid my hands in my pockets.

"I'm not sure," Jason answered, and he still hadn't looked at me. "But I have a good feeling about it. She and her husband—Darren's is a good guy, I like him a lot—they were surprised when I knocked on their door that day. Not because I looked like shit, or because I was dying, or because they thought I was some creepy stalker, but because…" He paused, and his voice trailed. He finally turned his head to look up at me standing behind him. "…You're not gonna believe this, Mr. Boone."

"Try me."

Jason stood up, close to the edge of the cliff, and he eyed me with a mixture of fascination and disbelief.

"They had seen my vlog," he said. "I didn't think anybody had seen it, really. But they had. Of all the people in the world, how could it have been Jillian?" He stopped, looked beyond me in deep thought, his brows crumpled in his forehead.

"Fate, perhaps?"

Jason smiled.

"Maybe," he said. "But not the—"

"You-can't-escape-it kind, a set path for everybody, an all-roads-lead-to-the-same-destiny."

His smile grew. "No, not that kind."

After a moment, Jason continued to look out at the water and the stars glittering above it in an inky-black sky.

"Jillian said she just stumbled across on the internet one day," he began. "And when she saw me in one of my videos, she thought I looked familiar." He chuckled. "I was surprised she'd remembered me from school at all, but she did. Anyway, um, turns out she and Darren are passionate about all the things I'm passionate about. He's a bigtime politician. And Jillian, well…she's…different, Mr. Boone. It's hard to describe, but she's just so full of love and life; she's the kindest person I've ever met. And it's *real*"—he looked back to meet my gaze—"not just somebody pretending to be kind, or expecting something in return; she's genuinely good."

After a moment:

"I know it's selfish," he said, "but I still wish it had been me who ended up marrying her." He sighed. "Anyway, I'm not sure what I got out of meeting her as far as the signs and all that; I mean, all we did in the short times we visited was talk. About life. About how shitty the world has become. About human rights and animal rights—you know, the stuff nobody likes to talk about because it could mean the difference between enjoying a burger and feeling guilty about it."

"How do you feel now, Jason?"

He turned.

"About what?"

I looked him up and down.

Then he looked himself up and down, he looked at the ledge he stood on, the long drop at the end, he looked out at Crater Lake, and something finally dawned on him.

He stepped away from the edge and motioned his arms in front of him, shook his head.

"Oh no, it's not what you're thinking," he said. "I didn't come here to…jump. I-I know it probably looks that way, but I promise that's not why I came. I-I don't feel that way anymore; I haven't in a while."

"I know, Jason," I told him.

He looked confused.

"You know? Well, okay then."

"But how do you *feel?*" I repeated. "On the inside. On the outside."

Then something else finally dawned on him.

He looked down at his hands as he opened them in front of him; he reached up and ran a hand over his face; he took a deep, undisturbed breath that wasn't painful for the first time in a long time. And then his eyes fell on me, growing more confused.

"I feel...good. But..."

"You died two hours ago, Jason." I stepped aside and a wedge of blue moonlight traveled behind me to rest on Jason's body sitting slumped against a tree just feet from the ledge.

He couldn't speak. He looked at his hands again, examined them with new eyes, flexed them, and then he touched his face with them, and his neck, and his hair.

And then he cried.

I let him have his moment.

Jason reached up and pinched the top of his nose with his thumb and index finger, trying to stifle the joyous tears.

"I'm...how did I not know?" His eyes kept moving between me and his body.

"A lot of people don't know," I told him. "Some go days, months, even years wandering this plane, living their life as if they were still alive, when what they're seeing and experiencing are just remnants of the life they left behind." Most of those cases were my fault, as I tended to let them wander for far too long.

"Is that what I was doing?"

"No," I said. "You were just enjoying the most peaceful moment you've ever known, for a little while longer."

It all had started to come back to him then; his eyes fell on his dead body for a longer time. "I remember now," he said, still focused on the body. "I knew I was going to die tonight. I don't know how I knew, but I just felt it, the certainty of it. Barely able to walk, I got on the first flight to Oregon. And then there was a man at the airport. I…" He paused in concentration. "He asked me if I needed a ride somewhere. He wasn't a cab driver, he was just a man. It was strange. But I didn't care because I was dying and what did it matter? I just wanted to live long enough to make it here. I wanted to die here, to see this place for the first time with my own eyes, to feel the wind on my face, the earth in my hands." He paused again, staring at the ground. And then he looked at me. "Seems time was on my side," he said. "I had just enough left in me to make it here—even to hike and climb all the way up here—and to sit here and die peacefully."

"It seems Time was," I agreed. "Sounds to me like Time even gave you a ride here from the airport."

Jason didn't understand what I'd meant by that, but that didn't matter. And I supposed it was a "kind" gesture for Morty to do such a thing. But I'd never tell Morty that. Unless I wanted to "mess with his head", in which case, I probably would eventually.

"Are you ready, Jason Layne?"

"Wait," he said, a third thing finally dawned on him. He pointed at me, his expression hardened with amazement and surprise. "I'm dead, but you can see me…"

"I am what you think I am," I told him. "I always have been."

Jason had trouble putting a sentence together.

Finally, he said, "You're Death?"

I nodded.

"And you were my…*psychiatrist*…?"

I nodded once more.

He looked confused.

"Um, how does that work exactly?" he asked. "You're Death, yet you convinced me *not* to take my life."

"Yes," I confirmed. "It's very difficult to understand, but that is the gist of it."

Jason opened his hands. "Hey, I've got time." He smiled. "I mean, I'm not sure where I go from here, but maybe you could explain it along the way?"

I thought about it. And then I shrugged. "All right," I agreed. "I'll tell you everything."

And that's what I did. I literally told him Everything. Everything that I knew, anyway. All about the Someone Elses and Morty Finch and my brother, Lucifer. I told him about The Game and the Beginning of Time and all about the terrible effects of suicide souls to which he was relieved he didn't choose to go that way. I told him about the place I was taking him and how because I liked him so much that his Afterlife would be much more comfortable than most, that I'd still use his soul to help balance me, but that he didn't need to worry. "Just sit back, relax, and enjoy yourself while you wait for The End," I'd told him. And then I told him about The End, and that it was not only inevitable, but closer than anyone living thought it was.

But in Jason Layne's end, he got what he had been searching for: questions answered, a better understanding of Life and his place in it, and more important, his place beyond it. I'd divulge, but, such information is privileged only to the dead. And to those who *know* they're dead.

There were only a few hours left before The Game would come to an end, and Morty and I would tally up—who was I kidding? There was no need to tally anything up. He would lose by many points. I couldn't see how he could catch up to me in under three hours, much less surpass me even by one point.

I was going to win—there could be no other outcome. Death would wear the belt, Death would be superior to Time. I was prepared to accept my trophy and make my speech and reap—no pun intended—the rewards and consequences of change. And as I sat alone in my room, contemplating things like consequences and change and how, no matter what, I couldn't avoid either, the back of my neck prickled with a familiar sensation.

I left my small, dark studio apartment and went to Brisbane's Bar on South Street where an almost-forgotten patient sat at the bar drinking a beer.

29

It was Saturday night, and the streets of New York City were packed with tourists and party-goers, and residents trying to make their way through them all without murdering them. Brisbane's was busier than usual, every chair and barstool occupied; the cook had help so that now three cooks were so busy working they rarely ever emerged from the heat of the kitchen; one waitress had also multiplied by five as they moved from table to table to the kitchen and back again with trays full of food and drinks balanced perfectly on their hands. And Frank, Brisbane's bartender and owner worked diligently behind the bar, refilling glasses and conversing with the regulars—including Morty Finch.

Morty sat on Joel's right—I sat on Joel's left—on the same barstool, the one with the best view of the flat-screen TV mounted on the wall; there was a cloud of generic full-flavored cigarette smoke around his head, and a woman at his side. Tall, slender, black hair cut short above her shoulders, olive-colored skin, deep-brown eyes. She leaned on his shoulder as she eyed a wad of rolled-up cash in his shirt pocket tucked behind a pack of cigarettes.

"It's good to see you again, Allister," Frank said. "Anything to drink tonight?"

I smiled.

"As a matter of fact"—I glanced over at Morty—"I think I'll have an Angel's Envy, neat." Yes, I chose it because of its name; I was in a boastful mood, I admitted.

"You know what they say about counting your chickens," Morty put in. He sat slumped on the stool, arms resting on the bar; he raised his whiskey glass to his mouth and took a big, aggravated gulp.

"You look like you've already counted my chickens for me, Morty," I taunted. Frank set a glass in front of me and then filled it. I took a small, confident drink, savoring the delicious taste and the warmth and the victory as it went down.

Morty grunted.

Joel, recognizing me after trying to figure out where he'd seen me before, looked over.

"Hey, aren't you that asshole psychiatrist?"

Morty chortled.

"I am," I said proudly. "Joel, right?"

Joel looked me up and down with aversion, and then he faced forward again, taking a drink from his beer. It seemed he had nothing more to say. Because he had more important things on his mind. Like catching his plane back to Missouri tonight after leaving the bar, then killing his wife and kids before turning the gun on himself.

Morty had read his mind, too.

"Won't change anything," I told him. "One point doesn't even come close."

"I guess not," Morty said, his eyes on the TV.

The woman with him never spoke; she was just another ornament waiting for the payoff of being his company.

"So, who won that game you two were playing?" Frank asked.

"Nobody yet," Morty put in.

I raised my hand, index finger pointed skyward. "But when that clock strikes midnight, I'll be wearing the crown."

Frank nodded, drying the glass in his hands with a dishcloth.

"What's the score?" he asked, always pretending, as he didn't believe this stuff.

"Eighty-one to Morty's twenty-two," I answered, because Morty wasn't going to. "So, you see why it's safe to call a victory before the hour is up."

Frank agreed, nodding.

Then he left us alone and stepped back over into the real world where patrons with more believable stories sat drinking at the bar.

"Are you still working on the private gated community?" I asked Joel.

He sighed with irritation, continued facing forward.

"No," he said.

"Oh, so you're working on something else?"

"Sure."

"What—?"

His head snapped around.

"What the fuck do you want?" His fingers tightened around the beer bottle in his right hand. "I'm not in your office," he pointed out, "so there ain't no need for you to be asking questions 'bout my life." Slowly, his fingers relaxed and he turned to face the TV again. "Leave me to my beer in peace, will you?" Plotting murder/suicides was mentally exhausting stuff, and it made him short-tempered. Well, more than usual.

I left Joel alone to enjoy his beer, and I left Morty alone to wallow in his loss, but as I sat there, staring at the TV but not seeing the news playing on the screen, I felt something I'd rarely ever felt before: concern.

Even one death you don't try to stop, and you can lose everything.

Nancy's words had been seared into my subconscious mind; even after reaping her soul and it putting me back together again, I could still hear her voice. But worse was that it wasn't just about winning. I felt genuine concern for Joel's family, just as Nancy had felt.

I closed my eyes and tried to shut it out, but it only got stronger, and I could see glimpses of Nancy's life weeks before she died. Nancy, knowing that Joel was a danger to his family, went to the construction site to speak with Joel's employer—the information she had on him at our office was just his first name and a fake number. She spoke to his boss, expressing her concerns without outright accusing him of anything too horrific, and attempted to get the personal information on Joel that could help her to contact Joel's wife.

"I'm sorry, ma'am," his boss had said, "but it's not exactly legal for me to give you that information."

But Nancy had a way of convincing people to do the right thing, and she talked Joel's boss into giving her his wife's phone number, who Joel had listed as his emergency contact.

"You didn't get this from me," his boss had said.

Nancy called Joel's wife later that day. She'd tried to convince the woman to take her children and leave, to go somewhere Joel wouldn't be able to find them—she even offered to pay for everything.

But the wife refused.

"Look, I don't know who you are," the wife had said into the phone, "but my husband's a good man, and a good father, and he'd never hurt his children." Nancy noted the wife said nothing about how Joel would never hurt *her*.

But Joel's wife was like so many other women in abusive relationships: afraid to leave, afraid to be alone, essentially brainwashed into thinking that the life they suffer is the only life they'll ever have, and so Joel's wife did not heed Nancy's warnings.

Every single day until the day Nancy died, she had checked in with Joel's boss to see if he was still on a job in the city.

"You really think he'd do something to hurt his family?" the boss had asked on the phone one day. "I mean, yes, I know Joel has a bad temper, but…all right, look, I believe you. I guess it's just a gut instinct, but I think you may be right."

A few minutes later:

"I can keep him here longer if you think that might help," the boss had offered. "We'll be done with the job in a week, and he's supposed to head back to Missouri then—"

"Oh no, you can't let him go back yet," Nancy had said. "I need more time to convince Patricia to leave."

"All right," the boss had said. "I'll put him on another job. I'll have to take someone else off, but I can manage."

"How much time does that give me?"

"Another month, at least. Maybe two."

And so, Nancy bought herself more time. And she used every bit of that time to do whatever she could to get "Patricia" to leave.

Unfortunately, Patricia was one of few who Nancy could never convince to do the right thing.

Even one death you don't try to stop, and you can lose everything.

I couldn't let it happen, even though I knew by the time he got home The Game would be over and I would've already won. Maybe it was just Nancy's soul, remnants of her human-self bleeding over into my consciousness, but I felt such a dire need to save his family. For Nancy? For myself? I could never know, and that never mattered. All that mattered was that I did whatever I could to stop it.

But what? Would I have to resort to lying and cheating and performing the Nevers, which would only make me an emotional wreck again? I didn't want to do that if I didn't have to.

And so I played my final card.

Lucifer walked into the bar, a toothpick dangling from his mouth. Morty looked away from the TV in the same instant, sensing his presence without having to see him.

"What's *he* doing here?" Morty grumbled.

"To help your loss be a little less pathetic," I answered.

"*Hmph!*" Morty went back to watching TV and drinking his whiskey. The ornament hanging from his shoulder let her attention stay on Lucifer longer than Morty liked, and he told her: "Pick your poison, princess", and then waved her off.

The woman sauntered toward Lucifer as he strolled toward us, but he passed her by without so much as a glance. Feeling slighted, and too embarrassed to run back into Morty's arms, she slipped away quietly and left the bar.

"You rang?" Lucifer said.

He stood behind Joel; Joel paid no attention to any of us, his mind so bloated and heavy with images of his future brutal crimes, to hear if a brawl had broken out in the bar behind him.

I glanced at Joel. "You said one freebie." I turned on the stool to face Lucifer. "This one is about to pull the plug on his entire family."

"But you're winning," Lucifer pointed out. "What does it matter what he does?"

"You gonna do it, or not?"

Lucifer shrugged.

"Sure," he said, and then he motioned with his thumb for me to move so he could take my place next to Joel.

He sat down beside Joel, and Joel instantly broke away from his thoughts to see Lucifer, giving him more attention than he ever gave me.

"Do you know what happens to murderers after they die?" Lucifer said.

Joel just sat there, wordless, confused.

"No." Joel had no clue why he'd even entertained an answer to such a strange question.

Frank made his way over with a shot of whiskey and placed it on the bar in front of Lucifer, knowing without having to ask, what Lucifer wanted, and then he walked away.

Lucifer sipped from his shot glass, the toothpick still dangling from his lips.

"What happens to them," Lucifer went on, "doesn't compare to what happens to men who murder children."

Joel turned on his stool to face Lucifer.

"What happens to men who murder children?" Deep-down, Joel's human mind tried to fight Lucifer's manipulation of itself, but to no avail. In this moment, Joel knew only the "man" sitting in front of him, and that that man somehow knew what Joel had intended to do. *And* that that man wasn't really a man.

"I have to kill them," Joel said. "I have to save them from this world."

"Are you sure?" Lucifer asked.

Joel took a swig from his beer, and he thought about it. "Yeah," he finally answered, nodding a series of nervous, unconfident nods. "Yeah, I'm their dad. I'm supposed to protect them." His dangerous personality came out then. "This country is turning to shit—the whole world is shit. We're being overrun by Muz-lams and niggers and wetbacks and chinks. I'll be Goddamned if I let my daughter get raped by them."

Lucifer took another sip.

"Are you *absolutely* sure?" Lucifer asked once more.

"Yes." Joel wasn't nervous or unconfident anymore—he was hell-bent.

"Well, all right then," Lucifer said, drank down everything in his shot glass, and then laid his hand on Joel's shoulder.

Joel's body shook and convulsed beneath Lucifer's hand, and the whites of his eyes rolled into view; if anyone had been aware of what was taking place right in front of them, Frank might've scrambled to call for an ambulance, and a crowd might've gathered around Joel. But no one could see what was going on but me, Lucifer, and Morty Finch, who was still uninterested in anything other than the TV.

Joel's hands came up in a desperate spectacle as he clawed at his face and neck—if his fingernails hadn't been cut down to the quick, he would've drawn blood, even flesh—and he cried out in pain, and the lights flickered in the bar, and the television cut on and off, and bottles of whiskey burst against the mirror on the wall. Joel fell from the stool onto the floor, writhing in pain, blood seeping from his fastened eyes and his nose and his ears and his mouth.

"Ahh!" he screamed. "*Ahh-AHH!*"

Lucifer stood over him, watching him, letting it go on long enough to get the point across, and I stood back and did the same, knowing what Joel was seeing, what he was experiencing, and what he would experience over and over and over again, every second of every day for all of eternity if he murdered his children.

When Joel's body couldn't take anymore and the fight in him failed to nothing more than a few desperate breaths and sputtering heartbeats, Lucifer released him from the torture of his own personal Hell.

Joel laid on the floor flat on his back, and he opened his eyes to stare up at the dark ceiling, and he couldn't move for a long time.

Lucifer crouched beside him—Joel tried to back away in fear, but all he could do was shake.

"W-W-What the fuck are you?" Tears streamed down Joel's face; his nostrils were clogged with snot and blood, his eyes were bloodshot-red, his pupils dilatated the size of nickels.

He didn't give Lucifer a chance to answer, and Joel managed to scramble to his feet. He took off running through the bar, slipping once and sending a waitress with a full tray of food onto the floor behind him; there was a *crash* as she fell, and then the door sprang open as Joel's hands slammed against it.

"What the hell?" Frank asked when he noticed the broken bottles and dripping whiskey behind him.

"Hey," Morty said to Lucifer and Lucifer turned around. "Next time, do it outside—can't you see I'm trying to watch the news?"

Lucifer ignored him.

He stepped past me and then stopped.

"He won't be killing his family," he said, "but he still might kill himself."

"Yeah, well..." I shrugged.

Lucifer went toward the door.

"What, you're not going to stay for my celebration?" I called out to him. "In twenty-two more minutes, I'll have beaten Time. You don't want to stay for that?"

"Nah," Lucifer said after opening the door. "Just make sure you hold up your end of the deal with John Macon's soul." His voice carried over the noise of the dining and drinking crowd.

"Yeah, well, you don't have to worry about that."

Lucifer nodded and left.

I sat on Joel's barstool next to Morty; Frank was too busy cleaning the mysterious mess to pour me another drink.

"So, what are we gonna do after this?" I asked.

"I dunno," Morty said. "Play another game—best two out of three, maybe?"

"I don't think so," I said, tapping my fingers on the bar. "I don't see how giving you another chance is going to change the fact that I won."

Morty grunted.

Several minutes passed. I had been watching the clock so intensely that when I felt the familiar sensation prickling on the back of my neck again, that I didn't immediately notice.

The gunshots outside woke me.

30

The patrons inside Brisbane's froze at their tables, forks suspended from hands and stationary drinks centimeters from lips. *Rat-Tat-Tat-Tat-Tat-Tat-Tat!* Another series of shots rang out, closer than before, and the static crowd fell apart, diving out of chairs and stampeding through the bar in every direction; some hid under tables, some tried to squeeze their way through each other down the hallway toward the restrooms, some fled to the kitchen looking for a backdoor.

Morty and I remained sitting at the bar, his interest in the TV replaced by the chaos. Morty looked delighted: eyes wide, a toothy smile that stretched across the room. "Oh, this is wonderful!" he cheered, and clapped his hands together once.

Morty's former dark-haired ornament burst through the bar's entrance, blood covered her abdomen, seeping through the breaks in her fingers as she held her hands over the wound. She didn't get five-feet in when she collapsed onto the floor.

Screams pierced the room, and the stampede switched direction, people who couldn't find a place a hide, jumped onto tables and leapt over the bar where Frank was hiding with a phone pressed to his ear, nine-one-one on the other end.

Joel entered Brisbane's Bar & Restaurant at precisely 11:57 p.m., armed with an AR-15, and he sprayed the building with bullets. I couldn't even hear the screams of the living anymore as the souls of the new dead were suffocating them in my ears. One by one, Morty stopped time for those with fatal wounds, leaving none to fight for their lives in the hospitals and later be called "miracles".

Except for Frank.

Frank was shot in the chest, and it should've killed him. But Morty liked Frank, and because he liked him he was spared.

At 11:58 p.m., Joel's gun and pocket had emptied of ammunition. He dropped the gun on a nearby table, reached behind his back and pulled a handgun from his jeans, put the barrel to his temple and he pulled the trigger.

In an instant, chaos became eerie silence, and gradually, during several minutes, the silence was replaced with cries and the footfalls of police officers who'd entered the building, guns raised on living patrons because they didn't know who the shooter was.

Morty and I stood in the center of the bar unseen, the room never darker than it was on this day, the floors slippery with blood and beer and food and littered with bodies, the walls a Jackson Pollock of blood and brain matter. And sitting in the corner, underneath the orange glow of a light in the ceiling above her was the Angel. Her expression remained untouched by emotion. I didn't know yet why she was there exactly, but I was soon to find out.

One by one I reaped the souls of Brisbane's patrons and the victims Joel had murdered outside in the wintry street. And with each one I felt a strange feeling creeping over me, stealing away my victorious mood and replacing it with doubt, though I wasn't sure why.

The three of us—Morty, the Angel, and me—stood in the middle of the snow-covered street outside Brisbane's, the sporadic flash of red and blue lights from police cars and ambulances and firetrucks bounced around on the buildings and the tall glass windows; people gathered in crowds all around the scene, held back by yellow-tape barriers; bodies were being covered with sheets; Frank was being wheeled into an ambulance on a stretcher.

"So," Morty said, "how many was that exactly?"

I counted in my head.

"Fifty-nine."

Morty's face lit up; he reached into his shirt pocket and pulled out a cigarette, pressed the filter between his lips and lit the end aflame.

"Fifty-nine?"

"Yeah, Morty, fifty-nine. What's your point?"

The Angel stepped up then, but she did not speak, although I knew she was going to soon, and I already despised her for it.

"We were eighty-one, twenty-two," Morty said. "Fifty-nine dead would make us even."

My mind scrambled to count the numbers, and yes, if the souls of the murdered even counted as points, then fifty-nine would've tied the score—but they didn't count.

"Fifty-nine dead doesn't make us even, Morty," I argued. "The score ends at eighty-one, twenty-three. Joel is the only suicide here." Even though I told him this, something in the back of my mind, and deep down in my gut, stole my confidence away.

"Oh, but if you recall the rules, Allister," Morty said with a twinkle in his eye, "then you'd know our game has ended in a draw."

"The rules?" I thought back on those two "simple" rules.

And then it hit me. And my heart sank into my feet. And I wanted to hit a wall but I wasn't standing close enough to one.

"Any death involving the suicide of one of your patients is considered a point for me," Morty reminded me.

"Yes," the Angel finally spoke, "the way the rule was worded would mean that *any* death, not just a suicide, that took place *because* of a patient that committed suicide, is considered a point."

"Yeah, I get it," I snapped at the Angel, and turned back to Morty. "So, then we went through all this for nothing? It ends in a *draw*?" I threw my hands up in the air beside me.

"Consequences," the Angel said. "What will *now* haunt you, Azrael, is wondering if you had not used the help of Lucifer, which, in turn, stopped the murder-suicide of Joel and his family, resulting in what happened here tonight instead. If your concern—caused by a *stolen* good soul—for the family had not been a factor, you might have been victorious. But because you chose to take the life of the one you called Nancy, your actions set in motion this outcome."

Without giving me any chance to respond, the Angel turned and walked away, through the aftermath of the carnage laid out on the street, past the red and blue lights and stretchers and hot, smoky exhaust of running emergency vehicles, and then she disappeared through a growing crowd of onlookers standing behind the yellow-tape barrier.

"Hey, I don't like her, either," Morty laughed, "but she *is* right."

My shoulders fell into a defeated slump.

"Why so glum?" he said. "It's not like you lost. You just didn't win." He pointed at me, and raised one bushy eyebrow. "I told you about them chickens, didn't I?"

"Yeah. All right, Morty." I slid my hands into my suit jacket pockets. "I have an important soul to reap. And then maybe to split. Though I'll probably just give Lucifer the whole thing since it'll drive me mad if I keep it. Haven't decided yet."

Morty nodded, puffed on his cigarette.

I started to walk away.

"Hey, Allister," he called out.

I stopped, but kept my back to him.

"You know what'll haunt you even more than wondering what the outcome would've been if you hadn't used Lucifer's help?"

I turned and looked back at him.

"What, Morty?" I asked, uninterested.

He smiled, and then with the cigarette dangling from his mouth, he said, "If I spared Frank for more than just because I like him."

That got my attention.

I marched right back over.

"Are you implying you could've won, but chose not to?" I refused to believe it. Or, did I?

Morty took a long drag, held the smoke in his lungs, and then let it all out in one majestic exhale.

"Maybe," he said.

I gritted my teeth.

"Hey, I guess you'll never know, because I'll never tell you."

I clenched my fists.

"What do you want, Morty?"

"I wanna play again," he said. "Higher stakes. Bigger rewards. I could do this forever, Allister"—he punched me gently on the shoulder; a grin deepened in his face—"and so could you, you gotta admit."

I looked around at the bloody scene, but I saw none of it really, as I had more interesting things on my mind than the chaos of mortals.

I hated them. Sure, I was as tethered to this world as any of them were, or as Morty and Lucifer were. But being tethered to it was the same as an addict addicted to heroin: I couldn't let go even though I knew it would kill me eventually.

"I'll think about it, Morty."

I left him on the street that night, and I went back to my apartment not too far from my office. And for the next year I continued to be the same Allister Boone M.D., except only I had become famous. People from all over the country—and the world—traveled all the way to New York City for a session with me. My new secretary, Darla, thirty-eight-year-old tattoo enthusiast who could never be targeted by the Angels because she was a delicious sinner who loved sex and alcohol and prided herself in telling the world they should do and say whatever they wanted because they have only one life, suggested I offer online sessions so people wouldn't have to travel.

"No," I rejected the idea. "If they want help bad enough, they'll spend the money and walk the miles for it."

And they did.

I worked seven days a week, twelve hours a day, and I loved it. Well, I loved telling them all what they needed to hear, rather than pushing cushions underneath their asses so it would hurt less when they fell. I *wanted* it to hurt. Not only for revenge that The Game didn't turn out like I'd wanted, but because I'd wandered this plane of existence for too damn long, disappointed—embarrassed even—by their stupidity, and their greed, and their senseless violence, which disrupted the peaceful era before they started walking on two legs and pissing on my goddamned shoes.

Not all of them were half bad, however, and some even made me proud. As proud as I could be, considering I was Death and that I, deep down, wanted them all to die already.

Even Jason Layne pulled off the impossible from beyond the grave. Turned out that Jillian Bowden picked up Jason's work from his video blog, and worked full-time to spread the messages he so desperately wanted the world to know. By the end of one year, Jillian-Jason Truth Talk had four million dedicated followers, many of which had been so inspired by Jillian's and Jason's messages, that they started their own blogs and vlogs and charitable organizations. Jillian also started a charity, named after and honoring Jason Layne—because she always gave one hundred percent of the credit of her success to him. Eighty-five-percent of her earnings went to the charity, which was then distributed to other reputable charities that helped give clean water to underdeveloped countries, animal welfare, children's cancer research. Darren Bowden, Jillian's "bigtime politician" husband, won a Senate seat last November, and was already making waves—and many red-faced enemies—with his unconventional approach to politics that had opened the minds of voters even in his rival party.

As always, I wasn't biased. It wasn't the charity work or the domino effect of positive, good things that happened because Jason Layne chose not to end his life early, that made me "proud". It was just the change of pace for once, the feeling of mortals doing intelligent things rather than shitting where they ate. Just as I needed balance, so did the world. And just as my scales had been tipped too far in one direction more times than I could remember, so had the world's.

Many of my living patients changed their lives, too.

Joanne Emerson, the typical, run-of-the-mill, self-pitying, selfish human, wasn't so self-pitying or selfish anymore. She still held a tight grudge against humans—who could blame her?—but she finally found the love she'd always wanted but had been denied all her life. Joanne challenged my advice, and she went to that address I'd written down for her. She had expected the place would be an animal shelter, and she thought it a clichéd and colorless thing to do. But when she followed the GPS and drove into the abandoned gas station-turned-dumpsite, she was shocked to find not one, as I had instructed her to find, but dozens of stray dogs of all ages living—and dying—amongst the rubble. She found dogs with broken and even missing legs, dogs with debilitating mange, dogs covered in so much hair and mud and feces she couldn't tell they were dogs upon first glance. She found dogs with gunshot wounds, machete scars, and one with an arrow stuck in its hip. She found several litters of puppies with bloated bellies that made them look like little pigs, and puppies with infections so they couldn't open their eyes, and deformities so they couldn't walk on their legs.

Joanne Emerson's heart broke that day for the first time in years. She began taking food and water to them every day. And two by two, Joanne took them by crates to get the veterinarian care they needed. And within a year, she had sold her house in the city, bought a smaller one in the country on twenty acres of land where she brought every dog she'd found at the dumpsite to give them the home they deserved. And to this day, Joanne Emerson helps stray dogs, and she fosters those there is no room for in the shelters. She finally found what she had been searching for, and she filtered all of her anger into something that made her genuinely happy, into creatures who appreciated her and loved her unconditionally.

Penelope Winters, the twenty-five-year-old daddy's girl from an upper-class family took my advice and called off her wedding. Her ex-fiancé, Anthony, found a woman more like himself and they traveled the world together, particularly to places they could help in building homes for poor families. They were a happy couple with little money—they worked along the way to pay for travel and food and housing. Penelope Winters, on the other hand, was never happy. She had everything she'd ever asked for—including a husband who didn't mind spending fifty thousand dollars on a wedding. But surrounded by money and material possessions and a father who continually catered to Penelope's materialistic lifestyle because he thought it was what made him a good father, she was the most miserable woman in northern Virginia. Nothing, no matter how expensive, was ever enough. She was "depressed". She did everything she could to feel better. She went to a new therapist, started new medications, didn't like the new therapist because she "didn't seem to really understand or care" about Penelope's problems, started yet another new medication. She went to yoga. She took several vacations—with her girlfriends, because her husband was always too busy "working"—but not even that did much to help her. She discovered that her husband had been cheating on her, so she threatened suicide, cutting her wrists just enough it made her look suicidal, but knowingly not enough to actually kill her, and—I have no idea what happened after that because I got bored with her fast, as I typically did with all her kind.

And Margot Henry. Ah, Margot Henry. She was my favorite. No, seriously. I gave her more shit than I gave anybody, but she never backed down from me, she never gave up. Out of all my patients, she was the one I was most proud of *because* she never backed down or gave up. She was the real deal, a person who, despite how hard it would be, *wanted* to be happy and would do whatever she had to achieve it.

Margot Henry did get that publishing deal she'd dreamed of—seven-figures—and she went on to help children learn to be accepting of their bodies, and of others. She started an anti-bullying campaign, and then she went even further to start a mentoring organization where volunteers just like Miss Henry became the friends that bullied children otherwise didn't have. Margot may never know this, but she saved two bullied children from committing suicide, within the first six months of her mentoring.

Margot did eventually lose a few pounds, after changing her lifestyle; not to look like society expected her to look, but to be healthy and to feel better on the inside. But Margot refused to lose too much. "I don't want to be skinny," she told a reporter in a TV interview one day. "If I'm skinny, and I look like everybody thinks I should look, how can these kids relate to me anymore? I'm staying just like I am, for them."

I struck a deal with the Someone Elses, ensuring Margot Henry would live a long life, untainted by their diseases and tragic accidents and numerous ways to curb their boredom.

And then there were my Casuals, but the only one interesting enough to recap was the Casual-Turned-Terminal.

Her dying cousin whom she didn't want to chip in with the rest of the family to help pay for his cancer treatment, made a "miraculous" recovery two months after *her* cancer diagnosis. She'd spent everything she had on her own treatment, and she never got that second new car. And then three months after she filed bankruptcy, she died.

Karma really is a bitch. No, really. She's actually an acquaintance of mine.

And I've been speaking with her a lot lately.

"Are you sure you want to do this?" Karma had asked just last week.

We were sitting on a park bench, surrounded by elm trees and sunlight, and in the distance bicyclists and joggers zipped past. Karma was, according to human perception, an unsightly woman, with pallid skin that clung to her bones like plastic wrap holding in a ninety-eight-pound frame. Her hair was yellow and stringy, and she looked like she never bathed because she didn't. Her teeth were rotting away. Like any of us, Karma could've chosen any body she wanted to inhabit in this world, but she chose that body because it was the opposite of what humans deemed beautiful. And Karma's sole purpose in this life is what one would expect it to be: she repays deeds, good and bad, in kind.

But the thing with Karma, despite looking like the drug addict whose body she took over, and despite being a bitch when she wanted to be, was that she was inherently good, exceptionally dangerous, and not in the same class as the Someone Elses. She was a class higher.

And she was now in league with me.

"Yes," I'd answered. "I'm tired of the back and forth of these mortals. I'm tired of their bickering, and spreading physical and emotional disease. I'm tired of the disrespect, the treatment of the world they live in, the complete lack of concern or even curiosity for their reasons for being here. I'm tired of their fucking free ride. I'm tired of the chaos—there's enough of it inside of me that I…"

"You what, Azrael?" She placed her hand on my shoulder.

A flash of red-black light crossed my vision and I shut my eyes, inhaled deeply as I tilted back my head—John Macon's Hell was… agonizing.

Slowly, I looked across the lush green of the park, and I said, "The chaos belongs to *me*. They are entitled to nothing. If war is what they want, then war they will have."

I knew John Macon's split soul raging inside of me had a lot to do with my change of…heart. I knew before I'd finally met up with Lucifer later the same day after the massacre at Brisbane's, that possessing a soul like that—half inside of me, half inside of Hell—would turn me into…something different.

And it did. It did.

Allister Boone the psychiatrist helping people for nearly two years because he didn't want their disgusting souls floating around inside of him, did a one-eighty and started talking them into killing themselves, instead. Allister Boone was no longer a psychiatrist—he was what he had been created to be: The Angel of Death.

Yes, John Macon's soul had a lot to do with it, but there was something else at play that far outweighed anything a split soul could ever do: the real me. I had finally had enough. I had finally untethered myself from this world, ready to set in motion its destruction, and ultimately its end.

I was ready to die.

My three companions had been harassing me for centuries to take my turn. But I was never ready until now.

And the only thing that excited me more was the war and destruction and death I would leave in my wake, and that I would get to bring them all down with me.

And who better to make The End more interesting than my old friend, Morty Finch?

"Higher stakes. Bigger rewards," I told Morty. "Are you ready for this?"

Morty smiled, tapped his fingers on the bar for another shot, and Frank limped over to fill his glass; he would never be one-hundred-percent after getting shot.

"Oh, I'm ready, Allister," Morty agreed. "What didja have in mind?"

I reached over and took a cigarette from the pack in Morty's shirt pocket and lit it with his lighter.

"This time," I said, "you'll work to keep mortals from killing one another, while I work against you to make them *want* to kill one another."

Morty grinned, thrilled by the idea.

"And you trust me to take their lives?" he asked.

"Yes. Because one rule will be that you must end any life taken by another, no matter how fond you are of them."

He thought about it, nodding with pursed lips.

"All right," he said.

Then he pointed at me. "But I get the Someone Elses."

"Fine," I agreed. "And I get Karma."

He shrugged, and accepted the arrangement.

"And my three companions on horseback," I added.

Morty froze. "You mean you're gonna—"

"Yes," I answered, exhaled a cloud of smoke. "Unless you can stop it."

Morty grinned.

"I accept the challenge."

ABOUT THE AUTHOR

Torvi Tacuski is a *New York Times*, *USA Today*, *Wall Street Journal*, and #1 Amazon best-selling author...under another name. While Torvi may be a fraud *sort of* hiding behind a literary veil, she is where she feels most comfortable, writing dark fantasy, speculative fiction, and satire.

All her life, Torvi thought she was Polish, but found out she's predominantly Welsh and Scandinavian. She loves *The Golden Girls*, *Xena: Warrior Princess*, nature, the universe, anime/manga, and fantasizing about the apocalypse. She despises socks, shitty people, staying up past 11:00p.m. and sleeping past 5:00a.m. She believes in God *and* science, is both spiritual *and* blasphemous, and has managed to tame her lifelong, debilitating depression and anxiety simply by taking "the red pill".

To learn more about Torvi, visit her here:

www.torvitacuski.com
Twitter - @TorviTacuski
Instagram: author_torvi_tacuski

36879167R00163

Made in the USA
Lexington, KY
18 April 2019